WHEN YOU LOVE SOMEONE

Susan Johnson

WHEN YOU LOVE SOMEONE

BRAVA

KENSINGTON PUBLISHING CORP.
http://www.kensingtonbooks.com

BRAVA BOOKS are published by

Kensington Publishing Corp.
850 Third Avenue
New York, NY 10022

All Kensington titles, imprints and distributed lines are available at special quantity discounts for bulk purchases for sales promotion, premiums, fund raising, educational or institutional use.

Special book excerpts or customized printings can also be created to fit specific needs. For details, write or phone the office of the Kensington Special Sales Manager: Kensington Publishing Corp., 850 Third Avenue, New York, NY 10022. Attn. Special Sales Department. Phone: 1-800-221-2647.

Brava and the B logo Reg. U.S. Pat. & TM Off.

ISBN 1-57566-811-4

First Kensington Trade Paperback Printing: January 2006
10   9   8   7   6   5   4   3   2   1

Printed in the United States of America

WHEN
YOU LOVE
SOMEONE

Chapter

1

Newmarket, May, 1788

She hadn't wanted to come to the Race Ball. But then when did she ever want to attend an entertainment with her husband?

Yet here she was.

Because her parents were dead and her brother needed a living.

And she would do anything to assure Will a future.

Dismissing the familiar encroaching melancholy that always overcame her when she allowed herself to recall the reasons she had wed, Elspeth reminded herself that there were many in the world in much more dreadful circumstances than she. And duty was a virtue, was it not?

"Get me another brandy and be quick about it," her husband snapped.

The world abruptly intruded. She heard the music once again, took note of the dancers sweeping by, looked down at the ugly twisted face of her husband gazing up at her from his Bath chair. Biting back the sharp remark on the tip of her tongue, she nodded instead and moved away to do his bidding.

* * *

"Who's that?" Lord Darley nodded, his gaze on Elspeth as she skirted the edge of the dance floor. "She's damned fine."

"That pretty thing is Grafton's latest wife."

"Another? How many is that for Old Hellfire?"

"Three."

The Marquis of Darley lifted his brows. "Is *that* the one who—"

"Put Grafton in that Bath chair? Yes, indeed. Some six months ago." Viscount Stanhope raised his brows. "It was the juiciest of scandals."

"Grafton had an apoplexy on their wedding night as I recall."

"And Lady Grafton's still a virgin. Or so rumor has it. Which may account for his watching her like a hawk. She's not allowed out without a duenna."

"Grafton's too old for a sweet little vixen like that," the marquis murmured, following Elspeth with his gaze. "Although he still likes to show her off from the look of her low décolletage. Where did he find her?"

"She's a vicar's daughter. Not your style, Julius. Excellent family but no money; some dust up over a small inheritance that should have come her way but went to a cousin instead, a younger brother who needed a leg up in the world. Grafton spied her at a hunt near his country place and the rest is history. She's a superior rider apparently; her father was a crack whip."

"*Was?*"

"He's dead, as is the mother. There's only a brother left and he's off to India with the Seventy-Third."

The marquis smiled faintly. "So she might be in need of some company."

"If only that were an original thought," Charles Lambton drily noted. "You and every man who's laid eyes on her thinks as much. But consider—even if it were possible which it's not—do you really want to bed a vicar's daughter?"

"It makes no difference to me if her father was a blacksmith."

Aware of his friend's democratic and unconstrained view apropos bed partners, the viscount said more precisely, "I meant she might be prudish."

"With a fulsome body like that, I'd suspect the lady is up to some degree of carnal amusements."

Charles shrugged. "Word has it she's refused all offers with a distinct coolness."

The marquis's glance swung away from the lady back to his friend. "She's been approached?"

"Of course she's been approached. If you didn't so pointedly avoid society, you'd be aware of the stunning entrance she made at Lady Chenwith's rout, not to mention her appearance as Iphigenia at Lady Portland's costume ball. Her costume was very revealing. Grafton stuck to her side like glue—his Bath chair not-withstanding—and she turned down every invitation to dance. Which were not invitations to dance exclusively as I'm sure you understand."

"Hmmm."

"Don't waste your time. She's unavailable. Unless you want to pay Grafton to watch perhaps," Charles quipped.

The marquis grinned. "Now there's a thought, old miserly wretch that Grafton is. On the other hand, politesse and tact is more likely to win fair maid. I believe I'll have to accept an invitation or so this week at Newmarket."

"Don't tell me you're willing play the gentleman for her. I thought only horses and debauch interested you. Lady Grafton's reputation is sterling by the way. Not your usual preference in women."

"She intrigues me."

"Don't they all." A blunt rejoinder, but then the men had been friends since childhood.

"We can't all be in love with our stepsisters," the marquis murmured. "And you must admit Lady Grafton's sexual allure is impossible to ignore. I haven't seen such showy, impressive breasts"—he winked—"probably since my wet nurse. You don't suppose she's pregnant with some stable boy's brat?" he drawled.

"Not unless the stable boy is a special friend of Grafton's. He keeps his wife on a tight leash."

"Like Selina."

"I'll thank you to keep your unseemly thoughts to yourself." Charles was still struggling with his unsuitable passion.

"Selina's not actually related to you."

Charles scowled. "We don't all view the world with the same elastic principles as you."

"You should ask her"—Darley smiled—"find out whether she's more adaptable than you—more flexible as it were."

"That's enough, Julius. You're speaking of the woman I love."

"Very well, but if you don't even try to play the game, Charles, you'll never know what she thinks. In my case, I'm going to bestir myself to make Lady Grafton's acquaintance and see what *she* thinks." Lord Darley smiled. "Thank you, by the way. I never would have come to this tedious affair without your insistence."

"And the promise of first bid on Run-To-The-Gold's next offspring," Lambton gruffly noted.

Another flash of perfect white teeth. "That, too. Now if you'll excuse me, I'll see if I can remember any of the virtuous, Biblical maxims beaten into me by my overzealous tutors."

Chapter
2

Lady Grafton had entered the card room and was waiting as a flunkey filled a glass with brandy when the marquis followed her in.

She was not, however, waiting alone.

She was surrounded by a jostling crowd of admirers.

On Darley's approach the throng parted like the Red Sea in deference to the marquis's skill at dueling, his erratic temper, his title, and last but not least—his great fortune that trumped all the other qualities in the hierarchy of aristocratic values.

Bowing gracefully as he reached her, Julius's smile was one of transcendent charm. "Darley at your service, ma'am. I understand you're a first-rate rider. If I might offer you the use of my horses while you're at Newmarket, I would consider it an unparalleled honor."

"How pretty of you," she murmured, not returning his smile. "But my husband brought my horses south. If you'll excuse me, gentlemen." Taking the glass offered her by the flunkey, she took a step forward.

Any other man but Darley would have moved aside.

In fact, all of them did—not that it mattered when the marquis alone blocked her path. "If I might escort you," he pleasantly said, putting out his arm.

She met his gaze with cool directness. "I'd rather you didn't."

A faint uptake of breaths in the surrounding press of gallants acknowledged her startling rebuff.

"I'm harmless," Julius murmured with a faint smile, letting his arm drop to his side.

"Pray allow me to disagree, my lord. Your reputation precedes you."

"Are you afraid?" His voice was suddenly pitched low, the words for her ears alone.

"Hardly." She, too, spoke in an undertone, not wishing to call attention to herself, particularly with a man like Darley who was a byword for dissipation.

"It's only a short stroll through a crush of people. How can it matter?"

His voice was gentle, his gaze oddly benevolent, his beauty at close range far exceeding whatever reports she may have heard in the remoteness of her country parish. But reports she *had* heard, as had any young girl with an ear for gossip. Lord Darley's scandalous exploits had inflamed the pages of *The Tatler* for years.

"Indeed, how can it matter," she abruptly agreed, tipping her head in the veriest acceptance.

He'd known all along that she'd accept his challenge. Something about the set of her chin gave him reason to suspect she had pluck. Although taking Grafton to husband required a certain degree of unflinching courage he didn't doubt. Lifting the brandy glass from her hand, he bowed gracefully and crooked his arm.

Placing her palm on the brown wool sleeve of his Jockey Club cutaway coat, she experienced a sudden leaping of her heart. Impossible, she thought, far from a woman of flighty emotions. But there—she felt it again as he turned his smile on her. And this time the tremulous jolt of sensation had nothing to do with her heart.

"You really should consider taking out my racer, Skylark, if you enjoy riding. He's incredible," Julius added. *Like you*, he thought, trying to ignore his body's violent reaction to the light impress of her hand.

"My husband wouldn't allow it."

"I could speak to him. Surely he wouldn't disapprove of you riding while you're at Newmarket?"

"Other than on my own mounts, I'm afraid he would. But thank you for your offer." She came to a halt just short of the archway into the ballroom. "Now, if you please, I'll continue from here alone."

"Certainly you're not in durance vile?" He'd meant to speak lightly, but found his tone more sharp than he intended.

"As a matter of fact I am," she crisply replied. "The glass if you please."

"Are you all right?" A sincere concern underlaid his query.

"I'm perfectly fine. But even if I weren't, it's no business of yours. Is that clear?"

"Yes, of course. May I call on you . . . and your husband, of course," he tardily included.

"No. Good-bye, my lord." And slipping the glass from his grasp, she turned and walked away.

"I gather you weren't successful in your pursuit," Charles observed as Julius rejoined him.

The marquis scowled. "The lady's a veritable prisoner, it seems."

"Didn't I say as much? Find some other quarry. Or simply stand still for the legions of women in pursuit." Charles's brows rose. "As in the current bevy about to descend on us."

Julius took note of the swarm of fashionable young ladies advancing their way, curls bobbing, cheeks flushed, a distinct sense of purpose in their step. "I'm leaving," he muttered. "Make my excuses. I find Caro Napier particularly annoying, not to mention Georgiana Hothfield and bloody hell . . . not Amanda—" Without a backward glance, the marquis bolted, the last person he wished to see forging ahead of the pack.

Just because he and Amanda shared an occasional night of ball-breaking sex didn't mean he actually wished to talk to her. Let some other buck entertain her tonight. He had things on his mind—such as golden curls and gorgeous pink breasts and chill blue eyes he intended to thaw.

Escaping through the terrace doors, he strode away and a short time later reached his race box on the edge of town. Entering his house, he waved away the footmen, strode to his study, poured himself a cognac and drank it down. Refilling his glass, he sat down by the fire and relaxed for the first time since he'd entered the Race Ball. Why anyone seriously involved themselves in society was beyond him. Tedious and predictable, the same people saw the same people night after night, week after week. One met the same women as well at every event and here at Newmarket where manners were informal and the usual crush reduced, it was more difficult to avoid being accosted by one's ex-lovers.

On the other hand, he decided, there were women like the delectable Lady Grafton who could accost him with his blessing.

Recall of her lush beauty brought a fleeting smile to his lips as quickly replaced by a faint grimace. Wasn't that the way it went— the females he didn't want he could have by the score. (His former urgent desires conveniently forgotten.) While the woman he found so enticing was unavailable.

Or so it seemed, he equivocated, unfamiliar with being thwarted.

Born into a great family, raised in privilege, gifted with good looks and accomplishments beyond the ordinary, Julius D'Abernon, Marquis of Darley, heir to the Duke of Westerlands viewed his place in the world with perhaps a forgivable lack of humility.

By his third cognac he'd dismissed whatever hindrances might exist in relation to Lady Grafton and was debating instead how to tempt her from her conjugal restraints. Surely, if Grafton was truly incapacitated, the lady might be grateful for a discreet opportunity to exercise her passions. She was glowing with life, a nubile young woman denied the pleasures of the flesh. To introduce her to amour would be gratifying.

That he normally found virgins dull he chose to ignore because Lady Grafton excited a rare, inexplicable desire in him. Her beauty alone, however bedeviling, wasn't reason enough for her unprecedented appeal. He'd amused himself for years with the great beauties of his day. Nor was the challenge of eluding a watchful husband out of the ordinary. Women of his class were expected to marry well, not for love. Once the required heir had been produced, they very often amused themselves outside the marriage bed.

So why was he so attracted? Why was he mooning over a pretty little blonde? Was she in such sharp contrast to his life of debauch that he was intrigued? Was the fact that she was a vicar's daughter enticing?

Or was some mute witchery at play?

Had she somehow, unspoken, made her wishes known?

He shook away the ludicrous notion, charging the absurdity to three cognacs in addition to the considerable drink he'd already consumed that evening. Even while dismissing such thoughts as ridiculous, he found it impossible to so easily dismiss the images of Lady Grafton filling his brain. He could almost smell her violet scent, see the splendor of her breasts, her slender waist, the curve of her hips. Her golden hair gleamed softly in his mind's eye, the diamond ear bobs in her pink lobes twinkled at him. Recall of the light touch of her hand on his arm fueled his lust.

She was fresh-faced, untried, a delight to the eye, and if Grafton had her on display, could he be faulted for taking the lure?

The answer was predictable; the world had been his from the cradle.

He'd call on her tomorrow.

And see what transpired . . .

Lost in his pleasant reverie of the morrow, the sound of a contretemps outside his study door went unheeded until Amanda abruptly burst into the room, brushing aside the footman who was attempting to refuse her entrance.

"Get out," she commanded, waving away the footman who stood in the doorway looking distraite.

Julius nodded. "Thank you, Ned. I appreciate the effort. I'll call if I need anything."

As the servant closed the door, Amanda kicked off her slippers, making herself at home with the familiarity of a long-standing friendship. "You'd think Ned was guarding the crown jewels," she said with a sniff. "Although," she added with a grin, "perhaps that analogy is apt." Walking over to the fire, she plopped down in a chair opposite Julius, leaned back and, surveying him from under her lashes, smiled. "You ran away tonight."

Instead of saying, *Get out*, he replied with an answering smile. "I had an appointment." The sudden realization that Amanda might be useful entered his mind. She could accompany him on his visit to Lady Grafton tomorrow. Surely old Grafton couldn't take issue with Lady Bloodworth visiting his wife. "I'm currently free however," he murmured. "Would you like a drink?"

"I'd like you," she purred.

"Here or upstairs?" His tone was gracious, on his best behavior with Amanda's cooperation at stake.

"I *should* be angry with you—bolting like that," she said with a pretty pout.

Ordinarily, she would have irritated him with her intrusion and pouty reproof. But his plans entrain, he found himself in a benevolent mood. "Let me put you in a better humor, darling." He patted his thigh. "Come, sit on my lap."

At the same time a gratified Amanda Bloodworth was rising from her chair, Elspeth was very near to losing her temper. She'd fetched her husband any number of brandies which did nothing to improve his acid temper; she'd politely turned down a dozen offers to dance when she would have *loved* to dance; she'd endured the lecherous advances of Grafton's equally hideous brother with stiff sufferance; and if her husband snapped at her one more time, she might very well throttle him in full sight of all the guests at the Race Ball.

She needed a drink, although she'd learned early in her marriage that alcohol and resentment were a dangerous mix. With her brother's future at stake, she prudently limited her drinking to an infrequent ratafia.

Grafton had purchased a commission for Will in the Seventy-Third after their marriage, as agreed, outfitted him commensurate with his rank of lieutenant and settled four hundred pounds a year on him. Contingent on her good graces, of course.

Which meant she was obliged to endure the burden of her marriage—at least until such a time as it was no longer required. Neither so self-effacing or docile that she would give up her life entirely and forever, she still had dreams of a future once Grafton succumbed to old age.

He couldn't live forever, she'd reminded herself on her wedding day. And fortunately the Fates had kindly intervened that night, although the period before her husband's collapse had been terrifying. He'd come into her bedroom very drunk, insulting her in the most vile language, threatening to whip her, snapping the quirt in his hand with the most menacing intent. Slobbering, red-faced, ripping off his clothes as he'd advanced toward her bed, he'd informed her in bellowing accents that he owned her body and soul.

As she'd huddled against the headboard, the quilt pulled up to her neck, not knowing if she should bolt or attempt to defend herself, her husband suddenly began gasping for air and turning blue, and collapsed just short of her bed.

A blessing she gave thanks for daily.

He'd survived his apoplexy, and his insults and discourtesies had become a constant, mortifying lesson in humility for her. But he'd been confined to his Bath chair once he'd recovered, and there had never been another attempt to enter her bedroom.

Grateful, she'd resigned herself to the purgatory of her marriage.

Although at times like this, even her *dream* for future happiness seemed elusive.

As elusive as the Marquis of Darley had been when the mob of ladies launched themselves at him, she reflected with a smile. Not that the marquis's companion wasn't handsome as well and perhaps equally a quarry. But even as she gave lip service to that nicety, she knew the ladies were after Darley.

When it came to male beauty and grace, the Marquis of Darley was the gold standard. Tall, broad-shouldered, lean and hard; his muscled arm had been like steel beneath her hand. And if his virile body weren't enough, his handsome face and his dark, seductive gaze were the stuff of legend. One look was all it took, rumor had it. And she understood why. He boldly offered pleasure with his roguish glance.

A soft sigh escaped her. Under different circumstances she might have responded to his advances tonight and indulged her senses. She might have allowed herself to experience a man like Darley—experiment as it were with the perfect pitch and sweetness of consummate performance. Surely, she'd held herself in readiness long enough. In fact, at twenty-six, many might say she was well past optimum ripeness—on the shelf in terms of fashionable allure. And until tonight when the rakish Darley had looked her way, she might have agreed.

She'd never known the sudden heat of longing, never felt a shimmering jolt of pleasure like she had with him. What would it be like, she wondered . . . to feel his touch, his kiss?

"Dammit! Have you fallen asleep!"

Jerked from her musing, she suppressed a shudder, her husband's claw-like fingers circling her wrist.

"I'm awake," Elspeth said, careful not to move. He disliked when she flinched at his touch.

"Fetch my cloak! We're leaving!"

Waiting until he released her wrist, she moved away without reply. It was safer not to respond to his churlishness. No matter what she said only added to his rancor.

But she made her usual cryptic notation in her journal that night before going to bed. A small numeral six, a smaller four. Six months, four days.

There was solace in her nightly tally.

There was comfort knowing some day it would end.

Chapter

3

Amanda rolled over and licked a slow path up the marquis's neck. "Are you awake?"

He levered open one eye. "I am now."

"Once more before I go?" she whispered, kissing him lightly.

Shaking away sleep, he debated his options. "What time is it?"

"Eight. Auntie Lou doesn't wake until ten. There's time."

Amanda was spending the week at her family's race box with only an elderly aunt as company. "After I have breakfast with Auntie, I'll dress and we can ride over to Grafton's place. Unless you've changed your mind," she coyly added when she knew very well why he was going and had every intention of benefitting from her agreement to accompany him there.

"No, I haven't changed my mind." He drew her close. "And yes"—he smiled—"there's more than enough time."

"I just love that your cock is always primed for action. How do you do it?"

He grinned. "Right now I have to piss."

"Then by all means hurry and do that."

"Yes, ma'am." He saluted playfully. "Any other instructions, ma'am?"

"None other than making sure I come in short order."

He glanced over his shoulder as he rose from the bed. "I doubt that's a problem with you."

"Do hurry."

"You're lucky I know you so well," he noted, strolling away toward the screen in the corner that concealed the commode. "Otherwise I might take issue with your orders."

She snorted. "As if you take orders. I know very well why you're being so accommodating, darling, and her name is Lady Grafton. So don't play coy with me. We're simply exchanging favors."

There was no argument to her blunt assessment and he wasn't about to dissemble. Facts were facts, just as a fuck was a fuck with Amanda. Fortunately, he just happened to be available right now. If someone else had caught her eye at Newmarket, he might have fewer options in his pursuit of Grafton's wife.

After pissing away the considerable brandy he'd drunk last night, he came out from behind the screen, washed with the hot water that had been brought in earlier that morning while they were sleeping and walked back to the bed.

"You're much too beautiful, darling," Amanda murmured, watching him approach. "There are times I resent you having everything—looks, money, a virile body beyond compare. Do you ever thank the druids or mythical deities for all the graces bestowed on you?"

His brows lifted faintly. "Since when have you become philosophical?"

"Since I've become a near-pauper," she replied with a small grimace.

"Ah."

"Don't say, ah, like that. I'm quite sincere in my compliments."

"Of course you are, sweetheart. How much money do you need?"

She made a small moue. "A little would help."

"I'll have Malcolm send you a bank draft."

"You're so sweet."

He laughed. "No, I'm not. But I have more money than I need. Now tell me, darling, are you in a hurry for a climax or just in a hurry to get started?"

Half dozing, Darley lay in bed after Amanda left, the previous night largely sleepless and Amanda's wake-up sex wildly tempestuous as was her wont. He wasn't certain she knew the difference between riding a horse and a man. Allowing himself a few more moments of rest before beginning his day, he contemplated seeing Lady Grafton again with pleasant anticipation.

Not that his pursuit was necessarily compelling; he was too worldly to view any woman as irresistible. But if Grafton's pretty little, virgin wife was looking for something to do while she was in Newmarket, he was more than willing to oblige her.

Stretching lazily, he ran his fingers through his hair, drawing it back behind his ears with a flick of his bronzed fingers. Then exhaling with the air of a man who knew his valet disliked being rushed, he threw his covers aside. Sitting on the edge of the bed, he tried to shake off his lethargy. Amanda could wear a man out. Not that he was complaining; she gave considerable pleasure in return. But he really needed coffee. And a bath; he reeked of sex.

Coming to his feet, he shouted for his valet.

Chapter

4

The marquis and Lady Amanda decided to ride cross-country to Grafton's. The spring day was bright with sunshine, a light breeze tempering the rising heat. Their horses, eager to run, pranced and curvetted as they mounted, and once they reached the outskirts of town, the riders let their mounts stretch their legs and gallop full out. Amanda was a superb horsewoman, Julius had been born to the saddle, and they took the first hedge so smoothly not even a branch quivered. As they rode full tilt over the green fields stretching for miles to the west, they gave themselves up to the sheer joy of speed and prime bloodstock beneath them, their powerful horses soaring over every fence with ease, clearing even the highest hurdles effortlessly.

As they neared their destination Amanda whipped her mount and shouted, "I'll race you to the gate!"

Darley's stallion was familiar with voice commands—neither whips nor spurs were used with the desert breeds—and at his low murmur, the sleek bay gave a snort through wide-open nostrils and leaped forward. Digging in, the powerful horse overtook Amanda's mount, easing back at Julius's soft command to keep pace with the smaller gray.

Laughing, her ebony curls windblown as she careened into Grafton's drive, Amanda shot a glance at Darley, his bay short of victory by only a nose. "I didn't think you were going to let me win."

Darley grinned. "Don't I always?"

Amanda's hat was askew, her smile merry. "I wasn't so sure this time."

"I wanted to see what your gray could do. The bookmakers would have paid on your win; it wasn't that close."

"Speaking of bookmakers." Amanda gave him an arch look. "What do you think your odds are with the young wife?"

"I'm a punter on this one. Small bets only. But nothing ventured, et cetera, et cetera." He shrugged. "If nothing else, it's a fine day for a ride."

"So your heart's not involved."

"Is yours with Francis?" Amanda's fiancé was an up-and-coming Under Secretary for the Exchequer.

"He'll be Prime Minister someday." They both gave non answers.

"And you'll be a prime minister's wife."

"So my mother assures me."

"Will she be happy then?" Julius had been listening to Amanda's complaints about her mother for years.

"More to the point, my father will be. He wants lucrative posts for my brothers. You know what it's like, Darley. Only wealthy men like you don't have to view the marriage mart with financial prospects in mind. I'm sure Lady Grafton understands about trading beauty for money. A pity she couldn't find anyone better than Grafton." Amanda smiled. "Consider—you'll be doing her favor."

"Should she agree."

Amanda snorted. "Humility from you, darling?"

"We'll see," he murmured. "It all depends on—"

"Grafton's level of incarceration, I expect. Surely, she wouldn't turn you down otherwise." Amanda had no ambition to exclusivity with Darley. Her sexual interests were varied.

"She might. I didn't get the impression Lady Grafton was the worldly sort."

"How charming." Amanda gave him a mischievous grin. "It's been a long time, hasn't it, Julius, since you've dealt with such virginal merchandise. It almost makes me jealous. Perhaps I should survey the field of young bucks here at Newmarket—or the grooms for that matter."

You already have, he could have said, Amanda's penchant for strong young men well known. "You're welcome to look over my stable lads," he politely said instead, because this wasn't the time to aggravate her. And his young lads could take care of themselves.

"Thank you, I will. Now, do you think Grafton will let us in?"

"Good question." He wasn't so certain he would.

"Should I charm him?" she lightly offered.

His brows flickered in sportive reply. "I would be grateful, of course."

"It's the least I can do to repay you for last night, darling Without question, you're the best cocksman in England."

A short time later, Julius and Amanda dismounted before the house and were met at the door by a young manservant.

"The Marquis of Darley and Lady Bloodworth," Julius said. "Come to see Lord and Lady Grafton."

"I'll see if my lord and lady are in."

"No need. We're old friends," Julius had no intention of being turned away. He gestured the man forward.

The servant had no choice, of course, as Julius well knew.

Moments later, the flunkey opened the drawing room door and announced their names.

Lady Grafton looked up from penning a letter and went pale.

Taking note of their hostess' stunned look, Amanda quickly said, "I thought I'd take the opportunity to call on you, Lady Grafton." Advancing into the drawing room with a warm smile, she added, "My family has a race box in Newmarket. I believe you know the marquis." She glanced at Julius who had followed her in. "I hope we're not intruding."

"No—that is . . . my husband is at the stables. I'll have him summoned." Elspeth turned to her maid as she rose to meet her guests, high color having replaced her pallor. "Sophie, have Lord Grafton called in."

"No need to interrupt his lordship," Amanda smoothly interposed. "We won't stay long. We were out for a ride and found ourselves near your house."

"I'm sure Lord Grafton would like to see you," Elspeth countered, signaling her maid to fetch the earl. She couldn't chance he'd find out later that she'd had guests without his permission. "Would you like tea?" It was impossible not to observe the social graces, although she found herself hoping her visitors might refuse.

"That would be lovely," Amanda replied with a smile.

"Sophie, tea as well," Elspeth ordered, trying to avoid eye contact with the marquis. She could feel her cheeks flushing with embarrassment. Or excitement. Or something else entirely.

"What a lovely view," Amanda exclaimed, walking over to the row of windows overlooking a bucolic vista of green fields and grazing horses. "Do you have a favorite mount you like to ride?"

Whether intentionally or unwittingly, Amanda's words incited an outrageously lewd image. Struggling to displace her wholly inappropriate thoughts, Elspeth found herself at a loss for words.

Aware of Lady Grafton's overlong silence, Julius smoothly interposed, "I've been trying to persuade Lady Grafton to take Skylark out for a ride."

Amanda spun around. "Skylark? You'll absolutely adore him! He's powerful and swift, yet gentle as a lamb. Tell her, Julius, how he took me over ten miles at top speed without even breathing hard."

"He has enormous staying power. It's characteristic of the Atlas Barb breed. You'd enjoy trying him out, Lady Grafton."

Elspeth tried not to misinterpret the marquis's comments. *Get a grip,* she told herself. Everyone was simply discussing horses and she was reacting like an agitated adolescent to the most benign remarks. "If it were possible, I'm sure I'd enjoy riding Skylark, my lord. However, we lead a quiet life since my husband's illness. But thank you for the offer. Won't you sit down," she politely offered when she would have preferred pushing her guests out the door and avoiding any further complications. From her husband and otherwise.

"Oh, look!" Amanda exclaimed, gazing out the window. "The most precious basket of violets! I adore violets!" Contriving a moment alone for Julius, she opened the terrace door and stepped outside to inspect the willow basket on the balustrade.

"Why did you *come?*" Elspeth hissed the second Amanda closed the door behind her. "I'm sorry—how rude . . . please forgive me," she stammered, blushing furiously at her graceless behavior. "I shouldn't have said—I mean . . . I don't know what came—"

"I couldn't stay away." Uncharacteristically blunt words for the marquis who only played at love. And if Grafton wasn't about to appear at any moment, Julius would have taken her in his arms and kissed away her trepidation.

"You *shouldn't* have come. He might—that is . . . you don't understand my . . . situation." Nervously surveying the door to the hallway, Elspeth visibly trembled. "My husband"—she took a sustaining breath—"is very difficult."

"I'm sorry." She was so obviously alarmed he felt a twinge of conscience—a rarity for him. This frightened child was clearly not equipped to undertake any amorous games. He shouldn't have come. "I'll fetch Amanda and we'll be on our way," he offered, moving toward the terrace door.

"No."

It was the merest whisper. His pulse quickened despite his new-found conscience and he turned back.

"God help me—for not having more restraint," she breathed, her hands clasped tightly to still their tremors. "I shouldn't be talking to you or even thinking what I'm thinking or—"

"Will your husband be here soon?"

She nodded, a jerky, skittish movement.

"We'll talk later, then," he calmly said when he wasn't feeling calm in the least. When he was contemplating taking the lovely

Lady Grafton to bed and keeping her there until he'd had his fill or couldn't move or both. "Please, sit down." Offering her a chair with a wave of his hand, he swiftly walked to the windows, knocked on a pane and beckoned Amanda in. Turning back, he smiled. "Don't be nervous," he gently said. "Relax. We're just here on a friendly visit. Tell me something about your father's parish. I understand he was a vicar."

The marquis's voice was incredibly soothing, as though they were indeed friends. She felt an instant lessening of her anxiety. "I suppose you do this all the time," she murmured, taking a seat. "Rumor has it, you're—"

"I never do this," he said. In fact, the mindless craving he was experiencing was so outre, he thought he might still be feeling the aftereffects of last night's drink. Taking a seat a respectable distance away, he added with an almost unbecoming brusqueness, "You affect me in a most unusual way." Impatient, his feelings stripped bare, the sensation was highly disquieting.

"I don't believe you, but thank you for the gallantry." Elspeth had had time to compose herself, to remind herself that she had quite literally everything to lose should she yield to the notorious marquis. "And please, allow me to apologize for my outburst," she offered, her voice calm again. "I can't imagine what came over me. Ah, here's Sophie."

The maid appeared in the doorway, followed by a footman bearing a tea tray, just as Amanda entered from the terrace.

Assuming Julius's conquest had been successful since he'd called her in, Amanda sat down next to the marquis in a well-worn chair that gave evidence of male comfort rather than a woman's touch. Offering Elspeth a disarming smile, she pleasantly inquired, "Did you plant the violets?"

"Sophie and I did. We thought they'd lend a touch of color to the terrace. Do you garden?" Once again in command of her emotions, Elspeth even found it possible to return Amanda's smile.

"As often as I can," Amanda mendaciously replied when she rarely stepped into a garden unless she and a lover were looking for privacy at a rout. "Provided my social calendar allows me, of course."

"I have considerable time since we rarely go out—other than to race meets," Elspeth explained. "Lord Grafton is committed to his stables."

And to his wife, Julius suspected, if he were capable. Even in a simple morning gown of sprigged muslin, Lady Grafton lit up a room with her beauty.

"Julius is obsessed with his stable, too, aren't you darling," Amanda noted, inspecting the young footman carrying the tea table with a practiced glance. "He spends a fortune on his horses. But then you're highly competitive aren't you, sweetheart?"

Elspeth found herself envious of Amanda's casual endearments directed at the marquis. When she should know better. When she had no right.

"Breeding racers is in my blood," Julius deprecatingly replied. "My father and grandfather started buying bloodstock abroad forty years ago."

"Julius travels to Africa and the Levant. Did you know that?" Amanda smiled at Elspeth as though they were confidantes. "It's all very mysterious and dangerous, but he loves it. Weren't you in Morocco last year?"

"Twice. The best Barbs come from the bled el-siba, the lands outside the sultan's control. I understand your father was a breeder," Julius observed. "I expect you still have some favorite horses."

"I'm afraid my father's stable was sold after his death." Elspeth poured tea into the cups set before her.

"I'm sorry."

"Our thoroughbreds all went to fine establishments. I was grateful." She handed a cup to Amanda, then to Darley.

"Bloody hell!" a booming voice echoed from the direction of the hall. "Why people think they can drop in uninvited is beyond me!" A moment later Lord Grafton appeared, wheeled into the drawing room by a brawny servant who conferred an apologetic look on Elspeth. "Who in blazes are you?" Grafton demanded, glaring at Julius and Amanda as though he didn't know very well who they were. Anyone who raced knew Julius, while any man with an eye for beauty couldn't miss Amanda.

"Lady Bloodworth at your service, Lord Grafton." Rising from her chair in a cloud of scent, Amanda approached the earl, the footman halting the Bath chair as she neared. "Darley and I were out for a ride and chanced to see your property. I apologize if we inconvenienced you," she purred, offering him her most seductive smile. "Since you have one of the finest stables in England," she fabricated, "we couldn't resist stopping in."

"Hmpf, can't say it's not up there with the great ones," Grafton gruffly noted, his head as easily turned by flattery from a beautiful woman as the next man. "What's your Christian name, gel?"

"Amanda, my lord. I'm in Newmarket for the Spring Meeting."

"The Duke of Montville's granddaughter, ain't you now?"

"Yes, sir," she replied with a pretty little bow. "At your service, sir."

"Which one's your pere?"

"Harold, Baron Oakes."

"Younger son, eh? Too bad, but then that's the way of the world. He has an asset in you, my sweet. A shame about your husband, but so it goes when you take on those high fences, eh? I suspect your pere has you on the marriage mart again."

"I'm currently engaged, my lord."

"Who's the lucky buck?"

"Baron Rhodes."

"Pitt's man."

"Yes, sir."

"At least he's not a damned scurrilous Whig."

"I'm sure he'd agree with you wholeheartedly. Could I induce you to show me your stables, my lord? My papa has always talked of your superb bloodstock."

"He has, has he? Well, don't mind if I do." An old roue who'd buried two wives, he'd not lost his eye for a good-looking female despite his infirmities. "Come, my dear, I'll give you a tour."

More interested in being alone with Amanda than concerned with leaving his wife in the company of another man, he signaled his footman to wheel him from the room without so much as a glance at Elspeth and Darley.

Perhaps his eyesight wasn't as good as it had been.

Perhaps he'd forgotten about the Marquis of Darley's reputation.

Or then again, maybe he didn't care about the marquis's reputation. He knew his wife wouldn't dare step out of line. As hostage to her brother's career, she knew who held the purse strings to Will's future.

Chapter

5

Setting his teacup aside, Darley spoke softly so his voice wouldn't carry to the maid seated in the corner. "Tell me your name."

Elspeth put up her hand in a small deterring gesture and turned to her maid. "Sophie, would you get us some warm tea?"

The neatly dressed, plump, middle-aged woman looked up from her embroidery. "He mayn't be gone long," she said with a frown. "Don't take no chances, now."

"Perhaps you could give me notice of his return." Leaning forward, Elspeth placed her cup on the tea table.

"Don't have to tell me that," the maid said with a sniff. "Course, I'll watch out. Although the old bastard should have died a long time ago, if you ask me," she muttered, setting aside her embroidery and rising from her chair.

"Sophie, please, consider—"

"Him?" The maid jerked her head toward Julius, the lappets on her cap fluttering with the vigor of her confirmation. "It's not as though the whole world don't know what you put up with," she fulminated, picking up the teapot. "Your husband's the devil's spawn and that's God's own truth."

A small silence fell as Sophie left the room.

At the click of the door closing, Julius smiled at his red-faced hostess. "An old family retainer, I presume."

"I apologize for Sophie's frankness. She was my nursemaid and still considers me her charge," Elspeth ruefully explained. "I'm afraid she's overzealous in protecting me."

"With Grafton she has reason for concern. His temper is well-known."

"Please, I wouldn't want you to think I'm suffering unduly. Many women are in similar marriages." She smiled faintly. "And I always have a staunch friend in Sophie."

"Would you like another?"

Her brows rose faintly. "A man of your repute interested in my friendship? Allow me to be skeptical." She doubted very much that Darley had chanced to pass by—nor that Amanda Bloodworth had spirited away her husband other than to accommodate the marquis.

"You don't know me." He wasn't so sure he understood himself at the moment, his normal carpe diem predatory instincts curiously tempered. "Now, tell me your name." His grin flashed. "I prefer not thinking of you as Lady Grafton."

"*I* try not to think of myself as Lady Grafton," she replied as candidly, the marquis's smile delightful regardless his motive. "My name is Elspeth Wolsey"—she grimaced—"or was."

"And you are prisoner now to your marriage?"

"Yes." She could be as blunt as he. What was the point in any event; her marriage was what it was.

"I would have thought you could have—"

"Done better? Is that what you were about to say?"

"I meant chosen more wisely."

"Really—from a man of your prodigally bad choices. Don't look at me like that. Your escapades and dalliances are in all the gossip sheets. And for your information," she said, a sudden crispness in her voice, "choices are limited in rural Yorkshire. My father's pension did not entail to his children at his death and my younger brother was in immediate need of a living."

He wished to say, *How much do you require for your brother's liv-*

ing? because his fortune was immense. But she was too gently bred to bargain with so callously. "I didn't mean to offend you," he said instead.

"People like you assume everyone has discretionary options. And why wouldn't you? Your wealth is legendary." She quickly lifted her palms. "I didn't mean to imply—that is . . . I'm not suggesting—"

"Is there a possibility," he gently interposed, taking advantage of the opening she'd given him, "that I could tempt you with some help concerning your—shall we say—options. No one need know. Your company would be greatly appreciated and my race box is close by."

Gracefully disposed in the chair so often used by her husband, the marquis was in striking contrast to the ancient, foul-mouthed monster to whom she was wed. Handsome as a god, his bottle-green coat, buff waistcoat, chamois breeches and crisp white linen set off his powerful masculinity to perfection. "Had I not so much to lose, I would let you tempt me—and gladly," she said, as susceptible to the marquis's allure as any other woman—perhaps more so with her lamentable marriage. "But I have no options, my lord. None at all."

He could have argued that statement, having from a young age understood that money buys most anything. But she had answered as a vicar's daughter would and he wasn't inclined to jar her proper world. "A shame then, that I didn't meet you earlier," he gallantly observed.

"And exactly what would you have done, pray tell? Marry me?" Her voice was light, teasing, perhaps as recompense for the misery of her position.

There was no answer of course, the thought of marriage anathema to him. "You needn't look so cheerful when I'm desolate," he charmingly offered.

"With all the women pursuing you last night, I'm sure you won't have any trouble alleviating your desolation." A mischievous intonation concealed her envy of that fashionable sisterhood.

"I'm pleased you find this so amusing." The little minx could flirt; should he be hopeful?

"Pray acquit me of guilt when you have a harem at your beck and call."

Not about to respond to intimations of harems, he said instead, "Should you ever change your mind . . ."

"I can't," she said with a small sigh.

"He keeps watch?" Although he might, too, with a wife like her—beautiful, virginal, with a body made for pleasure.

"Yes." She made a small moue. "As you know, a husband has considerable control over a wife—by custom and law . . . particularly when a woman is penniless."

How could he argue. Year after year, young ladies were brought to London for the sole purpose of procuring a wealthy match. Love was *rarely* a consideration. In terms of the marriage settlement, it was *never* a consideration. Although he couldn't be sure whether Elspeth spoke so bluntly of her lack of fortune in candor or for some more artful purpose. Was she indeed asking for money?

"If I could be of assistance with some additional funds, I would be delighted to be of service," he urbanely proposed.

Her eyes widened. "Heavens no!"

"I'd be more than happy to assist you."

"I wasn't bargaining, Darley."

Her gaze had turned cool. Apparently she wasn't after money. A shame, also a rarity. "I didn't mean to offend you. It's just that—"

"Women are after your money?"

If anyone should understand economics and the bedroom, she should, but this wasn't the time to debate issues of female dependence when he'd apparently been wrong. "There *have* been occasions," he suavely noted. "But this is not one. I beg your pardon."

She blew out a breath. "And I yours. I had no right to take offense. When it comes to choosing principle over money I can make no claim to virtue."

"You had your reasons."

"As perhaps your women friends do."

"I doubt theirs are so self-sacrificing."

"I'm no saint, Darley. It was sheer necessity."

"Is it possible we could be just friends—go riding together on occasion?" She intrigued him—for her directness more than anything. Not that he was immune to her sumptuous physical attributes, but she piqued his curiosity. She had none of the blushing reserve one would expect of a virginal vicar's daughter. "All modesty aside, I do have the best thoroughbreds in England."

She gazed at him from under her heavy lashes. "You don't actually mean that banality about being friends. And even if you did, I couldn't because of Grafton and"—she smiled—"I couldn't trust myself alone with you."

His smile was roguish. "I'm encouraged."

"Don't be. Grafton's very healthy." At Darley's startled look, she added, "I only meant I couldn't possibly consider a liaison while still married."

She *was* a damnable saint, he thought. Which meant he wasn't likely to get what he'd come for. Or at least not until Grafton died—not exactly the kind of instant gratification he craved. "I regret you're a woman of principle," he said with a grin. "But I must accept my congé with good grace." He came to his feet and bowed faintly. "Thank you for tea."

She chuckled. "You don't care to stay and bandy pleasantries over petit fours?"

"Not when we're both fully clothed," he murmured, his gaze amused.

"At least there's no question of your intentions." An errant lock of his dark hair had pulled free from the black silk ribbon at his nape. Tempting her to touch it.

"No," he agreed. "Although I regret having been rebuffed."

"I had no choice. I'm sorry."

"Not as sorry as I." With a roguish wink, he turned to go.

"Kissmebeforeyouleave."

He thought for a moment he may have imagined the whispered rush of words, but he turned back—a gambler at heart.

"I have my regrets as well, my lord," she said softly, blatant yearning in her gaze. "And mine can't be assuaged by a convenient harem."

He drew in a small breath of restraint; if she wanted a remedy for regret, he could accommodate her. Although he wasn't sure their palliatives would be in accord. Exhaling softly, he said, his voice taut with restraint, "I can't trust myself to stop at a kiss. Allow me to refuse." She didn't understand. He was decades beyond kisses.

"What if I didn't allow that?" She rose from her chair. "What if I kissed *you?*"

"You'd do so at your own risk."

No more than a few feet separated them—he was utterly still, she was flushed, her breathing erratic as though she might have run some distance.

"This isn't a good idea." He glanced out the windows, dangerous liaisons not without precedence in his life. "We might have company soon." Perhaps he had a conscience after all.

"Sophie's on watch and I've never been kissed," Elspeth confessed, the words running together as though racing against her better judgment. "Not that I'd ask just anyone, and obviously I haven't or I would have been kissed by now—at twenty-six," she added with a breathless urgency.

Did she truly say—twenty-six and never been kissed? The lustful possibilities stiffened his cock, his erection surging upward in an irrepressible frenzy. Could he fuck her before her maid or husband reappeared, he selfishly wondered? Although, if she'd never even been kissed, perhaps her first sexual experience should last more than the few minutes available to them in her drawing room. "Never?" he asked, as though matters of degree would temper his judgment.

"Never," she murmured, moving closer, telling herself she might not have such an opportunity again, that so splendid a man might never be so close, that she might die of old age without ever experiencing this—him . . . the piquant pleasure of kissing a glorious man like Darley.

Catching her arms as she reached him, Julius held her at bay, not sure he could deal with such fervid naivete. Or more to the point, deal with it civilly.

Looking up what seemed a great height, Elspeth held his gaze. "Please," she breathed. "Kiss me, then kiss me some more . . ."

Her eyes shone with the blue, untainted clarity of a summer sky, her plea resonating with such wistfulness he was momentarily daunted. "You're asking the wrong man." Unalloyed innocence was foreign to his world. "I can't be trusted with kisses alone."

She smiled. "There's no time for more. Come, Darley, am I asking so much?"

There it was again—the sudden shift—and he saw instead of innocence a woman of purpose. With her scent filling his nostrils, her nearness putting every receptor in his body on full alert, it would require a man of considerably more conscience than he to resist. "What if I wanted more than a kiss," he said, reverting to type. "What if I told you, you couldn't have a kiss unless I got something in return."

Inchoate longing like a drumbeat in her brain, feeling as though she might explode, she said, half-breathless and overwrought, "Tell me what you want."

He traced the curve of her jaw with a light fingertip. "Come to my race box tomorrow. I'll have Amanda take Grafton to the races."

"And now? What about now?" A strange, unquenchable urgency pulsed, coiled, flamed in the heated core of her body.

Smiling, he twined his fingers through hers and lifted her hands to his mouth. "You'll have kisses now," he murmured, brushing her knuckles with his lips. "And tomorrow—you'll have whatever you want."

He was offering her paradise. But dare she? He hadn't said take it or leave it, but she might never have this opportunity again, nor feel what she was feeling if she said no. "If I should come," she whispered, the raw, voracious desire coursing through her body making the decision for her. "What then?"

"I'd show you my race box and my horses," he gently said, understanding it was now only a question of when.

"What if someone should see—"

"No one will," he interposed. "I'll take care of everything."

"My maid—"

"I'll see that she's cared for," he intervened.

"My driver—"

"I'll send my carriage—wherever you wish to meet it."

"How long—that is"—she blushed at her presumptive request.

"As long as you want," he cordially said, as though they were discussing the timeline for some innocuous amusement. "Amanda owes me some favors."

"Really?"

Non-plussed, he debated the degree of honesty required to such an unpolished query.

"We can be together for as long as I want?" she sweetly inquired.

"Of course," he quickly agreed, relieved she hadn't been asking about Amanda.

She was being offered nirvana. Freedom. Pleasure. And more, she thought, trembling in anticipation of the sheer glory.

"You're cold." Drawing her close, he held her lightly in his arms.

"Not cold, Darley—hot," she said with a smile. "And excited and ravenous and any number of other sensations that make me tremble. I think a kiss would calm me," she sportively added.

"You do, do you?" he roguishly murmured. "Have I been derelict?" he teased, sweeping the room with a glance to assure himself of their privacy.

"More than derelict, my lord," she playfully pouted. "Positively behindhand in accommodating me."

The word accommodating did predictable things to his arousal and taking a deep breath, he said, "Only a kiss or two until tomorrow. Are we agreed?"

"I will agree to anything, Lord Darley, if you at last kiss me," she declared, reaching up, sliding her fingers through his hair, and pulling his head downward until his mouth touched hers. "Anything at all."

It was the worst possible choice of words. As his lips lightly brushed hers, he immediately began counting backward from a hundred—in French because this damnable kissing game was going to be torture. His cock was already aching, consummation was an entire day away and this darling puss wanting only kisses.

God willing, they'd be interrupted soon.

Before things got out of hand.

As the soft pressure of his mouth registered on her senses, as the velvety warmth of his lips skimmed hers, a shimmering heat melted through her body into every cell and crevice and fold, the delectable bliss beyond compare in her limited repertoire of sensual delight. But how nice it was to first experience these gratifying pleasures with the magnificent Darley. With a luxurious sigh, she gave herself up to bewitching sensation, sliding her arms around his neck, dissolving against his powerful body, savoring his hard, muscled strength. After six months with an aged husband, perhaps she was not only more susceptible, but more appreciative of a handsome, virile, young man.

Or then again, perhaps she was only responding to Darley like every other woman he'd kissed.

The marquis was on number sixty-four and beginning to sweat, Elspeth's lush, cushiony breasts compressed against his chest, her plump mons delectably obvious beneath the soft muslin of her gown. Holding her close, his hands at the base of her spine, he drew her pliant flesh into his rock-hard erection, gently forced her lips open and explored the sweetness of her mouth.

There was something else he wished to open more and gazing through his lashes, he rashly debated using the settee to assuage that impulse. Perhaps debate wasn't the precise word for he'd no more than thought the thought—the image of his aching cock buried deep in her virginal slit—than he took action. Slipping his arm under her legs, he lifted her into his arms and strode determinedly toward the Veronese green settee.

That she was panting feverishly, clutching his neck in an iron grip and eating at his mouth as though she wished to disappear down his throat only added confirmation to his own rash impulses.

He was past kisses; he was past reason. He was going to breach her virginal cleft.

And had not a sudden knock disturbed the strident dynamic, he would have.

Elspeth squealed.

His mouth absorbed the sound and a moment later, he raised his head and said, "Hush." His voice was remarkably cool considering the extent and violence of his sexually charged emotions. Depositing her on the settee, he moved to an adjacent chair, sat down, crossed his legs to conceal his erection and said, "Bid your maid enter."

Trying to still her trembling hands, she shook her head. "I can't," she whispered.

His nostrils flared and he drew in a breath. "Enter," he called out, the deep resonance of his voice echoing in the large room.

Poking her head in, Sophie gave her mistress a searching glance, her gaze shifting to Darley with a watchful regard. "They be a carryin' him up the porch stairs," Sophie said, pushing open the door and entering, the teapot in her hands. Setting it on the tea tray, she carried the engraved silver plate to Elspeth and placed it on a table in front of the settee. "Straighten your hair, sweetie, and have yerself a cup of tea," she quietly said. "It will calm your nerves."

Returning to her chair, she picked up her embroidery like an actor in a play.

When Grafton and Amanda entered the drawing room, Darley and Elspeth were drinking tea, which no doubt accounted for the flush on Lady Grafton's cheeks.

Chapter

6

"I gather you were successful?" Amanda's smile was conspiratorial as they rode down the drive.

"Not at first."

"But she couldn't resist your charms."

"I'm not so sure." He shrugged. "She just might have been ready for some adventure. She's twenty-six and never been kissed."

"My Lord! It's true, then—about Grafton and their wedding night!"

"So it seems," he softly drawled.

"Such naivete, Julius." Amanda arched one brow. "It could be disastrous in bed."

"If it is," he said with a faint smile, "you won't have to keep Grafton at the races long."

"You don't have enough money for *that* disgusting task," she said with a toss of her head.

"I'm sure I do."

Avarice twinkled in her eyes. "Is his absence worth diamonds?"

"Whatever your little heart desires."

Her gaze narrowed. "You're serious about this, aren't you?"

"Let's just say I find myself curiously fixated."

"Because of her virtue; it's a novelty for you."

He thought for a moment—Lady Grafton's virtue not necessarily an attraction, although her spectacular bosom couldn't be
discounted. On the other hand, he wasn't likely to go out of his
way for that reason alone. "Her courage in taking on Grafton intrigues me, I think."

"Please," Amanda protested. "Since when were you so high-
minded?"

He surveyed the green, rolling countryside as though an answer to his unusual desire lay in the bucolic landscape.

"You're not a man of principles, you know."

His gaze swung around. "I beg your pardon?"

"Don't look at me like that. I meant when it comes to seduction."

"I might take issue with you there as well. Am I not agreeable?"

"When it suits you."

He could have said as much about her. "The point is, I don't
know why the lady appeals, but she does," he said, not interested
in arguing about principle, or in fact, arguing at all. "If you'd be
kind enough to send Grafton a note asking him to accompany
you to the races, I would be vastly grateful." He winked. "Name
your price, of course."

She made a small moue, the thought of spending time with
Grafton repugnant. On the other hand, Julius's offer of monetary
carte blanche was impossible to refuse. "How long must I be
with Old Hellfire—for the early races as well or just for the afternoon ones? Did you and his virgin wife clarify your plans?"

"We didn't have time"—Darley's brows flickered in sportive
rejoinder—"consumed as we were with other—er—activities."

"I *thought* she looked flustered when we walked in."

"Elspeth has no experience with dalliance."

"Elspeth? Uttered in such a dulcet tone?" Amanda smiled
slyly. "Really, Julius, one might almost think this pretty little
thing has touched your reprobate heart."

"She affected an area slightly lower than my heart," he said, looking amused. "And had we not been interrupted . . ."

"It appears I saved you from disaster, then. Grafton would have shot you on the spot."

"On the other hand, had you appeared ten minutes later, I might have consummated my carnal desires and I wouldn't have to wait until tomorrow."

"You don't *have* to wait," Amanda murmured with a sultry glance.

He'd already considered the possibility and found it wanting. Struck by a sudden unease—he'd never turned down sex in his life—he almost accepted Amanda's offer to assuage that disquietude.

But he heard himself say instead, as though some alien spirit had taken control of his brain, "I should probably save my energy for tomorrow."

"You're joking." Darley could last for days.

"Actually, I haven't slept much lately." Which was true, but nevertheless an excuse.

"If you're going to put me off," Amanda pouted, "I might be inclined to ask for more than diamonds."

"Whatever you want, darling." He thought about offering her one of his stable lads but couldn't quite bring himself to serve as procurer. "Although I have you to blame for my fatigue," he dissembled. "You wore me out last night."

Her expression turned smug. "Why didn't you say so? That's altogether different."

"You already know you're the hottest little piece this side of heaven—bar none," he said, flattering her over-weaning ego. "And keep in mind, I'm not getting any younger."

"Nonsense! You're only thirty-three and the best stud in England." She gave him a considering look. "And I should know."

And you should know, he thought, well aware of Amanda's licentious amusements. "Perhaps you'd like one of my racers as further incentive," he offered, intent on getting home with all

possible speed, wishing to set entrain his arrangements for tomorrow.

She turned to stare at him. He didn't give away his thoroughbreds. He didn't even sell them. "You're in deep this time, darling."

"Hardly. Elspeth's dew-fresh, that's all."

"Take care or you might be caught," Amanda teased.

"It's sex," he said. "Nothing more."

"So you say," she archly murmured. "However, allow me to
dis—"

"My bay over your gray. I'll give you five to one odds." He preferred not discussing his interest in Lady Grafton. Tomorrow he
would make love to her and that would be the end of it.

"You lost last time."

"Care to try it again?"

She whipped her gray in answer, and seconds later they were
racing toward Newmarket.

Amanda's cooperation was essential to his plans.

There was no question who would win the race.

On the other hand, he would win as well—his prize a treasure
of another kind.

Chapter

7

Elspeth tossed and turned most of the night, telling herself countless times that she couldn't possibly go through with such a dangerous scheme, reminding herself that not only her own future was at stake, but Will's. And no matter how much she might wish to dally with the handsome marquis, doing so would be disastrous.

Fortunately they'd been interrupted yesterday before any firm agreement had been reached concerning a rendezvous, and now in the cold light of day, she was relieved she'd not committed herself to meeting Darley somewhere.

She really wasn't at all suited to amorous intrigue.

She was much more comfortable with a quiet, sensible life. And while her husband's rages had to be endured, he spent a good deal of his time with his cronies.

When Sophie came in with her chocolate and threw open the draperies and windows to the morning sun, Elspeth was able to say with a reliable sense of having made the right decision, "What a lovely morning."

"That depends," her maid muttered. "Seein' as how the earl has the whole household in an uproar. I had to make your chocolate meself. He's a primpin' and a hollerin' for his valet and driver and footman what pushes his chair. Goin' to the races he is—right early this mornin'."

The glorious image of Darley immediately leaped into Elspeth's mind, her pulse began to race and the notion of a quiet, sensible existence disappeared like vapor before a gale force wind. She glanced at the clock on the mantel, a thousand pleasurable possibilities jostling for precedence in her mind.

"It's early," Sophie said, taking note of Elspeth's glance. "Drink your chocolate while I ready your bath. The earl should be gone before long."

The marquis had done it! Was it really possible? "Are you sure Lord Grafton is going to the races?" Elspeth had been raised outside the sphere of wealth and privilege where apparently all things could be accomplished.

"A note came yesterday it did—perfumed it was, the butler said, and since then the old bastard's been talkin' about nothing else. It's the races where he's a goin'—there's no doubt o' that."

"Did anyone leave a message for me—I mean . . . I thought—"

"You didn't get no message," Sophie gruffly muttered. "And if you want my advice—which you don't— but I'll warn you for yer own good . . . stay clear of that there handsome rake."

There was no need to question of whom she spoke. "I know," Elspeth murmured, contrite if not wholly convinced with a full day of potential freedom before her.

"It don't look like you do know what with your cheeks flushing cherry red. I kin tell what's goin' on in yer head."

Elspeth quickly attempted to censure her thoughts. "For your information, I didn't sleep a wink for thinking about what I should or shouldn't do. In the end, I decided to be sensible."

"Your pa would be proud."

"I'm not so sure. Papa and Mama's marriage was a love match."

"The marquis ain't thinkin' about marriage, sweetie," Sophie brusquely retorted. "And love don't pay the bills, as your mama found out, God rest her blessed soul."

Her mother had died when Elspeth was twelve and Sophie

was right—her mother was a saint . . . making ends meet when there was never enough money. The day to day finances had fallen on Elspeth's shoulders after her mother's death—the vicar's view of money one of benign neglect. "And here we are"—Elspeth smiled tightly—"still paying the bills."

"It shouldn't have been your burden, but your pa always had his head buried in a book when he should have been smilin' at the old duke who gave him his livin'. It ain't one bit fair, but you done what you had to do. And God will reward you someday."

"Perhaps today," Elspeth calmly said, talk of rewards having turned her thoughts to more immediate avenues of recompense. "I think I'll take a walk once the earl leaves."

"Don't you go gettin' no ideas. Men like Darley are trouble," Sophie announced as though she could indeed see inside Elspeth's head. "And you have about all the trouble you can handle with yer nasty husband. One problem at a time's the way I look at it."

"But the marquis is unbelievably handsome," Elspeth said with a sigh, "and sooo charming."

"And he spreads that charm around from bed to bed the way I hear it. The cook knows his valet and Darley never sleeps alone she says. So don't fall under his spell. He'll only break yer heart." Sophie knew amour was just another form of amusement for the aristocracy, but Elspeth was out of her league with Darley. His name was a byword for vice.

"You're right, of course." But Elspeth's voice held little conviction.

"Someday, sweetie, things will improve. The old bastard can't live forever. And all the angels in heaven know what you did for your brother. You're goin' to get your chance at happiness—just wait and see."

She just hoped she wouldn't be too old to enjoy it when the time came, Elspeth wryly thought, but she took the cup of chocolate from Sophie, smiled dutifully and said, "I appreciate your advice—and your friendship. I'm quite resolved to deal with this in a responsible way."

"Don't you always, sweetie. You're an angel, ye are."

As Sophie bustled away to fill the copper tub in the dressing room with hot water, Elspeth sipped her chocolate and day-dreamed of some happy, but elusive future when she could do as she pleased. Perhaps it was every woman's dream, she thought, the role of women in society highly circumscribed—despite various factions who spoke up for women's freedom from time to time. Not that Parliament was listening in the least, nor judges nor any arbiter of authority.

And on that sobering note, she resigned herself to her fate. If she couldn't single-handedly achieve parity in the world of men this morning, she would at least have a blissful day of solitude without her despicable husband.

You see, she reflected, small pleasures were within her grasp even if the more spectacular ones like tumultuous affaires with gorgeous marquises were outside her purview.

Setting her empty cup aside, she slid down on her pillows, shut her eyes and half wished she had the courage to do what she really wanted to do. If she were brave she would ride to Darley's hunting box, knock on his door and invite herself in. If she were fearless, she would take advantage of her husband's absence, throw caution to the winds, ignore Sophie's warnings and grab with both hands the pleasure Darley offered.

The sound of the bedroom door opening and quietly shutting interrupted her reverie.

A maidservant with her breakfast, she thought, lazily lifting her lashes, a half smile of welcome on her lips.

"Did you sleep well?"

She sat bolt upright, her eyes flaring wide. Half in shock, half willing to believe in miracles, she stared at the intruder.

Darley lounged against her door, beautiful beyond belief, and if ever dreams came true, this was surely a bona fide example. Neither frightened nor panicked when she should have been, she found herself feeling instead as though she'd been given a present. "I slept—hardly at all," she said, thinking perhaps she should pinch herself in the event this was a figment of her imagination. "And you?"

"I've been up all night."

"How did you—that is . . . were you—"

"He's out in the drive; I came up the back stairs," Julius said, as though he could read her mind.

Perhaps that was normal in dreams, she thought. "You really shouldn't be here," she said, not fearful, simply stating a fact.

"I couldn't wait." He grinned. "Obviously."

"I should tell you to go." A sop to convention.

"It wouldn't do any good."

It was her turn to smile. "In that case, I won't."

He nodded toward the dressing room where the sound of water being poured could be heard. "You could bathe at my house and we could leave now."

She touched her nightgown. "Like this?" she said when she should have said something else entirely—like *No, I couldn't possibly.*

"I have a closed carriage out back. Sophie could pack you some clothes."

"She doesn't want me to see you." There. At last. Some defense against her treacherous desires. "She thinks you'll break my heart."

"She's wrong," he said gently. "You're more apt to break mine."

She was surprised at his reply.

He was as well; he'd never equated hearts with amour. Particularly his own.

A small silence fell.

Her lawn nightgown was revealing despite its buttoned collar and long sleeves, her pert nipples rising through the fine material, her plump breasts conspicuous under the light fabric. Any ambiguity about hearts and amour was easily dismissed with more relevant objectives in plain sight. "I'd prefer not wasting time today. The last race is at four." Tipping his head, he smiled. "If you don't mind."

"What if I did?"

"I'd have to persuade you to change your mind."

"Such confidence," she murmured, not sure if she was saying yes or no or still equivocating.

He shook his head. "Not confidence, my lady, only the most fervent wish." The sound of wheels on gravel, the crack of a whip drifted in through the open window and the marquis pushed away from the door. "That's his coach leaving."

Elspeth wondered at Darley's enormous appeal that he could speak so calmly of her husband and she felt no shame. Perhaps his matter-of-fact manner assuaged any guilt. Perhaps she'd been waiting so long for deliverance that he came to her in the form of salvation rather than disgrace. Perhaps the cult of sensibility so fashionable of late was in fact, true, and women were simply victims of irrepressible emotions. Or maybe his beauty alone exonerated her from any blame.

"Will he stay until the last race?" she asked, as though he had the answer to all things, as though he controlled the world like some mythical deity. Or maybe Ovid was right and it was convenient at times to believe in gods.

"I guarantee Amanda will keep him at the track until the last race," he said with a smile.

"Can you be certain?"

For the sum he was paying Amanda, she'd better, he thought. "One of my servants is with her," he more politely noted. "We'll have word should they leave beforetimes."

"You've thought of everything, haven't you?"

He grinned. "I was up all night."

"My sleepless night was not so productive. I only fidgeted and dithered and came undone."

"There's no need for agitation," he said pleasantly. "We'll go to my place and look at my horses. We'll ride if you like. Everything will be perfectly innocuous." He spoke as though they were old friends who went riding every day, as though they weren't virtual strangers.

"Innocuous?" she whispered.

"Perfectly," he quietly said, moving toward her. "We'll have tea if you like, walk in the garden. We'll do whatever you wish."

He'd stopped at the foot of her bed, the scent of his cologne wafting toward her, his dark hair gleaming in the morning sun, his smile offering her all she wished for. "You have a garden?" she said in lieu of the dozen more personal queries she wished to pose.

"My gardeners have a very nice garden." He smiled faintly. "I believe roses and lilies are their specialities." He didn't say he had gardens he rarely saw at all his homes because that would be pretentious and ill-mannered when she had been forced to marry a vile old man for lack of money. "Let me show you the flowers. Should I instruct your maid to pack for you or would you like to?" he added. He could placate her uncertainties and hopefully her desires more comfortably at his race box.

"I'll tell her," Elspeth quickly replied, but she didn't move.

He grinned. "Today?"

He was dressed casually, in breeches and a shirt; even his riding boots the simplest—as though he meant to pass as a servant. Yet he was every inch a noble—more—a veritable prince among men, and she could no longer resist his temptation. "Can we leave here undetected? I can't afford problems."

"No one will see," he replied with a certainty she found comforting.

Tossing the covers aside, she slid from the bed. "Wait here."

He could hear their raised voices or rather the old nursemaid's strident tones and Elspeth's softer replies, the words muffled at times, the more contentious phrases clear as a bell, the gist of the conversation obvious.

He was, apparently, not considered dependable by Sophie in matters of the heart.

A fair assumption if truth be told.

But then who of his male contemporaries were?

A short time later, Elspeth emerged from the dressing room, dressed in a fashionable pitch-colored riding habit, the new shade between green and black all the rage. She wore no hat, her hair drawn back into a chignon made less severe by the unruly curls framing her face. Her high color was obvious.

"I suppose you heard that," she said with a small grimace. "I apologize."

"I didn't hear a thing," he said, perjuring himself without a qualm since she was handing him a small satchel which meant she was planning on staying more than ten minutes.

"I just threw something on. I may have to change," she explained, her voice crisp, temper still evident in her tone. "I'll go first should we meet a servant on the stairs."

Perhaps the contretemps with her maid had been helpful, he thought, her new decisiveness apparent. She'd not appeared so certain when she'd entered the dressing room. "After you, my lady," he murmured, gesturing toward the door. Servants didn't concern him, but it would serve no good purpose to voice his opinion.

They met no one on the back stairs, the servants no doubt taking advantage of the master's departure to have their own holiday.

"This way," Julius said, as they exited the house and, leading her through the kitchen garden, they walked through a small orchard to his carriage waiting in the lane.

After seating her inside, he nodded to his driver, jumped in, tossed her satchel on the opposite seat and pulled the door shut.

"I've never done this before," she said.

He turned from securing the door latch and smiled. "Nor have I." In a curious way it was true; his experience with virgins nonexistent. "We're both in unfamiliar territory. But you're in charge. You set the pace."

She laughed. "How easy you make everything."

"And why not? I wish to please you."

"You have already."

"Good." Putting his legs up on the opposite seat, he slid into a sprawl. "So tell me what you wish to do?"

"Enjoy my freedom."

He glanced at her from under his lashes. "Meaning?"

She grinned. "To be perfectly honest, I don't know. I'm a complete novice."

"Would you like to inspect my stables?" he politely offered, not wishing to appear rapacious if by rumor and her own admission she was indeed a novice. "My horses are prime."

"Perhaps later."

"Very well," he softly said, suppressing his salacious urges with difficulty. "Later it is."

"Tell me about yourself," she said. "I know you so little."

Every woman said as much to him, but when in the past he would have given some flirtatious reply, he answered with a modicum of salient facts. He surprised himself with the degree of information he divulged, although perhaps her naivete required the soothing litany of people, places, and things to personalize their relationship.

"Now tell me about yourself," he said when he was finished. Maybe he even wished to know, although more likely it would pass the time until they reached Newmarket and his race box. Clearly she wasn't the kind of woman one could seduce in a carriage.

She would be more comfortable in a bed her first time, he suspected.

"And your brother," he politely added. "Have you heard from him lately?"

Chapter

8

Darley's race box was set in a manicured garden on the south edge of town, the original house Jacobean. That structure had been enlarged several times—the first addition during the Restoration, the second in Queen Anne's reign, the third only recently. The latest expansion had light, airy spaces, new conveniences like bathrooms, an indoor tennis court and the best stables in England.

Elspeth took in the sprawling structure as the carriage bowled up a winding drive, the old red brick mellowed with age, the windows sparkling in the sun, the ivy-covered walls giving it a country charm.

As the carriage came to rest at the back of the house, Darley pushed open the door. "I thought this would be less conspicuous for you. The front entrance is visible from the road."

"Thank you. I appreciate your thoughtfulness." Elspeth blushed. "Particularly when I'm not sure what to say or do."

He was reaching for her satchel and turned to smile. "Say whatever you like. And you decide what you wish to do," he added, as though he were casually offering her a choice of apple tart or syllabub, as though sex wasn't on the agenda, and she'd simply come for a visit. "For instance, the stables are close by if you'd like to look."

"I think . . . not . . ." Her voice trailed off, a tyro at exchanging urbane banter in irregular circumstances like this.

"I wasn't sure with you wearing your riding habit."

"I told Sophie we were going riding for lack of a better excuse." She drew in a slightly tremulous breath and clasped her hands more tightly.

"Fair enough," he replied, taking note of her white knuckles. "Why don't I show you some of the roses on the way in." His voice was mild, his offer deliberately mundane.

He was taking her inside as if she'd not expected as much, but his actual words conveyed an imminent point of no return. "This is all new to me," she whispered, not meeting his gaze.

The situation was unusual for him as well; he'd never had to coax a woman before. "I'll take you home whenever you wish," he politely affirmed. "*Now*, if you'd like. I wouldn't want you to do anything you didn't fancy."

He'd meant it in the most general way, no sexual connotation implied. Perhaps Amanda had been right. Perhaps Lady Grafton's virginity *would* be disastrous in bed.

The words *do anything you didn't fancy* struck Elspeth with a visceral urgency because she knew exactly what she'd like to do with Darley . . . or at least what her inexperience allowed her to imagine she'd like.

"It's up to you," he said.

He was lounging against the leather squabs, looking boyish in his white open-neck shirt and tan breeches, her satchel in his lap, his long slender fingers resting on the supple leather as though he had all the time in the world, as though her going or staying wouldn't disrupt his world. And a sudden, incipient need to know what he was thinking or perhaps simply prick his insouciance made her ask, "Do you want me to stay?" She may be a vicar's daughter and unsophisticated in the world of amour, but she was neither weak nor helpless.

"Very much." He sat up straight, his dark gaze direct. "Forgive me if I didn't make that abundantly clear."

"You appeared indifferent."

"I didn't want to frighten you off." He grinned. "You see how I'm out of my league with you."

"No more than I with you."

"So we're both treading lightly."

She smiled. "I suppose we are."

"*If* you come with me now, I promise you"—he flashed a smile—"whatever you want. On your terms."

She blew out a breath. "I'd be a fool to refuse, wouldn't I?"

"Let's just say I have a feeling I could make you happy."

He could make her happy simply by smiling at her like that. "So I should take the risk."

"There's no risk. You set the rules."

"I see now why you have such universal appeal," she replied, a soft teasing undertone in her voice. "What woman could refuse such largesse?"

He recognized capitulation even if she didn't and springing from the carriage, he held out his hand. "Let me show you the roses."

To that she could agree.

He knew as much and as her hand touched his, he said, "I think you need some tea."

Small steps, no rushing, he thought.

"Thank you. I would like that," she murmured, alighting.

It was kind of him to give her time.

He took her through a small walled garden ablaze with roses, the sweet fragrance and riotous color a veritable paradise of the senses.

He lifted his hand in a sweeping gesture. "I don't know one rose from the other. If you wish, we'll find a gardener."

"No thank you—that is . . . I'd prefer not—"

"Meeting anyone. I understand." In fact, he'd already made arrangements for his staff to stay out of sight. "We'll go in through the tennis court," he noted, opening a glass-paned door into an orangerie style space large enough to house a regiment, the banks of floor to ceiling windows on either wall allowing play in any weather.

"You must be very good," she murmured, awed by the extravagance.

"I can hold my own. Do you play?"

She shook her head. Their entire vicarage was probably smaller than this tennis court, not to mention Yorkshire had no indoor courts to her knowledge.

He smiled. "I'll show you if you like."

"I'll think about it," she murmured. While she wasn't entirely sure why she'd come here, nor yet certain she'd stay, tennis didn't figure in her plans.

Crossing the clay court, he opened double doors that led into a hallway lit from above by a glass barrel dome, carpeted in plush Aubussons and lined with portraits of his horses. To the right were a series of reception rooms, on the left his apartments, he explained, as he led her into a room he called his library. A great number of saddles, bridles, and whips were tossed on chairs and tables, racing calendars and stud books were scattered about, some open, others marked with paper tabs. A pair of worn riding boots lay on the carpet, a leather jacket was draped over a chair back, his passion for racing readily visible.

"Forgive the disarray. I spend a lot of time in here."

"It reminds me of my father's study, although not in scale." How many hours had she spent in that cozy room, she thought. How many evenings had her family perused the racing calendar and horse sales, trying to decide what new bloodstock they could afford, what races they might enter.

Overcome with a searing sense of loss, she forcibly looked away, gazing at the glorious display of white roses tumbling over the pergola outside. "Your gardeners are superb," she murmured, moving toward the terrace doors ostensibly to inspect the lovely view, more pertinently to hide the wetness in her eyes. "What spectacular roses!"

"The pergola leads to my stables," Julius noted, following her. "It's convenient."

As is everything in his life, she reflected, struggling to resist feeling resentful of the marquis's unencumbered existence. Blinking away her tears, she found it more difficult than usual to reconcile herself to her fate—the contrast in their lives so stark.

Her father hadn't been a vicar by choice—a younger son of a younger son had few other options save the army or navy. And now due to the vagaries of fortune, she was left to make her way in the world.

Perhaps she should consider the merits of a liaison with a wealthy peer like Darley in terms of repairing her finances. Rumor had it he was a generous benefactor. But it took only a moment to know she couldn't play the courtesan. No more than the role she would be assigned should she continue to stay here. And there beneath the pleasurable fantasy was the raw, unvarnished truth.

"I'm afraid this has been a dreadful mistake," she said, turning around. "I never should have come here."

His gaze flickered over her face. "You're crying."

"No, I'm not," she said, retreating a step, his closeness disconcerting. "It must have been the wind."

"Was it something I did?" he asked, ignoring her fatuous excuse.

She shook her head. "I just shouldn't have come. I apologize for putting you to so much trouble, but"—she made to walk around him, suddenly on the verge of bursting into tears. For no good reason. Or for a thousand reasons. None of which concerned him. "Please." She brushed his hand away as he made to stop her, forcing back her tears with an herculean effort. "I have to go," she whispered.

"Let me help in some way." He kept pace as she moved toward the door.

"It has nothing to do with you."

"With Grafton?"

She gave him a sharp glance, anger momentarily suppressing

her urge to cry. "Of course with Grafton and all the reasons there's a Grafton in my life. But, really, it's not your concern. Not in the least."

He stepped in front of her just short of the door and blocked her path. "I offered you money before. Don't take offense." Her eyes had turned stormy. "You wouldn't be obligated. I offer it as a friend."

"We're not friends."

"We could be."

"I doubt we agree on the meaning of friendship," she firmly said.

"Stay for tea, at least. I promise to keep my distance."

It was too much—his kindness, his extravagant offer of monetary assistance, his sweet smile and willingness to behave with scrupulous gallantry. She tried to refuse as politely as he'd made his offer, but her words came out in an inarticulate stammer thick with tears. And then, as if she wasn't embarrassed enough, she felt the first tears slide down her cheeks. Brushing them away with her fists, she tried to smile. "I apologize . . . for"—she hiccuped loudly. "I mean, how trying this . . . must be"—she choked back a sob—then another. Spinning away as the flood-tide broke, tears pouring down her face, she began sobbing uncontrollably.

Scooping her into his arms, he carried her to a chair, sat down and gently rocked her like he did his sister's children when they were unhappy. "There, there, don't cry," he murmured, thinking she reminded him of Betsy's youngest, blond and blue-eyed too, although Annie was only four. But at the moment, the lady in his arms was weeping with the same woeful fervor. He wished he could relieve her sorrow with the ease of childhood where a sweet or a new toy offered immediate solace. But Grafton was a much larger obstacle. And she didn't seem willing to accept money—a first for him. "Everything will be fine," he whispered, offering her soothing platitudes in lieu of more practical redress. "Everything will be perfectly fine . . ."

She shook her head against his chest and he smiled faintly at the similarity between young Annie and his erstwhile lover.

Candy clearly wasn't going to work here, nor toys, although Annie's new pony had stemmed a torrent of tears not too long ago. "Would you like one of my racers?" He was seriously altering the tenor of his life for this pretty maid; twice now, he'd offered up one of his horses in an effort to please her.

Why she intrigued him so, he chose not to question.

He simply wanted her and that was enough.

But rather than say yes, she cried even harder and holding her close, he gently soothed her as best he could, murmuring comforting phrases in a low, dulcet tone, wiping her cheeks with his shirtsleeves, playing nursemaid. Until, in time, her tears came to an end.

Looking up through wet lashes, she gave him a soggy smile. "I never cry. Really, I don't. I don't know what came over me."

"Was it something I said?" he teased.

She sniffled and giggled simultaneously. "I wish it were that simple. I apologize for ruining your day."

"You haven't ruined anything." She was sitting on his lap, the warmth of her bottom enticing, every nerve in his body on pleasurable alert.

"You're much, much too nice."

A smile slowly formed on his mouth. "Here's where I say I could be nicer still."

She couldn't help but grin. "And here's where I say I wish I could take you up on your offer."

He half lifted his hand to the silent room. "Who's to know?"

"Someone might walk by," she said, casting a nervous glance at the terrace.

If he read her reply right and he'd had a decade and more of reading female acquiescence, she wasn't precisely saying no. "The staff has orders to stay out of sight."

Her brows rose. "I don't know if I should be grateful or embarrassed for your forethought."

"Neither; we're alone, that's all. And so we shall be until I order otherwise. So you see," he said softly, "you have no further excuse."

"For what?" She gazed at him from under her lashes, a half smile on her lips.

It was the first openly flirtatious look he'd seen. "For giving me a kiss," he whispered.

"I shouldn't."

"No one will know—ever," he softly added.

"Ever?"

"Ever." Husky and low, the single word held the certainty of precept.

She drew in a deep breath that brought her fine breasts into even more prominence, exhaled and in a barely perceptible voice said, "Perhaps one, then."

"I'd like that." It wasn't a question of negotiating at this point. It was only a question of waiting.

"I'll kiss *you*."

He was pleased she spoke with less timidity, *more* pleased that she'd forgotten her tears. Lounging back against the sturdy red wool of the large Jacobean chair, he placed his forearms on the carved wooden arms and shut his eyes.

"You're teasing me now."

He heard the laughter in her voice and raising his lashes, took in her flushed cheeks, her shining blue eyes. If he hadn't been afraid of frightening her off, he would have reached out and touched her tempting-as-hell breasts. "I'm preparing myself for your kiss," he said instead, offering her a charming smile.

"As if you haven't had plenty of kisses before," she retorted with a little snort.

"This isn't the same." It was God's own truth. He felt as though he were as virginal as she and about to be kissed for the first time. Not that his jaded soul didn't understand such outlandish sensations couldn't possibly last—but for these fleeting moments the emotion was real.

"What's different?" she asked like women do, not content unless they decipher sum and substance of every word uttered.

"*You're* different."

"How?"

"I don't know. Exciting. New." He shrugged. "Don't ask me. I don't understand it myself." If he weren't so focused on the post-kisses interval, he might have felt a twinge of alarm at his rare involvement.

"I do. You excite me as well."

Which meant the pacing with such an ingenue was going to be frustrating. She wanted talk and kisses when he wanted to bury his cock in her succulent body at least an hour ago, if not yesterday. "Kiss me," he murmured, "and we'll deal with this excitement together."

As she leaned forward he braced himself, his hands closing over the chair arms. He felt her breasts press into his chest before her mouth touched his and he found himself holding his breath which was probably more shocking than anything that had hitherto transpired.

He forced himself to breathe.

It was only a kiss after all.

Cupping his face between her palms, she brushed his lips lightly, then not so lightly, having fallen under his spell at his first heated smile in the card room of the Jockey Club. His mouth opened under hers and she sighed in blissful happiness. Despite her best intentions, despite trying to deny her feelings, she'd been wanting him this . . . and more.

His warm tongue met hers in languid welcome and by instinct or long suppressed desire, with a throaty groan, she drew his tongue into her mouth. As inchoate prelude, perhaps, to all she craved.

It was a long, protracted kiss, lazy at times, at other times forceful, a delicate appetizer, ambrosia . . . occasionally a red meat kind of kiss that turned increasingly feverish. And impatient—for the lady had been too long denied.

On the other hand, having denied himself nothing, the marquis was now in the unenviable position of trying to adjust to an entirely new standard.

By sheer will alone, he dissuaded himself from tossing up her skirts, lifting her onto his rigid cock and burying himself deep inside her. With enormous restraint he curbed his intemperate urges.

He didn't want her to bolt.

Not until he had what he wanted. And she as well.

There was no question of his ability to bring her to climax or that he would.

He was very good at what he did.

She clung to his shoulders with a surprisingly strong grip, her kiss not so much a kiss now as a wet, frenzied gluttonous demand for more. Very near the brink whether she knew it or not, she was moving her hips in an undulating rhythm as old as time, her little breathy pants were warming his mouth and the scent of arousal filled the air.

Sliding his hands down her back, he gently cupped her bottom, adjusted her more conveniently in his lap and flexing his hips upward, made contact with her heated cleft.

She whimpered—a restive, needy sound.

Debating a move to his bedroom, he glanced at the clock, only to decide against it a moment later, not wishing to break the spell. Easing her around a few degrees, he made room for her legs by shifting his body to the left. The chair was large, made for long ago panniers, and there was room enough. Not that he intended to occupy the chair any longer than necessary when a sofa was available across the room. But for now, this would do.

He could almost feel her silken friction as he jammed himself into her throbbing flesh, almost feel the liquid heat of her body closing around him.

Almost.

But this was too new to her; he cautioned himself to patience.

Overwrought and seething, her senses inflamed, the small voice inside her head clamored, *It's not enough—not enough—not NEARLY enough!* Insatiable longing drummed through her pulsing flesh, a hard steady rhythm throbbed deep inside her. She ached for *satisfaction!* Plunging her fingers through his dark, heavy hair, she held his face immobile, her eyes wild with passion. "I can't wait! I can't, I can't, I can't!"

Offering up a prayer of gratitude to whatever gods prompted virginal young misses to revise their views on morality, he murmured, "Hold on," and rising from the chair in a surge of brute force and honed muscle, he strode toward the sofa. "You can stop me anytime," he murmured, when he knew she wouldn't, when a woman this inflamed required only surcease.

Easing her onto her back, he knelt beside the low divan, and leaning over, kissed her lightly. "Now, where do we begin?"

"Anywhere you want."

Hushed and needy, her simple pronouncement was erotic as hell, her carte blanche offer almost too much to resist—the possibility of exploiting her innocence damned tempting. Quickly jettisoning his baser impulses, he reached for the buttons on her jacket, hopeful they might explore the more physical dynamics of sex later. At the moment, the lady was too naive, he decided, slipping free a gold button.

"Let me," she said, brushing his hands aside.

"I won't argue," he said, sitting back on his heels. The buttons were impossibly small with loops instead of buttonholes.

"Your hands are very large."

And hers were small, he thought, the contrast provocative, as was everything about the virginal young lady. "The better to carry you around," he said with a wink.

"Thank you for coming to fetch me today." She met his gaze. "I wouldn't have had the nerve."

"I've enough for both of us." He grinned. "And I was damned impatient." Her jacket was open now, the dark wool framing the whiteness of her blouse, the outline of her chemise visible beneath the fine silk. Her breasts were spectacular.

"Impatience rather has me in its grip as well," she said, sitting up and shrugging out of her jacket, her former constraint apparently eclipsed by more potent emotions. "And I'm feeling desperately warm." She smiled. "I'm also feeling as though I've waited a lifetime for this."

"I'm gratified I happened to be available," he silkily murmured, his dark gaze slowly raking her bounteous form.

"Not as grateful as I, believe me," she said with a sunny smile, handing him her jacket without the faintest bashfulness, beginning to untie the jabot at the neck of her blouse. "And if you wouldn't mind my presumption," she went on, her cheerful tone suggesting she didn't really mind if he minded, "would you take off your shirt? I've never seen a man of your youth and vigor at such close quarters."

"Naked, you mean." At her reference to his age, the image of her wedding night flashed through his brain and he wasn't quite sure whether it was off-putting or added provocation.

"Yes, naked," she agreed in that same bright tone.

Since he'd never turned down sex in his life prior to meeting Lady Grafton, whatever reservations he might have had were swiftly discarded. Placing her jacket on a nearby chair, he pulled his shirt over his head, tossed it aside, held his arms open in a gesture of willingness and flashed a smile. "Anything else?"

Stunned at such raw masculinity, she couldn't help but stare. As he'd swept his arms out in a welcoming flourish, his powerful muscles had flexed across his wide shoulders and arms, down his lean, hard stomach, over the strong column of his neck, his virility so potent she almost wept with envy. If she needed any further impetus to enjoy Darley's amorous skills, the stark contrast between him and her husband sealed the bargain. He was breathtaking.

"Do I need permission to take off my boots?" he said, breaking the silence, his query politesse only for he was already discarding one boot.

"I'm not sure you need permission for anything when you look as luscious as you do without clothes."

"Partially unclothed," he amiably corrected.

"You're still ahead of me." Her voice was a seductive contralto. "I'm not sure that will do."

She was a natural, he thought. "Lift up your arms and we'll remedy that disparity."

She readily complied, and he slipped her half undone blouse

over her head. Placing it on her jacket, he turned back. "Now your chemise."

She suddenly crossed her arms over her chest. "Shut the drapes, please."

"There's no one outside."

"Still . . . I'd feel better."

"And I'd feel better not making love furtively in the dark."

"This entire encounter is furtive—is it not?"

"On the contrary," he said with a minute shake of his head— "it's the ultimate pleasure, like winning the Derby."

Clearly, he had a different perspective on illicit sex. "I worry . . . about being seen"—she hesitated—"by a servant." That and the fact that he was a relative stranger made nudity suddenly problematical.

"You won't see any servants and none will see you."

An unequivocal answer, as was his direct gaze. "And yet," she said, inhaling deeply, unsure and jittery.

He smiled. "Look, I'm not going away. Also, I'm perfectly harmless. You might as well uncross your arms."

In the grip of the proverbial cold feet, her rabid impatience of moments ago was superseded by a tumult of vague misgivings. "I keep thinking—what would Sophie say."

"She's not here, in case you haven't noticed," he drolly noted.

"I'm being silly, aren't I?"

His smile was tolerant; it was early yet. "You know I'm going to say yes. You're perfectly safe in my house."

"And Sophie's not here."

"Not unless she hiked five miles at top speed."

"You're right, of course." Elspeth dropped her hands into her lap. "And it *is* very nice here with you."

"Speaking of niceness," he offered, realizing she might require additional time to ease into her first sexual experience. "I believe I promised you tea."

She shook her head. "I don't want any. Perhaps a glass of sherry, although I'm so giddy, I don't need that either. You're intoxicating you know"— she fluttered her fingers toward his chest. "So utterly masculine, in fact," she went on, her words tumbling out in a rush, "last night I was dreaming of you and suddenly a very strange sensation—perfectly wonderful and glorious by the way—flowed through my—er . . . lower body in a delicious, rippling warmth. It was very pleasant."

He'd suspected her ardent nature at first sight; soon he'd see that she felt even *more* pleasant. "You climaxed during your dream," he murmured. "It happens all the time."

"Just like that? In a dream?"

"Just like that."

"Does it happen to you?"

With women a constant in his life, sexual dreams took second place to reality. "It has," he neutrally observed.

"Often?"

"I can make you feel ten times better than any dream." In lieu of further prevarication, he shifted the issue. "Guaranteed."

"Ten times!" A breathless, wide-eyed rejoinder. "I don't believe it!"

Reaching for the buttons on his breeches, he slowly smiled, "Let's see if I can make you a believer . . ."

He undid the buttons, slid his tan breeches over his hips, sat back, slipped them down his legs and tossed them aside.

Her previous view of erections having been confined to the equine variety—she surveyed Darley's upthrust penis with a novice's eye and breathless fascination. The engorged shaft was swaying faintly with his movements, the distended veins so prominent she could count his heartbeats. Would something that large fit in her? She drew in a nervous breath, even as a flutter of anticipation strummed through her senses, the carnal warmth rippling outward from her core as though in reassurance.

Beset by a curious fevered impatience she'd never experienced before, she found herself wanting—some illusive . . . tantalizing fulfillment—satisfaction of a kind not previously known. Sexual satisfaction she surmised. She wasn't without an understanding of the basic premise. And with the handsome Lord

Darley of amorous fame in her sights, why would not one be tempted. But this irrepressible craving that burned through her senses and overwhelmed all reason was stunning nonetheless. "Is it normal to feel this fierce, insatiable desire?" she murmured, even as her covetous gaze was drawn to his rampant arousal.

"Yes," Darley replied, in lieu of more complicated explanations, not in the mood for conversation. He'd never waited for any one lady so long. "There aren't any rules," he said with a faint smile.

"So I may ask for what I want," she cheerfully replied. "If I knew what I wanted," she added with a winsome smile. "You must teach me everything."

He almost lost control and tumbled her right there, the prospect of teaching her everything intriguing even a jaded rake such as he. With her offer of sexual carte blanche still bombarding his brain, he forced himself to speak mildly. "Why don't we start slowly. Like taking off your boots." Reaching over, he removed her boots, dropped them on the carpet, then rolled down her embroidered white silk stockings with a practiced ease and set them with her blouse.

"I was wondering," she whispered, wanting very much to touch him *there* on the gleaming head of his penis. "I mean . . . if you don't mind," she stammered, enthralled by the evidence of his virile maleness. "Could I?" she blurted out—pointing.

Tamping down his impatience, preferring fornication to anything so naive, he nevertheless deferred to her tyro status. "Be my guest," he offered, easing back slightly, making himself more available, telling himself virtue was its own reward.

But as her fingertips lightly brushed the distended crest of his erection, he abruptly recoiled, jolted by a powerful surge of lust quite out of proportion to the trifling event.

"Oh, dear, I hurt you," she said with alarm.

It took him a moment to answer with his erection surging upward in an explosive, headstrong frenzy. "No," he muttered, his nostrils flaring wide as he fought to curb his treacherous impulses. "I'm fine."

"Really?"

Her smile was so innocent, he seriously considered that he might have made a mistake bringing her here today. "Really," he said, lying through his teeth, not sure he could play the gentleman much longer.

Inhaling deeply in restraint, he debated his options.

With that deeply in-drawn breath, he inhaled the familiar scent of female arousal and his dilemma was solved.

Virginal miss or not, she wouldn't refuse him at this stage, or at least not seriously, regardless of what he chose to do. No longer afflicted by indecision, he offered her a practiced smile. "If you want me to tutor you today, why don't we start with lesson one—a kiss."

"I'm yours to command," she said with an answering smile.

"How nice," he said, as though they were engaged in a benign conversation. "If you have any questions," he murmured, politely, "you need but ask." And leaning forward, he gently framed her face with his palms, and kissed her chastely.

Sighing against his lips, she raised her hands, placed them on his shoulders and clung to him with a fierceness quite different from the mannered kiss.

His hard, taut muscles were an immediate, potent aphrodisiac to a woman who had only known an old, disgusting husband. How fortunate she was to be here, she dreamily mused, their honeyed kiss further warming her already overheated senses, a piquant intoxication consuming her thoughts. The glorious Lord Darley was actually kissing her. It was as if every overwrought, girlish dream had come true, the virtual fairy tale prince gossiped about in all the London papers, who stood stud to half the females in the country if rumor were true, was in her arms.

She was very much looking forward to the next lesson, she decided, squirming faintly against an indeterminate, but avaricious longing.

"Are you ready for more?" he whispered against her mouth, recognizing her fevered jiggle. Not needing an answer, he deftly eased her onto her back, slipped his hand under her skirt, kissing her rosy cheek, her pale, slender neck as he slowly slid his hand up her shapely leg, her warm thigh, and on reaching the gates of paradise, found them dewy-wet and ready for fucking. "See if you like this," he whispered, massaging the sleek, pulsing flesh with a masterful delicacy, up one side, down the other, around and around, ultimately coming to rest on the emerging bud of her clitoris.

Could one expire from the *sheer, thrilling* rapture, she wondered, every nerve in her body awash in shimmering ecstasy.

She didn't die, of course, although she began breathing in a decidedly erratic way as he continued to stroke her honeyed sex, her throbbing tissue swelling under the sorcery of his long, lean fingers, the taut nub of her clitoris quivering in arousal.

Soon, his fingers were saturated with pearly liquid, she was moaning, squirming feverishly against his hand, her nipples taut peaks through the sheer silk of her chemise, the flush of passion pinking her skin. He eased his fingers in a fraction more, intent on bringing her to fever pitch—only to come up against her virginal membrane.

There it was—not particularly welcome—but it had to be dealt with. He inhaled and blew out a breath. "This might hurt now."

"It—doesn't—matter," she panted, her hips undulating with increasing agitation, her gaze half-focused and skittish.

He lightly brushed the barrier with his fingertips. She didn't give evidence of discomfort. As for her willingness—that was abundantly clear. She was lubricated enough for an army, and as ready as she'd ever be to relinquish her virginity.

A queer notion—the premium put on virginity. He found it a perversely unappealing transaction.

But there was nothing to do but plunge forward—literally.

He chose not to undress her, trying to divest her of her clothing at this stage impractical. Shoving her skirt and petticoats up over her legs with a sweep of his hand, he rose to his feet and settled between her legs with a finesse acquired in countless boudoirs over countless years.

Through the fevered haze of her ruttish longing, she suddenly looked up and there he was, resting lightly between her thighs—broad-shouldered, powerfully muscled, all long-limbed grace and dark beauty.

"We'll go slowly," he murmured, his smile close, disarming in its sweetness. "Stop me any time," he added, not entirely sure it was possible, but uttering the platitude.

She nodded, beyond speech anyway—barely able to breathe. Shutting her eyes, she struggled against the hysteria threatening to overwhelm her, her body on fire, every nerve red-hot and seething, her senses seemingly melting away into some torrid oblivion.

"I won't hurt you," Darley whispered, trying to soothe her, mystified by tremulous virgins shuddering in his arms. "Take a deep breath, sweetheart. Relax."

Her eyes abruptly opened, his words instant balm to her seething emotions. "Thank you," she breathed, calmed by his low, husky voice, his equanimity. She took a breath. "I'm ready."

And because she knew better than most that life held no certainty and she might never be allowed this momentous passion again, she looked up at Darley with an open, wide-eyed gaze.

He found the intense blue of her eyes mildly off-putting.

Then she said, "I want to remember *every little thing*."

And he understood.

Even more unaccountably, he realized that this affaire was something uncommon for him as well. Lady Grafton wasn't just another seduction, although why was unclear. That he make her first sexual experience as pleasurable as possible was imperative.

A not impossible task for a man whose sexual talents were legendary.

Although, unfortunately, when it came to virgins, he was as much a novice as she. Impelled by sexual urgencies perhaps more ravenous than his partner's—he'd never had to curtail his desires so long before—he ignored any further speculation on preparedness and instead guided the head of his erection into her creamy cleft.

Only to find himself at an immediate impasse.

She winced as he pressed against her hymen.

Swearing softly, he eased back.

"Don't stop," she said on a small suffocated breath. "Please, don't."

"I should," he muttered, hesitating.

"No!" She tightened her grip on his shoulders. "Now, do what—"

Resorting to surprise, he plunged forward in the midst of her sentence, forcing his way through the fragile tissue, driving in swiftly, coming to rest a millisecond later in her hot, undefiled passage.

She shivered, her eyes glistening with tears.

"I'm sorry, truly I am," he whispered, feeling like a brute. But he didn't move.

"At least it's over," she murmured, shakily. "And I'm glad it was you."

He didn't know what to say. He should be grateful, he supposed, although, for him, it was a dubious honor. "You'll feel better soon," he said, no mannered reply coming to mind under such awkward circumstances. "Or at least I hope you will," he added with a small smile.

"Me more than you," she softly quipped.

He was gratified, her facetious remark portending better times. "There's no rush," he murmured, lying quiescent inside her. "I'm willing to wait as long as it takes."

"Now that you're"—she wiggled her hips ever so faintly— "here."

He smiled. "I don't recommend you do that again unless you mean it. I've been waiting for this for two days."

She snorted softly. "Twenty-six years for me."

He grinned. "So I should be patient."

He was encompassingly warm, powerful, all male and not only blissfully close, but at the moment, part of her, she happily thought, running her hands down his back, resting her palms at the base of his spine, feeling as though paradise was within her grasp. "I have a feeling it won't be too long," she purred, feeling the small heated tremors beginning to stir inside her.

He felt them, too, the ripples running up his rock-hard penis, a hot, dissolving liquid bathing his rampant length, her breathing taking on the familiar rhythm of arousal.

"Now?" he said, daring to move ever so faintly.

"Ummmm . . ."

Recognizing that enraptured sigh, he slid in a fraction more, advancing slowly at first, withdrawing only a marginal distance before sliding back in, increasing the scope of his movements by infinitesimal increments over the next few moments, eventually gliding all the way in and out, then forcing himself deeper and deeper still, until he was awash in her pearly dew, until she felt slippery hot around him.

Until she was screaming without knowing why.

He knew why—well-acquainted with that high-pitched, strident plea.

She was almost there.

Easing his hands under her bottom, he lifted her into his next downstroke, wanting her to feel the full extent of his prick.

She gasped, shut her eyes against the stupefying pleasure.

He drove in slowly once again, submerging himself to the deepest depth, holding his cock solidly against her womb, tightening his grip on her bottom and lifting her a notch higher, he gave her what she'd come for.

Her shriek reverberated through the room, raw, agonizing sensation exploding inside her as her first orgasm ripped through her body.

As if given license by that wild cry, Darley met her climax, pouring a seemingly endless river of semen into her hot, delectable, no longer virginal cunt. Two days worth of come as a matter of fact, which might have explained the prodigious amount. Or perhaps the vast well-spring of sperm was simply inspired by a nubile young virgin who had never been kissed.

They lay panting afterward, he resting lightly on his forearms, she in utter collapse beneath him. Having experienced the ultimate sensation, the sybaritic equivalent of basking in joy, whether she could breathe or not was currently of little import.

"If you . . . tell . . . me . . . it always . . . feels . . . like . . . this, I'll . . . never go . . . home," she gasped, her smile sunshine bright.

He grinned. "It does . . . so stay." Strangely, he meant it.

She winked. "If . . . only."

He glanced at the clock. "There's plenty . . . of time. You can come—a dozen times more."

She almost came right then—with him still inside her, surging larger even as he spoke. "You're . . . the most charming . . . man on earth," she breathed.

"And you're the hottest . . . little piece . . . I've ever seen." It wasn't a lie. She aroused him like no other woman. Not that he was inclined to introspection beyond the obvious advantages of the moment. "How does this feel?" he murmured, testing the limits of her vagina.

"Oh, oh, oh . . . yessss." Her eyes went shut against the exquisite sensation, her hips moving beneath him, wanting more, and short moments later, like rutting animals, they both came again.

He undressed her after that, any inhibitions about taking off her chemise long gone, and carrying her outside he made love to her in the cool, green grass under the rose-covered pergola. The scent of crushed grass tickled their nostrils, the dappled warmth of the sun warmed their skin, the voluptuous pleasure of amorous play and hot-blooded sex delighted and beguiled them.

When they were overly sticky with semen and her succulent juices, ignoring her protests, Darley took her to his bedroom. Carrying her through the silent corridors—not a single servant in sight as instructed—he brought her to his bedchamber where there was hot water and towels and tea set out on the table—waiting for them.

"How did you know?" she asked, as he set her on her feet inside the door.

"I didn't. This was just in case," he lied, this man who'd had women pursuing him since his adolescence. "Let me wash away the stickiness and we'll have some tea and sherry."

"And strawberries," she said, surveying the beautifully arranged table with embroidered linen and flowers and bowls of strawberries.

"And strawberries," he agreed.

Darley brought a new degree of enchantment to so mundane a task as her toilette, gently washing her swollen sex, kissing it to make it feel better.

Amazingly, kisses were exactly what she needed, although she'd not known such gratification existed. "You're spoiling me," she murmured some time later, her fingers laced in his hair, his tongue lightly caressing her clitoris.

He looked up, winked and before long, he spoiled her once again.

It wasn't as though he hadn't come his share of times that day, he reflected, lifting her legs from his shoulders afterward, easing off the bed, standing up and stretching lazily. And it wasn't as though he didn't plan on coming again, he reflected, gazing at the drowsy beauty in his bed.

He grinned.

Right after he rinsed out his mouth with some brandy.

As he carried the brandy and strawberries over to the bed a few moments later, she watched him, her lashes half-screening the brilliant blue of her eyes. Hopefully screening the adoration he inspired as well. Not that she didn't understand it was foolish to even consider falling in love with a man like Darley, a man who was a byword for vice. And yet . . . how vulnerable she was to his seductive charm.

"Open up," he murmured as he reached the bed.

Her body immediately did, addicted to him.

And then she took note of the strawberry he was holding and she opened her mouth as well.

He had but to command and she willingly complied, the pleasure he offered beyond compare.

He fed her strawberries and cream in another way as well, rewarding her at each spoonful consumed with another plunging downstroke until the strawberries were gone, she'd come countless times and they chose another game. That afternoon, they also sat at the table, drank tea and sherry, talked nonsense and horses and found pleasure in each other's company beyond the intimacies of sex.

But, mostly they played at love in all its endless variety, indulging their carnal urges with shameless delight.

Lord Darley found the role of teacher truly inspiring after all, although his fair and comely student, always ready to please, contributed in no small measure to his gratification.

It was all about sexual pleasure—serial, uninterrupted, unremitting.

And only the end of the races at Newmarket brought their idyll to a close.

Chapter
9

"Please, no, don't!" Elspeth pushed at Darley's chest. "You'll muss my hair and you only just fixed it and Grafton might be home already. He could tell in a minute if he saw my disarray! Don't, I beg of you!"

"One last kiss." Darley grinned. "I won't touch you."

"I shouldn't, I shouldn't—there . . . now no more." She reached for the handle on the carriage door, flustered and anxious and desperately in love like an untried young maid who had found true bliss in the arms of a handsome young man.

Not that Darley couldn't enchant women of any age, not that she wasn't more susceptible than most considering her wretched circumstances. Not that the marquis hadn't been on his best behavior.

"Come see me tomorrow or I'll come for you."

Arrested in the act of exiting the carriage, she stared at him with horror. "Don't even think of it!"

"I'll have someone take Grafton to the races again." It was just a question of money and if Amanda couldn't, he'd find someone else.

"He won't go out two days in a row. He never does."

"Watch me, ye of little faith."

"You're mad. It *can't* be done. And please, consider my position. I have my brother to support."

"I won't jeopardize you *or* your brother. And Grafton is just as likely to fall to Amanda's lure as any other man."

"Why would she do this?" Even as Elspeth spoke, she knew she had no right to take that tone.

"We've been friends a long time." His voice was deliberately bland.

"And she owes you favors." Stepping down to the ground, Elspeth half turned. "You must have been very nice to her at some point." She couldn't restrain her jealousy. "Although now that I realize how nice you can be," she coolly said, "I shouldn't be surprised."

"It's not like that. We grew up together," the marquis lied. Or half lied. He and Amanda had grown up together, but they'd slept together, too. Particularly after her husband died—her widowhood merrier than most. Not that he was inclined to divulge any of those details. "Amanda's engaged to Francis Rhodes who's making his way in Pitt's ministry. I happen to know people who could be of assistance to him. So you see, it's a mutual arrangement. She helps me and I help her. But I guarantee you, Grafton will *not* be home tomorrow. So make plans to join me."

Elspeth's brows rose. "Is that an order?" After six months of marriage, she didn't take kindly to male authority.

"Let me reword that. I would be honored if you would join me at my home tomorrow. Whenever your schedule allows. I, however, will be waiting for you at the crack of dawn."

How could she refuse a day in bed with Darley? How could any female? "I'd really like to," she said, opting for pleasure however transient. "And I don't wish to appear difficult; I'm only cautious for all the obvious reasons."

"I understand. I'll be discreet. Amanda will be discreet." He smiled. "But Grafton will be gone in the morning and I'll be waiting for you."

He was offering her paradise, and after so long in the wilderness, she couldn't resist—danger or not. "I'll try," she softly agreed.

"I'll have strawberries for you."

"Oh, God, don't say that," she pleaded. "Truly—I may not be able to."

"In any event, I'll be home. Come if you can."

A moment later, he watched her run through the orchard toward the house and felt a curious sense of responsibility, as though her innocence demanded something more of him than his usual fleeting regard.

And perhaps it did.

She was not the worldly female with whom he generally amused himself. And with that difference had come previously untasted delights—the game of amour forever changed. Her smile was more enchanting, her fresh young body more sweet, her beguiling willingness a form of sorcery all its own. And if he had a guinea for every time she'd murmured, "Thank you *so* much," with a soft sigh, he could have set aside a tidy sum.

The gate to the walled kitchen garden opened and shut, Elspeth disappeared from sight, and he suddenly felt bereft. Forcing away the unusual sensation, he knocked on the carriage ceiling, signaling his driver to leave.

He wasn't a grass-green adolescent, he sternly reminded himself. Nor was he prone to fits of emotion. And lovely and enchanting as Elspeth was, he was scheduled to be in London next week. Putting his feelings in perspective, carpe diem a way of life for him, he considered instead how best to approach Amanda. He wanted her to entertain Grafton for another day; she wasn't likely to do that for less than a king's ransom.

He smiled into the sunlit interior.

Fortunately he had a king's ransom and more.

As Elspeth slipped into her sitting room to find Sophie waiting, arms folded and looking grim, she announced, "Before you chastise me, let me say I've not been this happy in years."

"Hmpf. As if that happiness is goin' to last."

"It doesn't matter if it lasts or not. Is Grafton back?" Elspeth began unbuttoning her jacket. "I have to change."

"He ain't back. At least you had sense enough to come home in good time. You smell like a harlot."

"But a very happy harlot, I'll have you know," Elspeth said with a glowing smile. "Darley's unutterably charming."

"Everyone knows that there man has charm to spare. The question is whether you can keep your wits about you and not have him ruin your life. Now, I've said my piece and I'm done. I'll see to your wash water. And toss that riding habit out o' sight. I'll clean it up later."

"Thank you, Sophie. For everything," Elspeth softly added, half dreamy as she leaned back against the door.

Her old nursemaid turned from the threshold of the dressing room. "I hope you don't go gettin' any notions 'bout fallin' in love with that rake. I'm not so sure you're not in too deep already with that wispy tone o' yer'n."

"Don't worry. I know who he is and what he is. But allow me this, Sophie, for however long it lasts, because I'm really, really happy."

"Of course, my darlin' baby." Sophie's eyes misted over. That her little girl was happy again was worth whatever the price. "Now we'll get you cleaned up," she briskly noted, "so no one will suspect nothin'. With the earl gone, the servants all bin out o'sight anyway—takin' the day off I'd say."

"He promised to have Grafton entertained tomorrow, too." She couldn't help but smile at the lovely prospect.

"Darley's right smart if'n he can do that. Old Grafton don't budge from home much."

"I'm hoping it all works out," Elspeth cheerfully explained, beginning to unbutton the waistband of her skirt.

"No doubt," Sophie said with a smile, having done her share of sparking in her youth. "Now move, young lady, and get cleaned up right quick. I wouldn't want Grafton suspicious if'n you're plannin' on escapin' agin tomorrow."

Chapter
10

"You're joking!"

"Not in the least. I thought you might like to become an heiress," Julius said, with a lazy smile.

Intensely frustrated after sidestepping Grafton's heavy-handed ardor all afternoon, Amanda had come to Darley's immediately after depositing Grafton at home. They were on their third brandy, the sun was low on the horizon, and Darley had just offered her a blank check to keep Grafton busy for the entire week of the Spring Meeting.

"The little miss must be spectacular."

Darley shrugged. "Just interesting."

"Interesting enough to pay a fortune to cuckold her husband. Not that it couldn't happen to a more deserving man." She gave Darley a narrowed glance over the rim of her glass. "He's a dead boor."

"Then you deserve a bonus."

"I deserve a bonus *and* your undivided attention tonight."

"Name your price on the bonus. As for the other, I can't."

Amanda smiled slyly. "So she wore you out. Maybe you *are* past your prime, darling."

He'd never live down the gossip if he told her the truth—that he wasn't interested in casual sex tonight. "Didn't I tell you as much yesterday? The time comes for everyone."

"I'm not sure I believe it after our recent carnal romp." She shrugged. "But perhaps I'll take you at your word since you're willing to be so *extremely* generous."

"Extremely is the operative word. *If* Grafton takes a new interest in the races this week."

Amanda groaned. "You know I wouldn't have to do this if I didn't have such sizeable obligations."

"You shouldn't gamble with the Duchess of Devonshire. She plays too high. You can't afford it."

"She can't either."

"So I understand. But I'm willing to discharge your debts for you and I doubt the duchess's husband will."

Amanda's brows rose. "He'd have to know about them first."

"If I know, he knows. So name the sum you require and add the cost of a new wardrobe from your mantua-maker. I'll need you for five days, all told," he declared.

"I can't believe we're actually having this conversation. You've never been enamored and don't look at me like that; either you're enamored, Darley, or so simple some virginal young miss has turned your head. Which I seriously doubt—the part about you being simple. It's not possible for a rake of your stature to fall so low. So tell me what she has? I'm infinitely curious."

He sighed. "I don't know why she appeals. I'd tell you if I knew. Fortunately, I don't need a reason for what I'm doing. No more than you need a reason for throwing away money you don't have playing faro."

"Point taken. We're both selfish and impulsive."

He ignored her inference. "Tell my steward where to send the bank draft," he said, instead, lifting his glass in salute. "And thank you."

"Thank *you*. Did I mention Grafton is going to the soiree at the Jockey Club rooms tonight?"

"With his wife?" Straightening from his lazy sprawl, Darley held her gaze.

"He didn't say."

"Did he ask you if you were going?"

"I told him I might when I have no intention of doing so if he's going to be there. And there's no point in turning that charming smile on me, Darley. If I'm obliged to bear Grafton's baleful company all day at the races, I shan't for any sum of money ruin my evenings as well."

Amanda's tone indicated firm resolve. Nor could he ask so much of a woman who enjoyed amorous evenings more than most. "Perhaps I'll stop by the Jockey Club rooms later," Julius murmured. "It can't hurt to do my bit for the club coffers and play a game or two."

"And romance your lady love between hands?" Amanda coyly inquired.

"Not romance so much as"—recalling his refusal of Amanda's sexual overtures, he opted for a more politic reply than the blunt carnal word on the tip of his tongue. "In a way it is romancing I suppose," he said instead. "Considering the venue."

"Not that that's ever stopped you before." Her gaze was amused. "You have a reputation for finding the most convenient—or should I say inconvenient—places to fornicate. I doubt you'll ever live down the story about the little French duchess and you at Lucinda's masked ball."

"Can I help it if the door latch didn't hold?"

"Darling, why you even thought you were safe in Lucinda's bedchamber is beyond me."

Because he'd just fucked Lucinda and knew she'd returned to her guests wouldn't be a gentlemanly response. How was he to know she'd come back for her fan? "That all happened a long time ago."

"Lucinda still isn't talking to you. Nor her husband for that matter."

"If you wish to dredge up old scandals," he murmured, "might I mention the time you and Fairfax didn't have enough sense to—"

"Enough said," she quickly interjected. "Fill my glass and we'll lay our plans for tomorrow."

Chapter

11

Elspeth turned from the dressing room window, a small frown creasing her brow. "Help me think of some excuse to avoid dinner. I'm not in the mood for another evening of Grafton's rudeness."

Sophie shook her head and drew out a gown from the armoire. "He don't like excuses. You know that. Jes turn your thoughts to somethin' else during dinner. I doubt he'll notice you're a-musing seein' how he likes the sound o' his own voice best. Now, come, put on this gown."

Elspeth sighed. "I've only been married six months and it seems like six hundred."

"The way the earl's a-drinkin' he won't last long, sweetie."

"I don't know if I should pray you're right or chastise myself for being so unfeeling about another human being," Elspeth replied, moving toward Sophie.

"You're nicer than he deserves and that's a fact, and if it's any consolation to you, all the servants agree. The last wife locked herself in her rooms after a month and took laudanum until she didn't wake up one mornin'. At least you're keeping your wits about you. Look at the bright side, dearie. Mayhap he'll be in his cups agin tonight and fall asleep in his puddin'."

"I shall try to look at the bright side," Elspeth said with a small sigh. Although after an afternoon of such glorious pleasure, an evening in Grafton's company seemed almost insupportable.

"That's a good girl. I'll remind Georgie to keep fillin' the old man's cup."

"And I'll count the minutes until dinner's over." Telling herself there were many other women in circumstances no better than hers didn't have the same soothing impact as it had in the past. Having once tasted from the cup of happiness, she found her home life even more joyless. But she dressed and went downstairs as she should, as was her obligation. She couldn't, however, force herself to like it.

She'd no more than entered the dining room than Grafton announced that they were going to a soiree at the Jockey Club—the information eliciting a reaction in her of both delight and disgust.

That she might see Darley again filled her with elation.

On the other hand, she would be required to spend a long evening with Grafton. Not a pleasant thought when she'd anticipated a quick dinner and escape to her apartments.

"I want to be at the Jockey Club by nine," he brusquely added, snapping his fingers to signal the footmen to begin serving even before she'd reached the table. "And you'll have to change from that schoolgirlish gown. I detest it. Wear the new blue one with the pearl embroidery. Sit, blast it, we don't have much time."

It took every ounce of tact she possessed to acquiesce when she would have preferred throwing all the plates on the table at him. Reminding herself of all the civil maxims she'd been taught, reminding herself as well of the reason she was married to the rude, crude man she called husband, she sat. It won't be forever, she told herself. It can't be . . . or she'd go mad.

Shortly after ten, Julius and Charles entered the small assembly room at the Jockey Club and, standing in the doorway, surveyed the crowd. The crush was considerable, additional race goers having arrived in town for the match tomorrow between the Prince of Wales's black and Burlingame's champion roan.

"I don't see her," Charles said, scanning the throng.

"I'm not sure you're sober enough to see anyone."

"Since when have you become a presbyterian? We always drink through race week. Oh, I forgot," the viscount said with a conspicuous leer. "You were in bed all day with a virginal maid who'd rather do something other than drink."

"Keep your voice down," Julius muttered. It wasn't as though *he'd* told Charles of his rendezvous. Amanda couldn't wait to divulge the news when the viscount had stopped by.

"My lips are sealed." Charles made a broad, sloppy, crisscross motion over his mouth, nearly hitting Julius in the process.

"Why don't I find you a seat in the card room and I'll join you later."

"Won't be able to mount her here, my boy, even if you find her. Too damned many people."

"Thank you for the observation," Julius said drily. "There's Newcastle." He nodded toward the card room. "He plays high enough even for you."

"No point in playing for tuppence," Charles bluntly declared. "Damned waste of time."

Guiding Charles through the crowd, Julius deposited him at Newcastle's table, exchanged greetings with the table at large, and making some excuse about seeing some friends of his sister, he quickly retreated.

"Friends of his sister? Since when?" Newcastle said, his arched brows indicating his skepticism.

"Since he met some sweet young miss who shall remain nameless." Charles tapped the green baize tabletop. "Deal me in."

"If Darley's toying with her, she won't remain nameless for long," one of the men noted. "Not with his reputation. The broadsheets follow his every exploit."

"By the time her identity is discovered, he'll be on to the next one anyway." The man who spoke was smiling. "More power to him."

"Takes one to know one, eh, Durham?"

"They can say no if they wish." The Earl of Durham tipped his head faintly. "And I expect Darley's little lady is willing like all the rest. In fact, I wonder if he's tried that new girl at—"

"Darley doesn't need any help with his sex life," Charles interrupted, tossing two cards away. "I, however, need some decent cards. Give me two more, Newcastle—and make them good this time."

Conversation turned to whose luck was best, or rather what bets everyone was willing to place on the next hand, and Darley's newest pursuit was forgotten.

In the meantime, that new pursuit was standing stiffly beside her husband's Bath chair, half hidden from sight by a case of race trophies. She had a blinding headache from biting back the numerous responses she couldn't possibly utter as her husband harangued her for everything from standing too close to not smiling enough. Her smile was so stiff now she felt as though her face might crack as she listened once again to the earl lament the fact that he hadn't caught sight of Lady Bloodworth when she'd said with certainty that she would be here tonight.

"Dammit, go and find her!" he snapped, shoving Elspeth forward. "And be quick about it!"

She made her escape, seething with anger and frustration. Forced to serve as panderer for her husband, she bridled with indignation. Was there no end to her humiliation? How high a price was she required to pay for Will's future?

With a headache pounding in her brain so violently tears filled her eyes, she mindlessly pushed through the crowd, neither caring nor cognizant of her surroundings, wanting only to find some quiet corner in which to hide.

"Pardon me," she murmured without looking up, turning away from whomever she'd bumped into, desperately needing to escape.

"Come this way."

The voice was low and familiar, an arm was slipped around her shoulder, protecting her from the jostling crowd, and when she looked up and saw Darley's smile, she suddenly felt comforted.

"I've been looking for you," he murmured, as he guided her toward the adjacent hallway. "You've been hiding."

She grimaced. "I wish I could."

"Let me arrange it," he said with a wink. "Just give me the word."

She laughed, the joyful sound easing the chill in her soul. "What you can arrange is a quiet corner for me—for five minutes. I can't be gone long."

"Are you fetching him a drink again?" he asked, leading her down the hallway, the noise of the party fading behind them.

"I have orders to find Lady Bloodworth. Grafton thinks she's waiting to see him here, tonight."

"She's not, but we don't have to tell him that yet. Let's take advantage of your five minutes first." Opening a door, he waved her inside.

"Do you know where you are?" She surveyed the small office.

"Away from the crowd." He grinned. "And with very limited time."

"With my husband in the next room, there's *no* time," she quellingly noted.

"There's time for a kiss."

His smile was very close. "Don't tempt me."

"It's only fair. You're tempting the hell out of me." Her gown's décolletage was very low, her breasts on display as was the fashion, and the urge to gently lift the plump, soft mounds from their blue silk underpinnings was almost overwhelming. He gently brushed the satiny curves visible above the ruffled neckline, slipped a fingertip down her deep cleavage and felt her warm flesh close around it. "No one would know if I kissed these," he murmured. "I wouldn't muss your hair or bruise your lips or leave any evidence behind."

"Don't start, Darley." But the image he'd provoked was doing disastrous things to her pulse rate. "Really"—she pushed at his chest—"it's impossible."

Her hands on his chest were lightly placed, the likelihood of actually moving him with the delicate pressure she was exerting negligible. A fact duly noted by the marquis. "Nothing will show under your gown—even if your nipples like my kisses," he whispered, taking her hands in his, moving them downward, holding them at her sides. "That fall of lace"—he flicked a glance downward to her bodice—"covers everything."

"Darley—please . . . I can't let you . . . not now."

But her voice was hushed, her words equivocal as though timing alone was the liability and most compelling—she swayed toward him as if in invitation.

At least he took it as invitation.

Releasing her hands, he gently cupped her shoulders and eased her sleeves down her arms, exposing the rising swell of her breasts—perfect orbs raised high not by artifice or corsets but by robust nature.

"Stop—please, please, please," she whispered.

And if her hips weren't undulating against his erection in gross negation of her plea he might have. "This won't take long."

The deep, sonorous authority in his tone, the explicit denial however hushed vibrated in the pulsing core of her body and she shivered.

His erection surged higher.

Briefly censoring himself for responding so barbarously to her innocent longing, he fleetingly debated doing as she asked. Very fleetingly. But his engorged penis was rock hard and against that brutal surety, ethical considerations didn't stand a chance. Sliding his fingers between the lace bordering her décolletage and her lush bosom, he slipped his hands under her breasts and with swift deftness freed them from the confining blue silk. Balancing the opulent weight in his palms, he lifted them slightly, forcing them upward into huge, curvaceous spheres, watching as the nipples turned from blush pink to a deep rose before his eyes. "They want to be kissed," he whispered.

Eyes shut, she shook her head, as though child-like she could ignore her tumultuous desires.

"Look at them," he murmured, his voice soft as velvet. "Your nipples are taut and hard. They need to be sucked."

She shook her head again, her eyes still shut, but she was panting in little muted utterances that made it perfectly clear he was
right and she was wrong. And if time wasn't a problem, he might
have pressed her to acknowledge the truth. But the possibility of
someone walking in was considerable and more important, he
had plans beyond these transient moments. The lady could come
to terms with her carnal appetites in a more leisured milieu.

Tomorrow—at his race box.

When not only her lust, but his, could be adequately quenched.

In the meantime, he was more than willing to oblige the lady's
unrecognized desires and bending his head, he slowly drew a
nipple into his mouth.

She didn't resist, but then he was certain she wouldn't, and he
suckled her with infinite gentleness and finesse in deference to
her present fears. But when after a very short time, she jabbed
her fingers into his hair and pulled his head closer, he understood
gentleness was no longer required. He suckled harder, tugged on
the taut crest, nibbled and softly bit and just as he was about to
move to the other breast, her little breathy pants transmuted into
a suppressed wail—and before he'd even utilized his full repertoire—she abruptly climaxed.

How could she, how could she, how could she, silently shrieked
through her mind—with the sound of previously unheard violins
drifting into the room, with the possibility of detection imminent, with the very real chance of being *discovered* in the midst of
an *orgasm!*

Her knees went weak at all the possible disasters she'd *ignored!*

Catching her in his arms, Darley carried her to a wooden chair
while she trembled in fear.

"Someone might come in," she whispered.

"The door's locked," he lied. Not that he'd been unaware of the
possibility of an intruder. But unlike the lady—sexually aroused
or not—he always kept his wits. "No one can come in," he said,
sitting down and cradling her in his lap. And if they did, he was
relatively certain he could intimidate them.

Giving herself up to his comforting guarantees, she leaned against his chest and, emitting little sighs of pleasure, basked in the delicious afterglow of orgasm.

For a man who had refined personal gratification to an art, he found himself experiencing an uncharacteristic degree of pleasure as well—as though selflessly giving her the ultimate delight was enough. He felt a curious satisfaction quite separate from orgasmic release and he wondered whether a vicar's daughter exerted a special kind of sorcery distinct from lust.

"You're going to spoil me for the real world," she whispered, lifting her lashes enough to meet his gaze. "I'm not going to want to lose this feeling."

"I'll come for you early tomorrow." He grinned. "We'll have all day to satisfy your amorous inclinations."

"When is he leaving?"

"At nine." She'd made up her mind, he thought, when this afternoon she'd been indecisive—although an orgasm was the very best kind of persuasion.

"Then, I wouldn't wish to anger him. I'd better go." Sitting up, she began rearranging her bodice.

"I'll be waiting early," he simply said, helping to put her gown in order before lifting her to her feet. "Although I wish you could stay with me tonight."

"Wouldn't that be wonderful," she murmured, the sight of Darley's arousal stretching the fine wool of his breeches inciting a new throbbing between her legs. Quickly backing away before she did something outrageously stupid, she kept her gaze on his face. "If you'd stay here until I'm well away, I'd appreciate it. I can't afford any problems," she nervously added.

Whether he'd taken note of her crotch glance or was of a more practical bent, he calmly said, "I'll leave by the back door and go home. I only came here to find you anyway."

Flattery like that could turn a lady's head, Elspeth thought, tamping down the giddy enchantment warming her senses, telling herself sex was sex with Darley and it wouldn't pay to forget that cold reality. She turned at the door, however, because even if sex was just sex for him, he'd opened up a whole world of lush pleasure for her and she was grateful. "I forgot to say thank you." She couldn't help but smile. "I shall remember this soiree with great fondness."

"You can thank me tomorrow when there's more reason," he said, coming to his feet, his smile roguish.

She quickly shut the door and walked away, knowing if Darley had come any closer, she might have thrown herself into his arms and forgotten everything but hot desire.

The marquis circled the small room several times after she'd gone, out of deference to her wishes not to be seen with him, caught in the grip of a restive agitation as well. Hours yet until morning—damnably long hours until he could assuage his lust. Although something other than lust was at play here, too. Something more complicated than fevered sensation and explosive climaxes. Something he wasn't sure he wished to acknowledge considering his largely self-indulgent, profligate life.

He'd only just met her, he told himself, as though the newness and novelty was explanation for his unusual feelings. Or perhaps he was simply overreacting to her rare innocence and highly sensual nature.

That combination didn't come into his life every day.

There.

A sensible explanation for his sharp-set craving.

A logical reason for not being able to walk away.

With time though, he'd have his fill.

He always did.

And the Spring Meet only lasted a week.

Elspeth was terrified everyone in the assembly rooms would take one look at her and know she'd been indiscreet. Or if not a look, a smell—the scent of arousal still intense in her nostrils . . . the humid carnal reek drifting about her like vaporous dishonor. Taking care not to stand too close to her husband, she stopped distant enough to allow her scent to mingle with others in the crush. "I wasn't able to find Lady Bloodworth," she said, adding the information Darley had given her. "I was told by one of her friends that she's home with her aunt tonight."

"Hell and damnation!" Grafton scowled, his overgrown brows meeting over the ridge of his bulbous nose, his jowls quivering in frustration. "Damnable waste of time to come here. You." He jerked his thumb at Elspeth. "Wait in the carriage. I might as well play a hand or two of cards as long as I've bothered to come."

His discourtesy struck no distressing nerve tonight, Elspeth's entire body immune to the collective insult of the world in her current blissful state with pleasures past and future filling her mind. Thanks to the Marquis of Darley. Thanks particularly to his expert mouth and tongue, she thought with an inner smile, and to even more unrestricted access to his virile body tomorrow.

"What the hell are you smiling about?" her husband snarled.

Perhaps even inner smiles couldn't be contained when one was enveloped by bliss. "That's such a delightful tune the orchestra is playing," she pleasantly said, her butter-wouldn't-melt-in-her-mouth tone in accord with her pleasure-sated mood.

"Damned rackety noise if you ask me," the earl grumbled. Snapping his fingers for his footman, he jerked his head toward the card room.

As his footman wheeled the earl away, young Tom Scott flicked a glance at Elspeth's shoulder, tipped his head faintly and said, "There's a wrap in the carriage, ma'am—for the evening coolness."

Looking down, Elspeth caught her breath. A single dark hair lay on her shoulder, the trailing end tangled in the lace of her décolletage. Quickly plucking it up, she curled it in her fist.

She should throw it away. Evidence like that could be damning.

But she tucked it in her cleavage instead—in fond memory.

As for Tom, he was Sophie's favorite.

He could be trusted.

He was also very helpful; she'd cover herself in the shawl and cloak the odor of illicit sex on the carriage ride back home.

The only thing Darley would find helpful at the moment was an orgasm; he was going to masturbate the second he reached his race box. It was all well and good to be self-sacrificing and well-behaved for very brief periods of time.

That interval having come and gone, he was about ready to explode.

Immediately he entered his foyer, he strode to his library, walked in, shut the door and crossed the room to the divan where he'd so recently made love to the incomparable Elspeth. Without even taking off his boots, he sprawled on the sofa, unbuttoned his breeches and his linen small clothes   worn tonight in deference to the light wool fabric of his evening clothes that revealed more than utilitarian breeches. Impatient after his hindered encounter with Elspeth at the Jockey Club, his fingers moved swiftly, and wrenching out his aching cock, his hand closed around the stiff shaft. His grip had barely tightened for the first downstroke when he went off half-cocked like some puerile, horny adolescent and shot a catapulting spume of come across the carpet.

Now if only his randiness had been assuaged by that split-second climax, he might not have felt the urge to heave the nearest thing to hand—his new bloodstock book—at the window.

Fortunately, the iron mullions took the brunt of his rage, the book tumbling to the window seat below.

Swearing, he cast a black look at the clock.

Dammit, ten hours to go and he was still horny as hell.

Fuck.

He reached for the brandy decanter.

Chapter
12

Elspeth stayed in bed the next morning until she heard Grafton's carriage roll down the drive, half thinking by staying there she might resist Darley's dangerous temptation. Although if her sleepless night was any indication of his potent allure, she was waging a losing battle. But she didn't stir when Sophie came into the room, pretending to sleep, hoping she might somehow gain some inner strength by the sheer act of not moving.

If only she were able to stop thinking about how indescribably glorious it felt to climax.

If only she didn't want to feel Darley's strong, potent body over her and around her and in her.

If only. If only.

A little flutter rippled up her vagina as though in answer to her quandary.

An impossible-to-ignore flutter. A screaming-for-orgasm flutter.

She opened her eyes and glanced at the clock.

Five minutes after nine; she'd resisted five entire minutes.

Indication perhaps of Darley's sexual talents.

Indication as well of her numerous wet dreams last night.

"You're awake," Sophie said, standing at the foot of the bed with a breakfast tray. "Are you stayin' or goin'?"

"I was really trying to stay." Elspeth threw the covers aside. "Truly I was. All night and particularly since dawn." (When she could no longer sleep and consequently no longer dream, her fierce sexual cravings intensifying as a result). She swung her legs over the side of the bed and slid to the floor. "I'm going, though."

"Hmpf, as if I didn't know. Well, he's out there already, so you'd best make yerself presentable."

"He's here!"

"Out back of the orchard since the crack o' dawn," Sophie muttered. Although it pleased her that the marquis was as excited to see her little girl as she was him. And if an old woman was allowed to let her imagination go wild, she wanted even more from the marquis. Not that she'd gone completely daft, but it never hurt to hope. Grafton was old, he drank himself to oblivion every night and he'd already had one apoplexy. If there was a God, he'd have another. "Yer bath is piping hot, sweetie. And I laid out your nice yellow muslin seein' how it's a right sunny day. Ye go and enjoy yerself and don't have a care."

"Thank you, Sophie. I think I will," Elspeth cheerfully replied, her uncertainties neatly stowed away, her old nursemaid's acceptance the final validation to her day of frolic.

She saw him standing by a gleaming black phaeton when she walked through the garden gate, his calm strength visible even from a distance. He stood utterly still, self-reliant and assured, a man confident of his place in the world. And today he was hers, she thought with a small eager thrill that overlooked all but the rapture of the moment.

He caught sight of her and waved.

Her heart leaped and she waved back, tears of happiness stinging her eyes.

Not caring if he was seen, he hastened to her and she to him. And when they met, he swung her up in his arms and twirled her around and kissed her and told her how much he'd missed her.

It was all so perfect she started to cry.

"I'm sorry, I'm sorry," he whispered, coming to a standstill, kissing her some more. "I don't want you to be sad."

"I'm not—never, never—not with you." Hiccuping and sniffling, she tried to smile.

"Tell me what to do," he murmured, always at a loss with tears.

"Take me away."

He almost said where and meant it, the feel of her in his arms perfection, the thought of taking her away from her restricted world tempting.

Aware of his hesitation (men like the marquis dealt only in transience) she quickly covered her faux pas. "I meant to your race box, Darley." She managed a flirtatious smile because her happiness was at stake. "Did I frighten you?"

"No."

He'd answered without hesitation this time, she noticed, no further clarification required. "In that case, shall we go?" she lightly said, gesturing toward his phaeton. She wasn't about to give up what Darley had to offer, nor quibble over playing the role of co-quette if necessary. She understood very well that it was a man's world. Had it not been, she would have been living on a Greek isle long ago.

"By all means," he said with a smile, striding toward the phaeton, dismissing all the complexities with the ease of considerable practice. "I brought you something."

Was this where she said, *You shouldn't have, I couldn't, really?* And for a fraction of a second, she almost mouthed the words. But as they approached the phaeton, she saw a small black velvet box on the leather seat and instead, squealed in delight.

He laughed. "You haven't seen it yet."

"I'm excited, that's all." She couldn't say she'd never had a present in such a distinctive velvet box.

"It's just something small," he said, lifting her up onto the high seat. "Take a look."

As he walked around the carriage, she lifted the hinged top

and squealed again. On a bed of white satin lay the most gorgeous diamond and sapphire bracelet she'd ever seen. Of course she'd seen very few this close. None, in fact. The earl wasn't the kind of man to spend money on a wife's jewels, and her family hadn't been able to afford expensive baubles. "It's absolutely beautiful," Elspeth breathed, as Darley leaped up into his seat and gathered up the reins. But she understood, covetousness aside, she couldn't accept something so expensive. All the principles of a lifetime warned her off. "Much as I'd like to have something this lovely, I really can't—"

"Nonsense; it's the smallest trinket." He gave the matched pair of bays their head and the light phaeton sprang forward. Catching the jewelry box as it slid out of her lap, the marquis snapped it shut and handed it to her. "Wear it and think of me."

As if she wouldn't think of him without a diamond bracelet, she reflected, clutching the velvet box in one hand and the seat rail with the other. "We can discuss it later," she said in way of avoidance, more concerned at the moment with maintaining her balance on the high, perched seat. "If I'm still alive when we reach your house," she added, hanging on for dear life.

Holding the reins in his left hand, Darley slipped his arm around her and pulled her close. "Don't worry," he said with a grin. "I definitely want you alive. I have plans." His bays racing at top speed, he maneuvered a curve with finesse, his hand light on the reins. "This pair loves to run." He tipped his head and kissed her on the cheek. "Aren't they beauties?"

"I've been too busy writing my will now that I have a diamond bracelet to bequeath to notice," she muttered, willing the horses to remain sure-footed on the rough country lane.

"Practical woman," he said with a flashing smile.

"Keep your eyes on the road if you don't mind. And I'm not taking the bracelet; it was only idle banter to distract me from dying."

The vicar's daughter never ceased to amaze him. She was sincere about not keeping the bracelet. A radical departure from the women of his acquaintance. "Why don't I slow down." Darley's skill with women wasn't entirely the result of practice; he was intuitive if he chose to be.

Within seconds, the horses were sedately cantering, the hedgerows and trees ceased to fly by in a blur and Elspeth's pulse rate was considering returning to normal. "Do you always drive hell-for-leather?" she asked, releasing her white-knuckled hold on the seat rail.

"I like speed. That's why I love racing. And thoroughbreds."

"And winning all the prominent races." Darley could live well on his race winnings alone.

He shrugged. "I like to win. Don't you?"

"My options are more limited than yours."

He gave her a narrow-eyed glance. "They don't have to be. Let me give you a loan if you won't take funds outright. You'll have options in your life, your brother will be solvent; you might find independence to your liking."

"All it takes is money. Is that it?"

"Don't get touchy, darling. No one needs a fortune, but a certain competence helps."

"And you're the banker for all the improvident ladies in your life?"

"Not usually," he said, because most of the ladies in his life were married to other men and didn't need his money. Sexual amusements came second only to gambling in the aristocracy.

"So I'm the only poor church mouse," Elspeth testily remarked.

"I don't like seeing you with Grafton. You should have a damned sight better life." His vehemence startled him. "Although I'm in no position to give unwanted advice," he added, reining in his aberrant emotions. "Forgive me."

"Could we just not discuss this?" Her voice was cool.

"Yes, of course." His was equally cool; the solution to her problems could have been handled very simply with a bank draft.

"Thank you."

"You're welcome."

The pounding of the horses' hooves, the muted creak of the phaeton springs were suddenly loud in the dappled sunlight, a palpable tension in the air.

"I don't know about you," she finally said, "but I get out so seldom, I dislike quarreling on my holiday." She offered him a conciliatory smile. "Paix?"

He smiled back, forgiving her easy. "It was my fault entirely."

"Yes, it was. You're too wealthy, Darley. That's your problem. Oh, dear, I shouldn't have said that when I meant to be—"

"Submissive?"

"I beg your pardon." Her blue gaze turned heated again.

"Darling, stop, stop—I apologize . . . for having teased you, for my wealth, and anything else that displeases you."

"I might require something more than an apology." She half smiled, back in good humor again after such a blanket concession. "Something more substantial."

"How substantial?" he drawled, innuendo in every syllable.

"The issue isn't how much but when," she replied with a sportive flicker of her brows.

"We *could* stop here."

"If only I shared your exhibitionist tendencies we might," she drolly noted.

"Then I'm afraid you'll have to wait."

She pouted prettily. "Not too long I hope. Did I mention I dreamed of you again last night?"

He almost pulled the phaeton off the road right there, the thought of her wet dreams, of her hot, sweet pussy needing him, almost irresistible. "The grass is cool; I guarantee no one will see us." He nodded toward a clearing ahead.

She made a moue. "I just wouldn't be comfortable."

Having had considerable experience with making women forget about comfort in a variety of locales, he debated arguing with her. But she wasn't an exhibitionist, she'd said. On the other hand, he definitely wasn't a monk. "Hold on," he said crisply, cracked the whip and set his pair into a tearing gallop.

* * *

As the phaeton careened into the drive behind Darley's house, they saw a coach and four being unloaded, the team being led away, and several servants in the process of transferring trunks and parcels inside.

Recognizing the coat of arms on the coach, the marquis groaned and immediately began making alternate plans that didn't include visiting with his sister and her two children. In fact, he was in the process of turning the phaeton and answering Elspeth's query about the coach's owner, when a female voice called out, "Julius, darling, over here! Julius—halloo—halloo—over here!"

Bringing the phaeton to a halt, he silently ran through a number of possibilities that might ease the moment, none of which fully served the purpose. "Would you like to meet my sister?" he asked, opting for bluntness.

"God, no—I couldn't! Don't look at me like that—it's impossible!"

"Betsy's understanding as hell. Really. She won't mind at all."

"But I will! Good God, how embarrassing, not to mention scandalous!"

"She's not concerned with scandal. Nor should you be."

"These encounters may happen to you every day of the week, but they don't to me! I can't be blase about meeting someone I don't know under these—highly irregular circumstances."

It had been a very long night, a longer morning waiting for nine o'clock, and when it came to winning, Darley preferred *winning*. And right now that meant *not* wasting a perfectly good day in bed with a very desirable woman simply because he'd forgotten his sister was coming up for the races.

Normally, Betsy's visits didn't interfere with his life, his liaisons conducted outside his home. With the exception of Amanda who prevailed on their long-standing friendship to walk in uninvited, he made sure his paramours understood his privacy was sacrosanct.

"Uncle Julius," a high-pitched little girl voice proclaimed. "You're back! See, Harry, I told you he'd be here!"

"Unka Ju, Unka Ju," a second childish voice cried. "Look, look at me!"

At their shouts, the marquis observed his niece and nephew, their heads just peeking out from behind the remaining luggage on the coach. "I have to go talk to Annie and Harry," he murmured. "I'll be right back."

"And then we'll leave."

He nodded. "I'll be back in a minute."

"What about them?" Elspeth pointed at the spirited team.

"They're trained to wait. You're safe." Jumping to the ground, he looped the reins around the whip and walked away.

Easy to say, Elspeth nervously thought, surveying the powerful bays and then the distance to the ground, debating how best to save herself should they bolt. But a moment later, her worries about safety faded into oblivion against a much larger fear. Darley's sister was walking from the rose garden and she was headed directly toward the phaeton.

Chapter

13

"Hullo." Betsy smiled. "I thought you were Georgina Blake. I saw your blond hair. I'm Betsy, Julius's sister. It's a lovely day for a drive, isn't it?"

Her smile was like Darley's. Warm and intimate even to strangers. "Yes, it's a lovely day," Elspeth replied and then fell silent, not sure how to converse with a member of Julius's family when she was about as far outside the family circle as one could be.

"Don't let us deter your plans. Julius always forgets we're coming, but he's easygoing when it comes to guests—although I'm sure you know that. We'll find our own entertainments. Ah, they found you," she said, turning to Julius who was approaching, the children holding his hands. "We came early." His sister laughed. "You forgot we were coming at all, didn't you?" She looked up at Elspeth. "As usual, I might add." Redirecting her gaze to her brother who she resembled in coloring, her diminutive form and prettiness a female version of the D'Abernon good looks, she said, "Don't worry, Julius, we can manage very well here without you. Don't let us interfere with your plans." Obviously he was engaged in some illicit assignation if the lady wouldn't give her name. The girl didn't wear a bonnet, although her gown was elegant. Was she some country girl with a hand-me-down gown? A married one apparently with that ring on her finger.

"We were just stopping by for a minute. Why don't I see you at dinner tonight?" Julius suggested.

"Will you be at the races? Prinny's telling everyone he's going to win."

"Perhaps later," Julius noted, stooping down to talk to the children. "Tell your mother to show you the cabinet in the library—the one with the glass doors. There's something in there for both of you."

"A present!" Annie screamed.

"A toy!" Harry shrieked.

"You'll have to go and find out for yourself," Julius said, coming upright with a smile, the children already streaking off toward the house.

Annie was outstripping her younger brother; Harry was shouting for her to wait, his little toddler legs churning like pistons.

"I'd better go supervise." Betsy grinned. "Before they wreck your library. Have a nice drive."

"I'll see you this evening," the marquis said. "Tell cook your wishes for dinner." With a nod, he walked to the phaeton and leaped into his high seat.

Betsy waved and turned to follow her children.

"That was embarrassing," Elspeth murmured.

"I came back as quickly as I could when I saw Betsy moving your way. You should have introduced yourself." He'd been close enough to hear the women's conversation. "My sister understands the ways of the world."

"Or more aptly, understands your way of life."

"I doubt even Yorkshire is sheltered from the conduct of the Ton. I'm not the only one, believe me." He could have said your husband is out with a woman as we speak, but chose politesse instead. "I know an out-of-the-way little inn where we can enjoy some privacy now that Betsy has altered our plans."

"I'm not sure. Someone might see me."

"It's up to you. But it's a very small village that happens to be on one of my properties. I know everyone and everyone knows me."

"And you bring women there all the time."

"I go there fishing."

"Forgive me. I shouldn't take issue with your style of pleasure," she said, embarrassed by her fit of jealousy when she'd known Darley for a total of two days. "I must seem very naive to you."

He didn't say he was familiar with female jealousy, no more than he said hers was oddly charming. He said instead, "I like your naivete. One sees very little of it in the Ton. And if it eases your conscience, I can offer you complete security from prying eyes. Meg and Beckett who run the inn are salt of the earth people who only see goodness in the world. That's probably one of the reasons I go there so often and fish. Where else can I find such genuine incorruptibility. Certainly not among the haute monde."

"I can't picture you fishing."

"Then we'll fish—I'll show you. In fact," he said with a twinkle in his eyes, "perhaps I might induce you to consider the merits of making love in the green grass beside a gently flowing river."

She smiled. "You make it sound very idyllic."

"I can make it more than idyllic," he said with a roguish grin. "I can make it orgasmic."

"Yes, you can." She looked away for a moment, letting the green countryside, the warm sunshine and birdsong flood her senses. "At the risk of appearing completely ingenuous," she said, turning back to him, "you can do any number of things to bring me happiness. I don't wish to alarm you with my candor," she quickly added, his eyes taking on a shuttered look. "I know very well the pleasure you offer is impermanent. My circumstances allow no more in any case. So there, I've said my piece and I'm done. And if you still wish to take me fishing or anywhere else this fine sunny day, I'm available."

Such frankness didn't often come his way. The ladies with whom he amused himself understood the rules. One of which was to never expose your true feelings—an indictment perhaps of the brittle world in which he lived. And now here was this art- less young woman revealing herself as simply as a child. Not that she was child-like in any other way. Not that he would turn down her company while he still had breath in his body. And to that end, he said, "I'm not alarmed—I'm flattered, and if you like, why don't we test the bed in the Red Lion first and go fishing second?"

Her smile was pure sunshine. "I'd like that."

"We'll have Meg make one of her incomparable strawberry tarts to go with the fish we catch, and with luck, my cache of hock there is still sufficient to add to our luncheon."

"You think of everything, don't you? I was afraid I was going to have to go hungry."

"If you want something, just ask. If you want Meg to make you some special dish, we'll have her do it. She's a very good cook; she was mine in London before she met Beckett." He smiled. "I probably shouldn't have had Beckett bring me fish from Bishop Glen so often and I'd still have my cook. And for your information, I haven't brought a lady there before." He wouldn't have had to say it; with anyone else he probably won't have. But she encouraged a simple honesty with her forthright manner. And at base, he found he wished to please her.

"You don't have to say that."

"It's the truth."

"Really?"

"Ask Meg."

"I couldn't. But thank you. What a nice thing to say."

But a short time later, after they'd exchanged greetings with the proprietors of the Red Lion, agreed the weather was lovely, the fish were jumping, Darley's room was ready at the top of the stairs, the marquis said, "Tell her, Meg. Tell her I've never brought a lady here before."

"He ain't never and that's the truth," Meg said, taking even more notice of Elspeth. Not that she hadn't scrutinized her closely already since Darley had made it known on more than one occasion that his room at the inn was his own private hermitage—no guests were allowed. "He bin comin' here for near on a decade, he has and always alone."

"Am I exonerated?" Darley quipped.

"I stand corrected," Elspeth said, feeling as though she was very near to paradise.

"I'll expect an extra kiss or two," he teased, bending to drop a light caress on her cheek.

Elspeth blushed, cast a swift glance at their hosts and blushed even more as they beamed their approval. Beckett was tall and thin, his wife short and plump—evidence of her profession no doubt—but they both clearly doted on Darley.

"Am I embarrassing you?" he whispered, his mouth warm on her ear.

She nodded, her cheeks on fire. But it was impossible to discount the rush of delight she was experiencing.

"We're going to rest for a time and then go fishing," the marquis said, directing his remark to their hosts. "And if you'd make your famous strawberry tart, Meg, we'd be grateful."

"Beckett will bring up a bottle of yer hock, me lord. And the tart will be done in no time. And if'n you don't go fishin', we have some fresh trout from this mornin' all set to cook up fer you."

"The fishin' is right good though, my lord," Beckett said. "'Specially down around the bend in the river. You might want to test the waters."

"We shall. Absolutely. I promised the lady a lesson in fishing. Did I not, my dear?"

"Yes," Elspeth replied in a near inaudible whisper, not as degage as Darley, too new in the ways of amorous intrigue to play the role of wanton with ease.

"This way, darling." And with a nod and a smile for their hosts, he took Elspeth's hand and drew her toward the narrow stairway.

His room was at the top of the stairs, the ancient door made for men of smaller stature. "After ten years, I've learned," he said with a grin, bending his head to navigate the low lintel, pulling her inside and shutting the door. "See what you think of Meg's gardens." He indicated the bank of windows tucked under the eaves with a sweep of his hand. "The view is grand as well. You can see the church spire in Halston five miles away." Dropping into a sprawl on the rustic four-poster bed, he exhaled a satisfied sigh. "I think Betsy did us a favor."

"This is a lovely little inn," Elspeth agreed, moving across the scrubbed pine floor to the windows.

With a single guest room, extremely private as well, Julius mused, pleased there was no possibility of interruption here. Newmarket didn't offer such absolute privacy; Charles in his cups was unpredictable as was Amanda any time.

When Elspeth reached the windows, she gasped in astonishment. A vast carpet of color lay before her eyes, a riot of flowers sweeping across an open field—as though nature had so planned it. "It's absolutely gorgeous! And what a lovely view." She half turned from the window. "I can see why you come here."

"I like the peace and serenity. After too long in London, I crave a tranquil abode."

"And you fish?"

"And sleep and eat."

"When your excesses have left you depleted."

"What do you know of my excesses?"

"You figure rather prominently in *The Tatler* and *The Bon Ton* magazine. Everyone in England knows of your amusements."

He smiled. "Even in Yorkshire?"

"We must have *some* excitement in our lives."

"So a vicar's daughter has met me before in the gossip sheets."

"You're *so* much more exciting in person."

"Am I." He looked amused.

"I couldn't sleep last night, Darley, for wanting you." She glanced at the bed. "And now I have you all alone."

"In a very private room."

"To take my pleasure of."

"Then my long sleepless night was worth it."

"There's so little time, my lord," she whispered. "And so much to do . . ."

"So many orgasms you mean." His voice was husky and low.

"If you don't mind . . ."

He hadn't moved, except for a certain portion of his anatomy that had its own agenda. "So we shouldn't wait for the hock?" he gently said.

"I don't think I can."

Her voice was breathy, her closeness intoxicating. "I'll let Beckett know." Rolling off the bed, he strode to the door, pulled it open, and shouted, "No hock right now!" Shutting the door, he turned the key in the lock. "Just to be sure," he murmured, tossing the key on the bureau. "Now come here, darling," he whispered, "and I'll give you everything you want."

The small room, the remote locale, the utter privacy was like being granted permission to luxuriate in every forbidden pleasure, to bask and swim and wallow in the halcyon glory of carnal delight—Darley's promise of "everything" like adding dry kindling to the flame of her desire. "We're all alone." Pulling the ribbon holding her heavy tresses loose, she shook her curls free.

"Utterly." He wrenched his neckcloth open.

"No one will bother us." She shed her slippers, one, then the other, the green leather a splash of color on the pale flooring.

"No one." He was used to this, his coat already discarded, his shirt stripped free.

His powerful, nude torso seared her retinas; she was lost. "Do you mind? If we rush?" she whispered.

He grinned. "Leave your gown on if you wish."

"I can't. The wrinkles will show. And then he'd"—nonplussed and trembling, she wavered—indecision and fear a sudden crushing weight.

He could have pointed out that the muslin was wrinkled already, the sheer fabric easily crushed. "Let me help," he said, instead, moving nearer, keeping his voice softly reassuring against the bewilderment and doubt in her gaze. "Turn around, I'll unclasp the hooks; we'll make sure not to wrinkle your gown."

She obediently turned, grateful for a solution, wanting him desperately and, reaching her in a few strides, he deftly unhooked her gown. Nudging her arms up, he lifted the yellow muslin over her head and carefully draped it over a chair. "Meg will iron it for you if you like."

She swung around, threw her arms around his neck and holding him in a death grip, melted against him. "Thank you, thank you, thank you for judgment and reason when I have none. When I can't think of anything right now but holding you and feeling you and having you inside me. When I could fall off the end of the world right now and I wouldn't care as long as you made love to me first."

Her artless candor did disastrous things to his control. It surprised him, this man of superb self-mastery. Being able to wait was his speciality—one the ladies adored—and now he was like a callow youth . . . ready to explode. "I'm not so sure my judgment is any more steady than yours," he said, easing her backward the few feet to the bed. "I need to feel you now."

"Then we're in perfect accord." Falling back on the mattress, she wrenched up her petticoats, spread her legs and met his gaze, her eyes hot with longing. "Have I mentioned how I'm utterly taken with you?"

"Try taking this," he whispered, opening his breeches with blurring speed, pulling her to the edge of the bed and sliding inside her in one sleek thrust, burying himself deep with a throaty groan.

Her blissful sigh matched his and lacing her legs around his back, she said, "Now, give me more."

It was a frantic, out-of-control coupling, driven by lust and savage need, an incendiary, selfish fucking, with both partners heedless of all but consummation.

She came first. Or he waited for her climax to begin and he followed her into an orgasm with such synchronized swiftness, they both lay panting in unison at the end.

He said between rasping breaths, "I'll finish undressing you in a minute."

"Don't bother," she gasped. "I've been thinking of nothing else all night. Not to mention waiting twenty-six years for"—she caught herself before she said *you*—"this," she whispered.

His cock surged upward at breakneck speed, the idea of twenty-six years of pent-up desire inciting a prodigious lechery. "I'll undress you later," he whispered. In an hour or so, he thought, not inclined to stop fucking anytime soon. That he would have found a virginal miss this ripe and horny and desperate for sex in this quiet countryside was not something to temporize about even fleetingly. Not that he was prone to speculation in the throes of lust no matter who his partner.

Fornication—headlong and hot-blooded—that was the ticket.

Not having had Darley's experience, Elspeth had no way of putting her passions in perspective. She only knew she wanted him with heedless, impetuous longing. She only knew that the pleasure he brought her was so shockingly beautiful, she felt transported beyond the mundane world.

As though Darley could, single-handedly, bring her to paradise.

More familiar with carnal sport, Darley was solidly fixed in reality, although the nature of that reality was uncommonly good, he had to admit.

Stripping off his breeches a moment later, he pushed the lady upward into the middle of the bed and dispensed with her petticoats, chemise, and silk stockings in record time.

"Are you warm?" she whispered, holding her palms to her flushed cheeks.

"Fucking hot," he whispered, settling between her legs in support of that statement. "Spread your legs wider," he ordered in a husky rasp.

He pounded into her in a frenzy, like a battering ram, withdrawing with quicksilver speed so he could plunge in again and feel her lush tightness close around him, so the unchecked violence she inspired could be assuaged.

Or marginally assuaged.

He couldn't get enough of her that day.

Or she him, her raging desires as rampant as his.

They mated with brute force and strange, suspended moments of calm.

They met in fury and gentleness.

They felt sweet joy and the most frantic hysteria.

They felt dizzy with—if not love—something very like it.

Not that either would dare to acknowledge anything so outre.

So inconceivable.

Chapter
14

Much later when their hearts had stopped beating like drums, when they could think beyond the heated moment, when sex no longer commanded their every impulse, they took the simple lunch of bread and cheese Meg had packed for them and went down to the river.

They lay on the cool grass of the riverbank, kissing and touching and murmuring sillinesses to each other, he feeding her and then she him. Sipping cool hock between kisses.

"I don't want to leave," Elspeth murmured. "I think I'll stay right here and never go home."

"I'd keep you safe. You could disappear and no one would find you."

"Ah . . . temptation. And you'd come to make love to me and keep me happy?"

"Every day, every hour, every minute." For a man who had experienced every sexual sensation, the measure of his involvement was not only astonishing but without precedent. "I'll bring you whatever you need. Give me a list each day and I'll fill it."

"I only need you to fill me—always and ever . . ."

"Now?" As if he'd not climaxed a dozen times already, his erection was at full mast, his craving insatiable.

"Yes, yes—now and in five minutes and two minutes . . .

please, please, please." She rolled over on her back, opened her arms, raised her hips and smiled a sultry temptress smile. "I'm ravenous for you."

He plunged inside her a moment later, felt her pulsing flesh close around him and finally understood after countless women and endless debauch what pleasure was. It was lucid and luminous and lunatic all at the same time. It was the emptiness of the cosmos, the minutia of a single breath, the sense of having reached—after a long, arduous voyage—journey's end.

They spent the remaining days of race week at the Red Lion, although in a modified format from the one they so playfully fantasized. They could not so cavalierly dismiss Elspeth's conjugal obligations nor the unyielding perimeters of the daily race schedule at Newmarket. But within those confines, several hours each day were entirely theirs.

They made love in endless variety, each touch and caress, every sensation made more exquisite for the fleeting nature of their time together. Joy was fragile and precarious, sweet as honey. And they gathered their rosebuds while they may as lovers had for millenniums before them—with never a word of tomorrows.

At intervals in their amorous play they would leave their cozy hermitage under the eaves and go fishing or walk occasionally in the colorful, scented garden; they'd eat Meg's delicacies and drink Darley's hock; they'd lie in the sun and talk of nothing and everything like lovers did—wanting to know all the insignificant details of each other's lives.

Darley had never allowed anyone to see him so exposed.

Elspeth had so long restrained her every thought and word, that she felt like a prisoner set free in some wondrous fairyland. "If I talk too much, tell me to stop," she'd whisper. "Truly do."

He'd laugh and kiss her some more and say, "Tell me what your mother was like or what your favorite subjects were in school" or, more often than not—"what horses you prefer . . . then and now."

For beneath the amorous passions that captivated them and

held them in thrall, ran an equally ardent devotion to racing and prime bloodstock—the touchstones of their lives. They spoke at length of bloodlines and pedigrees, of breeding "soundness"; they discussed the issue of good trainers and training, of the best yearling sales and prime race meets. It was a congenial, harmonious meeting of minds and thoughts and purpose.

Elspeth wondered briefly whether their mutual passion for horses accounted for their fantastic rapport in terms of ardent affection. But then, she'd discussed horses her entire life with any number of people and never felt this way before.

It was Darley, pure and simple—his stark beauty and sleek, powerful body, his unutterable charm. While his reputation for pleasing women in bed was not only well deserved, but much appreciated.

A shame that she would soon be leaving Newmarket.

Would that her life were different.

She knew better of course. She knew it was foolish to dream unattainable dreams. She'd had these few days with Darley and for that she would be grateful. He had family obligations in London next week, he'd said, the opening of the Season requiring his presence in town. Her obligations were equally fixed. Grafton would be returning to Yorkshire for the local race season immediately after the Newmarket meets.

But rational understanding did little to counteract the terrible sense of loss and finality she felt as she readied herself to leave the Red Lion for the last time. And try as she would, she couldn't curtail her sadness.

At first the marquis tried to ignore Elspeth's tears for he had no relief to offer other than sympathy for her plight. She'd refused to take any money from him, although he'd tried often enough. Nor could he offer her any hope of meeting again. He didn't make those kinds of plans. He never had.

"I told myself I wasn't going to do this," she whispered, sniffling loudly as she drew on a glove. "It's really quite outrageous of me. There." She sniffled again. "I'm quite recovered."

He was standing near the door waiting. "I'm not good with

adieus," he said, honestly. "But I very much enjoyed this week."
Several thousand pounds worth, as it turned out, Amanda's price
having risen each day as Grafton increasingly pressured her for
sexual favors. "Do you and Grafton come into town for the
Season?" It was the merest politesse, for he knew better.

"Never," she said, taking a deep breath, patently aware of
Darley's discomfort. "And I, too, enjoyed myself this week. I'm
deeply grateful for your company." She found herself able to smile
as she reflected on the glory of that companionship. "You've been
a very good teacher."

He suddenly found himself displeased by her comment.
Would she find someone else to teach her more once she was
home in Yorkshire? Or did she know enough now to become a
tutor herself? The lady had a natural bent for amorous play there
was no doubt. But then, so did many women he knew and just
because a pretty horse-mad lady had amused him for a few days
was no reason to make any changes in his way of life. He sensibly
curbed his pique, his voice smoothly urbane as he said, "I couldn't
have had a better pupil." He too, smiled. "I shall remember this
week with great fondness."

Nothing could be plainer. How coolly he'd spoken. But then
amorous liaisons were commonplace in the Ton, sex no more than
a transitory amusement. And Darley, more than anyone, was a
byword for those libertine activities.

She'd simply been his diversion this week.

But it was time now to go.

Picking up her other glove from the dressing table, she shoved
her hand into the embroidered green kidskin and moved toward
the door. "Will you thank Meg and Beckett for me when next
you see them?" She could be equally urbane.

"Of course," he said, opening the door and bowing her out.

The servants had conveniently departed for the village after
luncheon, curtailing the necessity of any embarrassing small talk
or farewells. Darley thought of everything, Elspeth noted. But
then, he was well-practiced at the game.

The drive back was awkward, conversation a matter of exchanging trite banalities concerning the weather or the passing landscape. Elspeth found herself biting back recurring observations on the sunny skies, her mind blank of scintillating chatter.

In the course of the journey, the marquis found it necessary to constantly curb his impulse to say, "Come visit me in London. I'll send my coach for you." That he was even thinking such thoughts was unnerving for a man who had made it a practice to keep his sexual diversions temporary. That he was even tempted to offer such an invitation went against his every instinct. His jaw was set in a hard line by the time he pulled his bays to a stop in the lane behind Grafton's property, his foremost thought escape.

Elspeth was similarly inclined and the instant the phaeton rolled to rest, she jumped to the ground. She couldn't possibly deal with Darley touching her as he lifted her down. Nor did she wish to leave herself open to the gaucherie of having to kiss him good-bye—or have him kiss her.

What was the point of kisses anyway.

It was over.

She forced herself to act like an adult—to smile up at him and wave. It might even have been a jaunty wave. "Have a pleasant Season in London. And thank you again for a delightful holiday."

He nodded. "You're welcome."

He hadn't smiled—not now, not once on that seemingly endless drive. Nor had he said thank you himself, she thought, turning quickly and walking away so he wouldn't see the wetness in her eyes. Although that wasn't likely she realized a second later at the sound of the marquis's carriage bowling away at top speed.

Running through the orchard, she entered the kitchen garden, quickly shut the gate behind her, and out of sight of the lane and the house, collapsed onto the grass and uncontrollably sobbed.

How was she going to survive the agony of her marriage after having experienced a week of bliss with Darley? How was she going to endure the unending days and weeks and months as prisoner to a vile, repellant, odious old man? How could she sustain the demanding pose of wife to Lord Grafton when he constantly oppressed her in a hundred fiendish ways? What if she couldn't? What if she succumbed to his malevolence like his previous wives and took her own life?

Never, a firm strong voice inside her head pronounced with absolute conviction, the sound so like her mother's voice, she glanced up as though she might see her beloved parent. Instead she saw butterflies flitting from flower to flower, felt the warm sun on her face and a flutter of hope stirred in her breast. Hadn't her mother always been optimistic even when life seemed the darkest? Hadn't she taught her to see good in everything? And had *she herself* not known that Darley was as elusive as the colorful butterflies darting among the flowers?

Her life had always been less frivolous than his and it was no different now for having known him. She had married for Will; she would persevere for him because he deserved a better future than the one he'd been left. Although in her father's defense—how could he have known their uncle's will would be altered to benefit Cousin Herbert who appeared opportunely at Uncle Dwight's deathbed?

But that was all water under the bridge, she reminded herself sternly. With luck, Grafton might drink himself to death before she was too ancient or Will might return from India more prosperous than when he had left and save her. Many an English officer before him had accomplished as much in the land of maharajas and pigeon-size rubies and diamonds. On that hopeful note, she wiped her face with her skirt, straightened her shoulders, drew in a deep breath and pictured Will as she'd last seen him in his uniform, smiling at her with that boyish smile that lit up a room. He'd always been the sunshine of her life—lighthearted and gay, never morose, the eternal optimist—much like their father who had never despaired even in their most dire periods of monetary distress.

If only their father hadn't always been so deep in debt to Tattersalls, the sale of his stable might have realized a profit. If, if, if. If wishes were horses, she ruefully reflected.

But no amount of wishful thinking was going to solve her

problems. She must simply muddle through until such a time as Will returned—hopefully richer than when he set out.

Darley's cool farewell had been sobering.

She understood more than ever that her fate was entirely in her own hands.

No shining knight was going to appear to offer succor.

Nor some good Samaritan to free her from her conjugal bonds.

She was responsible for herself—*and* Sophie . . . and as well as one could across the continents . . . for Will.

Chapter
15

On her return to Grafton Park, Elspeth rode for hours each day, avoiding as much as possible the need to interact with her husband. He was busy with his grooms and trainers in any event, getting all in readiness for the local race season. But she was required to appear at dinner each evening, an ordeal she faced with dread. Grafton was often drunk and abusive, and no matter how she requested to be excused once the meal was over, he insisted she stay and pour him his port or play the piano for his entertainment, or simply listen to his ramblings.

She hadn't thought it would be so difficult to readjust to her former existence. She'd thought she could go on with her life, putting away her memories of Darley to recall with fondness from time to time like one might childhood remembrances. But nothing so facile had occurred. She hadn't been able to walk away and disengage. In fact, thoughts of Darley swirled through her mind with increasing frequency as time went on—as though having experienced bliss, her discontent came into sharper focus.

She reminded herself that she was only one of legions of women who had come under Darley's spell. She couldn't allow herself to dwell on useless fantasies. She was where she was

while the marquis was back in the social whirl of London. And
the sooner she forgot about him the better.

Sophie watched her young mistress with increasing concern
following their return from Newmarket. Elspeth was losing weight,
although hours in the saddle each day were reason enough for
that loss. But she had little appetite as well and despite Sophie's
offerings of cakes and sweets in hopes of whetting her young
charge's appetite, Elspeth showed little interest in food. In fact,
the moment Elspeth woke each morning, she'd throw aside her
covers, drink her chocolate, dress for riding and make for the stables as if the devil himself were licking at her heels.

And so the days at Grafton Park went apace, Elspeth's riding
schedule altered only when Grafton's ponies were running at the
local meets. On those days, she and Sophie had to be dressed and
standing on the front portico at nine where their small carriage
awaited them—as did Grafton's larger coach.

Lord and Lady Grafton never traveled together. The earl's
coach conveyed his bath chair, his valet, chairman, his traveling
liquor cabinet and himself. Very much the country squire, he
preferred the company of men. Pretty manners he left to the
Macaronis in the Ton.

Not that Elspeth was averse to driving alone. Nor did she take
exception to going to the races other than having to sit beside
Grafton in his box. He insisted she play her wifely role when his
horses were on the track. In the intervals between races, she took
the opportunity to visit with old friends. Her classmates from
Dame Prichard's School for Females, all married now and having
children, were a constant source of local news and gossip, although she found herself taking a new and unusual interest in
their babies. That fascination was directly related to her yearnings for Darley of course. She understood perfectly well—as she
did the more sobering reality that anything having to do with
Darley and babies was pure whimsey.

In the course of that green English spring, she never missed her nightly tally in her journal, the mounting sum giving her the courage to face another morning, another day, another tedious evening with her husband.

And so her life would have continued had Elspeth not received a letter one day in June that changed everything.

Chapter

16

Elspeth had just come in from the stables and was stripping off her gloves as she ran up the stairs to her apartment. She couldn't afford to be late for dinner. Grafton was a martinet for punctuality.

As she reached the top of the stairs she caught sight of Sophie waiting for her in the open doorway of her sitting room, her face ashen. Alarm bells rang through her brain. Sophie was not given to drama. "What is it?" she called out, desperately praying it wasn't about her brother.

"A letter come for you." The maid held up a folded sheet of paper much the worse for wear, the wax seal long since lost.

It was obvious she'd read it. "Tell me," Elspeth said, coming to a stop at the entrance to her rooms.

"There was fever on board Will's ship."

She clutched the doorjamb to keep from falling, her worst fears realized. "Is he"—she stopped, unable to say the words.

"He was set ashore in Tangier," Sophie explained. "Along with the others who"—Sophie hesitated.

"Weren't expected to live," Elspeth softly finished. Twin spots of color flared on her cheeks, the contrast ghoulish against her bloodless skin. "When was the letter written?" Her voice was barely audible.

"Three weeks ago."

"We must go to him." Her mouth was set, a sudden resolve ringing through her words. Dropping her hand from the jamb, she briskly moved past Sophie into the room. "Start packing," she said over her shoulder. "I'll tell Grafton at dinner," she added, striding toward her dressing room. "Bring sensible clothes—nothing grand." She suddenly stopped and spun around. "He hasn't seen the letter, has he?"

Sophie shook her head. "Addie brought it up. She wouldn't have told anyone."

"Good." Some of the servants' families had been Grafton retainers for centuries and despite the earl's sour temperament were loyal to the household. Others sympathized with Elspeth's plight—Addie among them. "Tell Charlie to ready our carriage. Don't look at me like that. I know it's not mine, but we'll send it back when we reach London." Charlie could be trusted. He was her groom on her daily rides—a kindly man and an ally.

"The earl won't let you leave."

"He can't stop me. But I'll give him the courtesy of asking," Elspeth said, resuming her progress. Throwing open the doors of her armoire a moment later, she pulled out the first gown she saw. Tossing the silver tissue evening gown on a chair, she began unbuttoning the jacket of her riding habit. "We leave tonight—the moment Grafton slips into a doze."

Elspeth walked into the dining room as the clock was striking seven. Grafton didn't keep city hours. He dined early.

As she slipped into her chair at one end of the long mahogany table, the earl signaled the footmen to begin serving.

"I won't abide tardiness," he growled, scowling down the length of the table. "See that you're not late tomorrow."

She hadn't been late, but there was little point in arguing. And since she didn't plan on being there tomorrow, she said instead, "The going was soft coming home through the south meadow. The wet ground delayed us."

"See that it doesn't happen again," Grafton warned, tucking into his soup with a loud slurp.

She looked down at the barley broth that was a staple at each meal, the earl having been told by his doctor that it prolonged life, and found herself experiencing a small elation despite the fearful nature of her recent news. This would be her *last* bowl of barley broth she had to pretend to eat. This would be the *last* evening she had to sit across from her despicable husband and mind her manners. This would be the *very* last time she would count the minutes until she could escape to her room.

Tonight she would set out to find her brother, rescue him and, with luck, never return to this hellish place. Perhaps Will's illness would turn out to be opportunity in disguise. Perhaps, they could find a small cottage somewhere when they returned and she could teach, or open a village school. She would be content earning a modest living. And Will was a young man of parts. If he didn't wish to be a schoolmaster, he could find some other livelihood.

His purchased rank in the army could be easily disposed of. Her brother might realize a goodly sum for his uniforms alone and if his horses had been set ashore as well, they could race them. As part of her marriage settlement, she'd insisted Will have a string of top-notch ponies for the polo matches in India.

Buoyed by her new optimism, ignoring all her previous hopes for a grand career for her brother, she found herself considering her brother's sickness as a supreme example of fate intervening.

As to the possibility that Will might not survive or may already have passed away, she refused to contemplate anything so fearful.

With the courage of her new convictions bolstering her resolve, she gazed down the table at her husband—already red-faced from drink, his shirtfront stained from his soup—and spoke with a deliberate calm. "I received a letter from my brother's commanding officer today," she said. "Will has taken ill and has been placed ashore at Tangier. I would like to go there and bring him home."

Grafton's soupspoon dropped from his hand, clanked into his bowl and looking up, he stared at her with incredulity. "Tangier?" he bellowed, spitting soup over the table. "Don't be ridiculous!

It's a heathen, pestilent place! I won't hear of it!" Even if he hadn't been irate that she'd had the audacity to make such a request, after several glasses of wine, his voice always took on a thunderous note.

"I can't simply leave him there. He needs care. He needs clean country air to bring him back to health." She wouldn't allow herself to lose her temper. If nothing else, she would present her case with courtesy and logic.

"Your brother's probably dead by now! You'd be wasting your time and *my money*! I absolutely refuse to let you go and that's final!"

Elspeth went pale and, clenching her hands in her lap to keep from screaming, she sat in rigid silence. Will *wasn't* dead. He *wasn't*! How *dare* Grafton say something so hateful! And if she'd had any small, niggling reservations about leaving her marriage, Grafton's vile comments had effectively dispelled her misgivings. Nostrils flaring, she drew in a breath of constraint and signaled the footman to take away her soup bowl. She would never eat another spoonful of his noxious barley broth.

She glanced at the clock as a footman refilled Grafton's glass, and another set the next course before her. Seven-fifteen. Well aware of the laws that allowed a husband complete control over a wife, she would nevertheless leave tonight. Picking up her fork and knife, she cut off a small portion of Dover sole and lifted it to her mouth.

Then she settled in to wait until her husband passed out.

As the meal progressed, she wondered if the footmen were conspiring with her for they were keeping the earl's wineglass full. Had Addie or Charlie said something to them? Not that she dared look directly at any of the servants. Not that she dared do anything untoward that might raise suspicion. In mere hours she would be free of Grafton Park.

Eat, drink. Remain calm even while her heart was beating like a drum. Smile and pretend one last time.

Although once the meal was over, once her husband had fallen into his usual drunken stupor, her first order of business would be to obtain money for their journey. She couldn't quite decide if she would reimburse the earl or consider the money duty pay for six months hard labor. But whatever she decided, she *would* need a considerable sum.

Fortunately, she knew where he kept his cash.

As the earl ate like a trencherman and drank himself insensible, Elspeth made her plans, counting the number of post stops between Yorkshire and London, estimating the hours they would be on the road. Should they take time to sleep at an inn or push on?

If the earl pursued them, it might be best if they drove straight through.

Of one thing she was sure. Once Grafton passed out, he wouldn't wake until morning.

At the very least, they would be guaranteed a twelve-hour head start.

When her husband's chin finally fell to his chest and his snoring took on the steady cadence of deep sleep, she rose from the table, politely bid good night to the footmen and walked from the room. Once in the hall, she glanced left and right and seeing no one, proceeded to her husband's study. Slipping inside the room, she quietly shut the door behind her, locked it, and went directly to his desk.

She'd had to stand before the massive oak desk often enough, waiting humbly for him to dole out her pin money. Although having lived through the humiliating experience on several occasions, she knew exactly where to look. Moving behind the desk, she opened the drawer and was gratified to see a leather purse within. Now she wouldn't have to carry the money upstairs wrapped in her skirt. Swiftly thumbing through the bills, she noticed a small lacquered box shoved to the back of the drawer. Lifting the lid, she found it stuffed with very large banknotes.

She hesitated, moral dictates of a lifetime restraining her.

Passage to Morocco would be expensive, however—*very* expensive.

Only the wealthiest of nobles could afford to travel abroad.

And Will could be dying alone in a strange, far-off land.

She scooped up the banknotes, jammed them into the purse,

pulled the drawstring tight, shoved the drawer shut, and swiftly crossed the room. Cautiously opening the door, she surveyed the corridor, and once assured no one was about, she stepped into the hall, eased the door shut and walked toward her apartments with what she hoped was an air of assurance.

If anyone should cross her path before she reached her apartments, they wouldn't be likely to ask her about the purse. At least not to her face.

But that didn't mean they might not try to rouse Grafton.

She started to run and didn't stop until she'd gained the security of her sitting room. Trembling with fear, she dropped into a chair, waiting for her breathing to return to normal, needing time to compose herself after having become a thief for the first time in her life. A few moments later when no one came knocking on her door, she reminded herself of the importance of her mission, and rose to her feet.

Walking into her dressing room, she tossed the heavy purse on a table. "We have funds," she said, smiling as Sophie looked up from the portmanteau she was packing. "Next stop: London."

"Provided he don't catch us first."

"He won't wake until morning." After six months of marriage, of that she was certain. "Does Charlie have the carriage waiting?"

"Anytime after half past seven, he said—after he asked who's gonna drive us."

"Oh, dear." Elspeth frowned. "I never thought about a driver."

Sophie smiled. "He's been thinking about leavin', Charlie said. I said mayhap he might like to see Morocco."

"Really?" Elspeth's expression brightened. "Did he say he would?"

"Couldn't let us go that fur piece alone, he said."

If Charlie accompanied them, their enterprise suddenly took on a new certainty of success.

Elspeth softly exhaled.

Until that moment, she hadn't realized how worried she'd been.

Chapter
17

They decided *not* to stop at the posting inns. Charlie had suggested carrying horse feed with them when they'd discussed the possibility of pursuit and they chose to rest and feed the team in quiet, out-of-the-way areas. Also, Grafton's horses were too expensive to leave at some post stop. As for their meals, Charlie purchased whatever food they required in local villages while the ladies remained inside the carriage with the shades drawn. Since the carriage bore no coat of arms, they traveled south in relative obscurity.

Two days later, it was nearing sunset as they entered London. Feeling that the docks would be unsafe with evening coming, they found a modest inn near the Tower Bridge. In the morning they would find passage to Tangier.

Grafton's carriage and team had to be returned now, although Elspeth and her companions were at odds as to the best method of accomplishing the task. Charlie was reluctant to hire an unknown driver who might abscond with the horses and equipage. And while Elspeth understood Charlie's concern, she was adamantly opposed to the suggestion she solicit Darley's advice on a driver.

"I don't care if he's the only person we know in London,"

she'd replied whenever the subject had come up. "He wouldn't welcome the intrusion and I *don't* wish to ask him."

"Yer only askin' for the name of a trustworthy driver," either Charlie or Sophie would point out with the objectivity of the uninvolved.

He wouldn't perceive it that way, Elspeth wished to say, conscious that a man like Darley would look askance at a former lover knocking at his door. "I'm sure we can find a respectable livery stable in a city this size."

But neither Sophie nor Charlie were sympathetic to her quibbling over what to them was a sensible solution and Elspeth found it increasingly difficult to sustain her position.

"Consider," Sophie proposed as they deposited their bags in the small second floor room at the White Hart. "You needn't even see Darley. We'll stay here and send Charlie. *He* can ask for a driver's name." The possibility of Grafton charging his wife for the theft of his precious horses weighed on the elder woman's mind.

"Why didn't you say that before!" Elspeth exclaimed, relief flooding her senses. Darley so muddled her brain, she'd not been able to think of something so simple. "Thank you, Sophie. What a relief," she added, glancing at Charlie who was laying a fire against the coming coolness of evening. "Charlie, you wouldn't mind asking Darley, would you? Although, you must be discreet and not mention my name—*if* possible."

"I don't even have to say yer in town, ma'am," he said, meeting her gaze before striking flint to tinder. "I'll get us a driver and that's that."

Elspeth smiled. "Wonderful. Perfect. Everything's settled, then."

"Although if the marquis might see his way to puttin' up our team tonight, it would save us the trouble of finding a livery stable," Charlie noted.

Elspeth groaned. "I dislike imposing on him." Not that it wasn't common enough when traveling to house stock with people you knew. Perhaps she was overreacting to something quite ordinary.

"Very well, use your own judgment," she capitulated with a small sigh.

"I won't embarrass you none, ma'am." Setting the flickering flame to the kindling, he watched it ignite, then came to his feet. "I'll be back in no time with everything right and tight, my lady."

Charlie's habitual calm was steadying in her world gone mad. "I'm very grateful," she murmured, trying not to cry. So much was at stake with Will's health in the balance, their journey barely begun. She tried to smile. "You have money, now."

"Yes, ma'am."

"And some notion of the general direction in which—"

"I'm right fine, ma'am. Don't you worry none. I'll find him easy enough."

The innkeeper's directions were excellent, the gentry all residing in close proximity to Whitehall and Green Park, and soon Charlie was bringing Grafton's rig to a stop before Darley's lodgings in St. James Square. The streets were still bustling, the full spectrum of humanity from servants to aristocrats enjoying the balmy summer air.

Tossing the reins to a street urchin, Charlie walked up to the green door, lifted the polished brass knocker, let it drop and, waiting, surveyed the town house's three-story facade. The shutters were newly painted, the windows sparkling clean, the red brick a soft rose hue in the glow of late afternoon.

When the door opened, he looked up into the haughty visage of a tall, portly butler who gazed down the sharp beak of his nose with an air of disdain. "Deliveries at the back door." He began shutting the door.

Charlie put his hand out to stop the forward motion of the door. "I'm here to see the marquis on business so be right quick about it or your master will have your hide."

"Lord Darley is away from home," the butler said, curtly. "Remove your hand from the door."

Swiftly plucking one of Grafton's guineas from his pocket, Charlie held out the gold coin. "The whereabouts of the marquis's sister would suit me as well." He'd heard of Elspeth's meeting with Betsy from Sophie.

"Lord Darley is not with her." But the butler slipped the coin from Charlie's grasp with the finesse of considerable practice and his expression altered marginally from frigid. "Lady Worth is at Westerlands House in Portman Square." He opened his mouth, shut it, and apparently deciding a guinea was worth an additional scrap of information, opened it again and added, "She's with her parents while Lord Worth is in Paris on government business."

For another guinea, Charlie suspected the butler might even divulge the marquis's current location. Lady Grafton wouldn't appreciate the unnecessary exposure, however, so Darley's sister would have to do. "Much obliged," he said, and let his arm drop.

The door abruptly shut, curtailing any further speculation apropos the butler's mercenary tendencies, and Charlie was left on the stoop facing his reflection in the brass knocker.

Chapter

18

As Charlie made his way to Portman Square, the occupants of Westerlands House were having tea in the drawing room. The duke and duchess were being regaled with the latest gossip, their daughter having attended the Duchess of Devonshire's rout the previous night. Since everyone who was anyone was there, Betsy was bringing her parents up-to-date on all the scandal.

"Prinny was there dancing attendance on Mrs. Fitzherbert who hasn't been seen in society of late—for various and sundry reasons, as you know."

"She must have forgiven him for his profligacies with his brothers these months past," her mother observed. "Although what choice does she have."

The Prince of Wales had been entertaining his brothers—the Duke of Hanover, back from Germany after six years, and the recently anointed Duke of Clarence, returned from his second tour of duty at sea. All three men had been engaged in every debauchery and dissipation know to man for several months now, their retainers universally bemoaning the young princes's depravities.

Betsy shrugged faintly. "She has none, of course, although she and Prinny seemed quite taken with each other last night." The

Prince of Wales had secretly married the twice widowed commoner against the laws of the land and the advice of his friends two years ago.

"Mrs. Fitzherbert might have had Prinny's attention last night, but not for long I suspect," the duchess noted. "The prince's affections are capricious as everyone knows." Her mouth quirked in a small smile. "Apropos such men; was Julius in attendance last night?"

"No, nor has he been anywhere save, Langford since he returned from Newmarket."

The duchess made a moue. "He's keeping company with Amanda, no doubt."

"Of course. When he wearies of the world, he turns to her. He finds her comfortable."

"He best not consider marrying the gel," the duke grumbled from the depths of his chair, glancing over his newspaper at his wife and daughter.

"You needn't fear Julius will marry anytime soon," Betsy observed. "Nor is Amanda likely to be his choice should he ever take the plunge."

"At least the boy still has his wits about him." Giving the paper a snap, the duke went back to his reading.

The duchess gazed at her daughter, one brow faintly arched. "I hope you're right. But I heartily wish Julius would find someone else to amuse him. Amanda's rather too headstrong for my taste."

"You needn't worry, *Maman*. Julius tires of everything in due course—Amanda included. He's simply brooding over an affaire of the heart at the moment and Amanda serves as distraction."

"Seriously? Julius?" The duchess's eyes widened. "My goodness. Who is this woman?"

"A complete unknown—a young married woman he met at Newmarket. Completely ineligible, of course. But from a few of his comments as well as his behavior since Newmarket, I'm of the opinion he's blue deviled over this chit."

"Are you sure? Julius serious about a woman?"

"Perhaps serious is too strong a word, but interested certainly."

"Keep in mind, darling," her husband murmured from behind his newspaper. "I had no intention of marrying before I met you."

"You see, *Maman*?" Betsy said with a grin. "Perhaps there's hope for Julius." The story of her parents' accidental meeting at a fall hunt was a much told tale.

"A shame the dear boy couldn't have found someone more eligible," the duchess said with a sigh. "I don't suppose the husband is old and frail?"

Betsy shrugged. "Old certainly. As to frail—in a manner of speaking, yes and no. It's old Grafton's wife causing Julius to brood."

The duke dropped the paper to his knees. "Old *Hellfire*?"

"None other."

The duke's heavy brows came together in a scowl. "How many wives has the damned reprobate had?"

"This young lady is the third."

"She must be some guileful trollop to marry Old Hellfire after two of his wives have gone to their graves."

"On the contrary, Papa. She's a vicar's daughter left impoverished on her father's death with a young brother to launch in the world. I suspect it wasn't an easy choice for her."

"I'm not sure I like the sound of it—impoverished or not," the duke grumbled. "Old Hellfire couldn't have been the only available man she could have turned to. How much do you know about this woman? Might Julius be in the grips of an ambitious female?"

Betsy hooted. "Papa, consider your son's legendary record when it comes to ambitious females. Have *any* been even remotely successful?" Darley had been the target of every managing mama and cunning puss since he'd reached manhood.

"Point taken." The duke returned to his paper.

"You must tell me what this unusual woman is like." The duchess leaned forward to set her teacup on the table. "Where did you meet her? What does she look like? She must be very pretty to entice Julius."

And had not a footman entered the drawing room at that moment, the duchess would have had her questions answered.

Instead, the flunkey announced, "Lady Grafton's coachman is at the back door asking to see Lady Worth."

Everyone came to attention as though the king himself had been announced. "Tell him I'll be right there." Quickly coming to her feet, Betsy said, "It must be something of import that caused her to send him here. I understand the lady is shy by nature."

"Shy, indeed," the duke snorted. "An ambitious woman has sent her calling card if you ask me."

"Now, darling, give Julius some credit for his judgment," the duchess murmured.

"Ha!" the duke exclaimed, taking pithy exception to his wife's fond disregard for their son's profligate life. "His good judgment is confined solely to his bloodstock, my dear."

"Yes, darling, I'm sure you're right," she tactfully replied, waving her daughter off. "Do hurry, Betsy. I'm alive with curiosity about this woman who's bedeviling our Julius."

Chapter

19

Left cooling his heels on the stoop outside the servants' door, Charlie wasn't sure whether he would receive a response or not. Before the door had been shut on him for the second time that night, he'd been flatly informed, "Lady Worth don't talk to no coachmen what she don't know." Only by invoking Lady Grafton's name had his message gained the necessary respect to have it delivered.

Perhaps.

As the minutes ticked by, he became less and less sure.

Maybe the man had simply walked away and left him. Silently cursing the rudeness of London servants, he decided that if no one returned soon, he'd go around to the front door and try again to gain Lady Worth's attention.

She was their last hope in this city of strangers.

To his great relief, the door suddenly opened and a smiling, well-dressed woman stood before him. "Do come in," she said, kindly. "I'm Lady Worth."

"Beggin' your pardon, ma'am, but I'm fine right here. I only came to ask a wee favor for me mistress. We be needin' the name of a respectable livery stable. If'n you might ask one of your grooms, we'd be right grateful and I'll be on me way."

"Of course. I'll get that information for you, but do come in while I have a groom brought in from the mews. Parker—get one of the grooms," she ordered, standing aside and waiting for Charlie to enter.

Short of being rude, he had no choice, and stepping into the house, he followed her down the hall to the kitchen.

"Would you like a cup of tea while we wait? Do tell me why Lady Grafton is in London?" Without waiting for his reply, she said, "Tea, Dolly," to a young maid, and offered Charlie a chair. "You must give me directions to Lady Grafton's lodgings so I may call on her."

"I were told to just ask for the name of a stable, me lady," Charlie replied, remaining standing. "I ain't allowed to say no more."

"Nonsense, I shan't bite. Is your mistress staying with friends? Sit, please."

"I ain't right sure the name o' the place where she be," he said, sitting reluctantly.

"If Lady Grafton is in town, I insist you tell me where she is." Offering Charlie her most charming smile, she took a seat opposite him and pushed a cake plate toward him. "Have some Dundee cake. Come now, you needn't champion Lady Grafton's privacy. I'm sure she wouldn't mind if I call on her."

Even if it were possible to defy a lady of rank—which it wasn't—Lady Worth's winning smile was impossible to ignore. As was what seemed a genuine interest in hearing that Elspeth was in town. Telling himself he hadn't had *specific* orders pertaining to Lady Worth—only to Darley, he debated his options. Elspeth had been near tears when he'd left, the burden of not knowing her brother's condition weighing heavily on her, the fear that he might be dead a constant threat to her peace of mind. Lady Worth's visit might brighten his mistress's spirits or at least transiently distract her thoughts. "We be at the White Hart near the Tower Bridge," he offered. "But we be leaving on the morning tide."

"My goodness! Then I must go to her directly! As soon as the groom comes in with the information you need. Better yet, use our stables. Is your equipage here?" She was speaking briskly, each word uttered in a sharp staccato. "Drink your tea while I go fetch my cape. We'll have my coach brought round and yours sent to the stables. Everything will work out perfectly," she finished with a smile, coming to her feet in a rustle of silk. "Don't move. I shall return shortly."

Suddenly wondering if he'd been the cause of an unwanted visitor for Elspeth, Charlie frowned at the cup of tea that had been set before him.

"She be a kind'un. Don't worry none," the young maid Dolly said, smiling shyly.

He blew out a breath. "I hope you're right." But what was done was done. He couldn't take it back. The horses were cared for and any of her stable staff could recommend a driver. How much harm could come from a visit from Lady Worth when they were leaving directly in the morning?

As Betsy rushed breathlessly into the drawing room, the duchess set her cup down so quickly the tea sloshed over the rim.

"I'm driving over—to visit . . . Lady Grafton," she gasped, having sprinted up from the kitchen. "She sent her coachman over . . . for information on a stable—for her team and carriage. I offered ours. Don't look at me like that, Papa. She's really very nice—as you'll see tonight for I intend to invite her to stay with us. She's sailing in the morning in any event so she won't be here long."

"Sailing where, for heaven's sake?" her mother inquired, making plans to receive their guest even as she asked her question.

"I don't know. We'll find out."

"We'll put her in the Queen's Room," the duchess murmured. "It's away from the noise of the street."

"The Queen's Room!" The duke tossed his paper aside. "This is some chit who may or may not have bamboozled our son! She doesn't require the Queen's Room!" The room had been designed around a splendid portrait of Queen Elizabeth, its cachet further enhanced by an Antonio Zucchi interior.

"Consider, darling, Julius is apparently enamored. She must be special."

"Hmpf. Your special and his special may be two different things."

"Speaking of Julius," Betsy said, bending to give her mother a kiss on the cheek, "send him a message and inform him of our guest."

The duchess's eyes sparkled. "Will he come?"

Betsy grinned. "We'll see, won't we?" She turned to leave.

"A pony says he doesn't," the duke muttered.

Betsy shook her head. "I wouldn't lay a bet either way. Not with Julius."

As the door closed on their daughter, the Duke of Westerlands looked at his wife. "Is Betsy interfering too much?"

"Julius can choose to do what he likes as he always has. As for the young lady, if she's sailing tomorrow, whether Betsy's interfering or not matters very little."

"I suppose you're right," the duke grumbled. "But I'm still not sure she's worth the Queen's Room."

Chapter
20

Very shortly, Charlie was following Darley's sister as she ran up the inn stairs to the second floor room the innkeeper had designated as Elspeth's. He would have preferred going first and warning his mistress, but he hadn't been given the opportunity. And he knew better than to take precedence over a countess, no matter how friendly her disposition.

Betsy knocked and without waiting for a reply, opened the door and walked into the room. Perhaps she and Darley had much in common when it came to wanting what they wanted. Or perhaps great wealth allowed them to indulge their impulses.

Elspeth shot to her feet at the sight of Darley's sister, the color draining from her face, every imaginable variant of the word disaster flooding through her brain.

"Surprise!" Betsy cried, the single word immediately qualifying as the understatement of the century. "How wonderful you've come to London! You must stay with us, of course," she murmured, moving forward in a cloud of perfume to give Elspeth a hug.

Engulfed in her scented embrace, Elspeth shot a censorious look at Charlie while trying to fabricate a graceful refusal to Betsy's invitation. But numb with shock, her brain was incapable of generating a diplomatic excuse.

Taking Elspeth's lack of response as an affirmative, Darley's sister proclaimed as she released Elspeth, "That's settled, then. We'll have such fun. You can finish your tea at our house," she added, taking note of the tea and buttered bread set on a nearby table. Waving at Sophie—who had observed the encounter with mixed feelings—she added with the authority of rank and fortune, "Pack, my good woman. We leave immediately."

"I couldn't, really I couldn't," Elspeth protested, red-faced, filled with panic, forcing herself to speak before it was too late.

Betsy smiled. "Of course you can."

"Much as I appreciate your generosity"—Elspeth hesitated over her choice of words—"we can't. We're—that is . . . we're traveling incognito."

Betsy merely smiled again. "I shan't tell a soul you're in town."

In desperation, the thought of being a guest of Darley's sister terrifying in all its numerous implications, Elspeth divulged the news of her brother's life-threatening illness in hopes of making her refusal more intelligible. "So you see, I'm afraid I would be poor company. Will is very much on my mind."

"And well he should be," Lady Worth murmured. "You must be worried to death. But being alone at a time like this only increases your anxieties." She patted Elspeth's arm. "If you're apprehensive about running into Julius, you needn't be. He's out of town." Not exactly a falsehood since he was at the moment. As to how long he'd remain at Langford, she couldn't be expected to know. "Come, now. It's silly for you to stay in these cramped quarters when we have an entire house with no one there but my parents, myself and my children."

Elspeth almost fainted on the spot. How could she possibly meet Darley's parents? What would she say? I made love to your son at Newmarket, but am otherwise unacquainted with him. Or maybe: I left my husband, stole his money and am running away. "To be perfectly honest," she said, choosing to refuse with a blunt explanation that even someone as open-minded as Lady

Worth was bound to find offensive, "I've left my husband and prefer the anonymity of this inn."

"You left Grafton?" Betsy clapped her gloved hands. "Good for you! The world, too, will applaud your decision. Not that I don't understand your wish for discretion," she went on in a conspiratorial murmur, "but no one need know you're staying with us. There now. Everything's settled. Come, we'll talk in the carriage while your maid packs your things."

"No—no, please . . . I couldn't. We're leaving so early we'll disrupt your entire household."

Betsy brushed aside her objections with an airy sweep of her hands. "That's even more reason why you should spend your single night in London in more pleasant surroundings. We're dining en famille tonight. It's completely informal," she remarked, taking in Elspeth's travel-stained gown. "Darley so enjoyed your company at Newmarket." She winked. "I have a feeling he misses you."

Brother and sister were both equally charming, Elspeth decided, capable of telling one what one most wished to hear. And whether Lady Worth was motivated by mere politesse or something else, Elspeth found herself wishing with complete illogic that her comments were true.

"I enjoyed our friendship at Newmarket as well," she replied, weeks of lovesick longing and dreams of Darley attesting to the fact.

"Julius tells me your family was horse mad. Why don't I show you his collection of bloodstock books? I'm told every aficionado of the turf is vastly jealous of Julius's racing library."

Every thoroughbred owner and breeder knew of Darley's expansive collection. But few had seen it and now she was being offered access to the treasure. Furthermore, short of grabbing the bedpost and refusing to budge, Elspeth realized her chances of remaining at the inn were nil.

Nor could the opportunity to see Darley's childhood home be discounted.

Lastly—and perhaps most pertinently—she was touched by Betsy's openhearted warmth at a time when her own life was in complete, utter chaos.

And if Darley was out of town, other than the awkwardness of meeting his parents, what harm would come from spending a night at Westerlands House?

It was only one night.

Tomorrow, they'd be on the high seas and whatever transpired in the course of the evening—embarrassing or not—would be no more than a memory.

Rationalization was operating at full capacity.

And perhaps a small measure of wistful hope was functioning as well.

Or maybe she was just feeling sad and alone and Betsy's kind offer came at an opportune time. "I've spent my whole life with horses," Elspeth noted, her decision made. "I should enjoy seeing Darley's bloodstock books."

"And drink a glass or two of champagne?" Betsy merrily observed with a flashing grin.

"I should enjoy that as well."

"Then we're off." Betsy held up her hand. "I hope you don't mind children at the dinner table. They adore joining us."

"I shouldn't mind in the least."

Betsy put out her hand and slid her fingers through Elspeth's. "Why don't we go ahead and have a nice coze while your maid assembles your things."

How long had it been since she'd had a friend to talk to, Elspeth thought, feeling a sudden wave of loneliness roll over her. But forcing herself to smile instead of cry, she grasped the sweet hand of friendship offered her.

The women were laughing before they reached the top of the stairs.

Chapter
21

After dressing, Betsy had joined Elspeth in her room and, lounging on a chaise while Elspeth finished her toilette, she chatted as though they were old friends. She offered up all the current gossip making the rounds in London's drawing rooms, talked of her children and husband as well, and on occasion, her brother.

Whenever Julius's name came up, Elspeth would invariably blush, but she also stored away each little scrap of information against some future time when she could relish them at her leisure. She understood her yearnings were futile, even more—ridiculous—but still, she cherished every revealing detail about the man who had come to mean so much to her.

"Did you enjoy the bath?" Betsy indicated the adjacent bathing chamber with a flick of her wrist. "The tub comes from a Roman palace, or so I'm told. Some ancestor took a fancy to it and had it shipped back to England."

"I was quite overwhelmed." Elspeth's brows arched into perfect half moons. The tub was green marble, the taps of gold and crystal, while the luxury of hot and cold running water was unheard of in Yorkshire. "Thank you for sending the maid to explain all the equipment."

"After traveling, I know how I welcome a bath."

"Indeed, it was wonderful." Elspeth swept her hand downward. "I do apologize for my frock, however. We were planning on rough accommodations on our travels. My wardrobe is devoid of grand gowns."

"You look perfectly lovely. Muslin becomes you—unlike so many ladies who are too matronly to carry off the new shepherdess fashions."

Elspeth smoothed the skirt of her simple French-gray frock, standing patiently as Sophie tied the blue silk bow at the back of her waist. "A color such as this was meant to withstand more primitive conditions than London. The port where Will was set ashore is little more than a bivouac, I understand."

"We must have the cook pack you some victuals for your journey, then—and drinking water no doubt would be useful as well. Morocco is desert, is it not?"

"I'm not sure. Although I shall find out soon enough."

"There ye be, sweetie," Sophie said, patting the bow into place and smiling at her charge. "Ye look right pretty."

"Ready, then?" Betsy rose to her feet in a froth of cerise silk.

Elspeth took a small breath. "I confess, I'm very nervous."

Betsy had deliberately delayed their meeting until Elspeth could cast off her dusty traveling gown, wishing for her brother's sake that his paramour be seen in the best light. "There's no reason in the world why you should be nervous." Betsy smiled. "*Maman* and Papa will find you charming." In fact, Lady Grafton was stunning—all golden hair and wide-eyed innocence . . . not Julius's usual style, but definitely a beauty. "As for my children, I warn you, they are spoiled and demanding and not in the least well-trained," she declared, her smile that of a doting mother.

"I'm forewarned, then," Elspeth said, a teasing note in her voice. "Although I thought them sweet children when I saw them that day at Julius's."

"They simply adore their uncle. He's much too extravagant with them, but curbing Julius is impossible as you no doubt know. There, now I've gone and embarrassed you. Forgive me.

I'm afraid I have a tendency to speak my mind rather too often. Come, the champagne is waiting."

Just as the ladies were entering the drawing room in London, Darley's valet was knocking on the door of the marquis's bedchamber at Langford on Thames.

"A message for you, my lord!"

Lying in the shambles of his bed where he and Amanda had been largely installed for the better part of a fortnight, Darley opened his eyes marginally, glanced at Amanda who had come awake at his valet's interruption and shouted back, "Go away!"

"It's a message from the duchess, my lord!"

"*Merde,*" he muttered, not in the mood for family matters. "Read it to me!"

"It's sealed, my lord!"

His mother only sealed letters that were for his eyes only; her usual invitations for her numerous routs and dinners were left open for his valet or secretary to read.

Which meant he'd have to get out of bed. Sighing softly, he swung his legs over the side of the bed, came to his feet and padded across the Turkish carpet to the door. It wasn't a true crisis, he knew, or his mother would have sent her personal groom with the message.

Running one hand through his ruffled hair, he opened the door, and standing nude on the threshold, held out his hand.

Without expression, his valet dropped the letter into his open palm.

"Thank you, Ned. You needn't wait for an answer." Shutting the door, Darley walked to the terrace windows where enough light still remained on this summer evening to make out the script. Breaking the seal, he unfolded the sheet and read:

My dear boy,
    I thought you might like to know that we have Lady Grafton as our guest tonight. She is in London alone and for only a single

*night. She sails on the morning tide to bring her brother back from
his sickbed in Morocco.*

*Affectionately,
Maman*

He stood there, the words searing his brain, the thought of
Elspeth at his parents' both provocative and disturbing. Was she
pregnant, was his first thought. He'd deliberately avoided issues
of paternity by amusing himself with sophisticated women—*except* for the virginal Lady Grafton. Had she come to make demands through his parents? Or was it possible there was some
more benign reason why she was a guest at Westerlands House?
More to the point—demanding women not uncommon in his
life—did it matter whether she was in London or not?

He'd been standing with the note in his hand for so long that
Amanda pushed up on her elbows and gave him a searching
glance. "Bad news?"

"No—it's nothing . . . just one of *Maman's* dinner parties." He
dropped the note on a nearby table. "For some reason, she thinks
I'm interested."

"And are you?"

He didn't answer, gazing out the window into the growing twi-
light with a faint frown.

Not familiar with being ignored, Amanda wrinkled her nose.
"Have you fallen asleep over there or have you taken a sudden
interest in your garden?"

Darley slowly turned his head. "Did you say something?"

"Be a dear," she murmured, sensible enough not to provoke
Darley when she was enjoying her holiday on the Thames, "and
pour me another glass of claret."

He gazed at her for a moment, then abruptly smiled. "One
glass of claret coming up. Would you like more cake as well?"

"Perhaps a tiny little piece."

He laughed. "Does that make six or eight?"

"Does it matter?"

"Not in the least." Her very small pieces had added up to almost an entire cake since their luncheon in the garden. But ever gracious, he poured her claret, cut her piece of cake from the remains they'd brought inside and delivered both to her with an exquisite bow. "For your pleasure, my lady," he murmured, setting the items on the bedside table.

"You may offer me something else for my pleasure as well," she purred, her gaze traveling slowly downward until it rested on the object of her affection.

He grinned. "Why am I not surprised?" Climbing over her, he fell into a sprawl at her side and inquired, blandly, "Sex first or claret and cake?"

Amanda's gaze moved from the bedside table to Darley's rising erection. "This first," she said, reaching for his cock.

As the heat of her mouth closed over the crest of his penis, Darley found himself suddenly unconcerned with any quandaries precipitated by his mother's invitation to dinner, the immediacy of sensation overpowering such irksome dilemmas. That he'd been drinking for a fortnight contributed as well to his lazy indifference to events beyond the confines of his bed—or more pertinently—his cock. And Amanda had an endearing ability to take almost his entire length into her mouth. It was a gift, he reflected. A damnably fine gift. Shutting his eyes, he concentrated on licentious sensation.

After she'd swallowed some time later, Amanda pivoted upward, lay across Darley's chest and murmured through the salty taste of him, "Did you like your orgasm, oh lord and master?"

His eyes opened marginally, his gaze amused. "Are you my maid this time or my governess? Or do we have a new game to play?"

"I was thinking if you liked my services, my lord, you might allow me to serve as upstairs maid more often," she murmured.

"I'm not sure you're experienced enough," Darley drawled, picking up on his role with ease. "Has the housekeeper explained the nature of your duties?"

Amanda offered up a winsome gaze. "She said only that I was to do whatever you asked."

"So if I were to ask you to say—wake me like that every morning—"

"I would be honored, my lord." Her voice was wispy, deferential.

He suppressed a smile, Amanda and deference normally polar opposites. "The hours could be long," he noted, his expression suitably severe. "I'm a hard taskmaster."

"I'm getting wet just listening to you," she whispered, rubbing against his chest, her nipples hard as jewels.

"You're not allowed to get wet unless I sanction it," he said, with a proper imperiousness. "My maids must practice self-denial."

She shot a glance at his cock. "*You* don't practice self-denial."

"How dare you chastise me." There was a ruthless edge to his voice. "I could have you discharged without a reference."

"But would you?" she asked in a dulcet murmur, wiggling her bottom with a restive impatience, Darley's low growl reminding her of how aggressive he could be if he wished. Or if she did.

Pushing himself up on his elbows, he brusquely shoved her away. "What makes you think I wouldn't, you brazen trollop?"

"Ask your steward," she said. "He'll tell you how good I am."

"I don't care if you're fucking half my household," Darley snapped. "If you don't please me, you're out the door. Is that clear?" Amanda liked to be dominated. It had something to do with her older brother although he'd never cared to hear the details. But nothing got her wetter and hotter than curt orders from a man.

"I'll do *anything* you say, my lord, if only you'll let me stay."

"Then get on your hands and knees and lift your little bottom high enough to give me easy access. And I don't want you to cry if it hurts."

"Oh, please, don't hurt me," she begged, plaintively.

"Just do it," he growled.

She scrambled to obey, displaying herself as directed.

Sitting up, Darley surveyed the lush, pink bottom conveniently positioned, Amanda whimpering softly, begging him with tragic fervor not to hurt her. Was her earnestness real or in play?

He wasn't sure.

Nor did he care.

Coming up on his knees behind her, grasping her hips, he rammed his cock up her slippery wet vagina, any issues of possible pain quickly put to rest—as he'd suspected. And with masterful diligence and suitable drama, in due course, he made certain that his erstwhile, apparently insatiable, upstairs maid understood the full extent of her duties.

Amanda shouldn't have been surprised when Darley gave her a light kiss afterward, rose from the bed and announced, "I'm going into London." She'd known as he was having sex with her that his thoughts were elsewhere. Not that he hadn't performed with his usual expertise. Not that he hadn't let her come as often as she wished, nor had several orgasms himself. But his eyes had shut from time to time against some inner vision and she wasn't sure whether she should be grateful or resentful of that scene playing behind his eyelids.

Since he'd been in top form, she chose not to quibble over the impulses motivating him. Since she'd been the recipient of his highly charged passions, who was she to complain over the reasons why? But she rolled over to follow his progress as he walked away, and out of curiosity asked, "Why are you going to London?"

He opened the armoire and pulled out a shirt. "To please my mother, I suppose."

"Such filial piety. I'm impressed."

"Betsy and the children are at the house, too."

As they have been these many weeks, she thought. "I see," she said, instead, their long relationship partly the result of her talent for knowing when not to be difficult. "Will you be back soon?"

"I don't know." Tossing the shirt over his head, he slid his arms into the sleeves. "Stay if you wish."

"There's no point in my staying if you're not coming back."

He looked up from buttoning a cuff. "Suit yourself. My plans are uncertain." Sometime in the last hour, he'd found himself unable to resist seeing Elspeth, pregnant or not. And if, indeed, she was leaving in the morning, his window of opportunity was limited. Whatever had brought her to his parents' home could be dealt with, while *his* reason for going there was simple. And decidedly carnal.

Slipping on his breeches, he buttoned them as he walked toward the door. Pulling the door open a moment later, he shouted loudly enough to carry down the corridor and into the entrance hall, "Have my horse saddled and brought round!"

Before his valet appeared, red-faced and out of breath, the marquis was already dressed, booted, and searching for his gloves, the drawers of the tallboy pulled out willy-nilly.

"You should have called me, sir," the man panted, surveying Julius's casual open-neck shirt with a pained look. "I would have put out your evening clothes."

"My parents won't care what I wear. Is my mount ready? It is? Good. Where do you keep my gloves?"

"Here, my lord." The valet whipped a pair of riding gloves from a bow-front chest and handed them to Darley.

Turning to Amanda who was watching him with unusual intentness, Julius ignored her speculative gaze. "Thank you, darling, for a lovely holiday. Ned will see to anything you require. *Au revoir.*" With a bow, he walked away, slipping on his gloves as he exited the room.

Julius hadn't sounded like a man who was returning soon. Nor did he appear to be a man who had dressed with such speed only to see his parents. His mother's note was still on the table where he'd dropped it; obviously its contents weren't confidential when he'd left it exposed. Or so she rationalized as she rose from the bed, walked over and picked it up.

Lady Grafton's name leaped from the page.

As Amanda read on, her brow furrowed.

So the little chit was in London—*and* mysteriously at Westerlands House—more strangely yet—Julius had been sent for.

The burning question was why?

She didn't believe the tale of a sick brother for a second.

Although it was extremely clever of the lady to ingratiate herself with Darley's parents.

If she were a betting woman—which she was—she might be tempted to take odds against Darley on this one. The little baggage had come to London alone, obviously concocted some admirable story to gull Julius's family—and the peerless piece de resistance was her apparent assertion that she was in town for only one night.

Tempus fugit.

Now or never.

What wonderful bait!

Chapter
22

Langford was in the suburbs, the distance to Westerlands House an easy drive and a swifter ride—particularly for a man in a hurry.

Particularly when he rode prime horseflesh bred to run.

Particularly when the rider was focused on the lady awaiting him at the end of his journey.

The marquis told himself his exaggerated interest in seeing Elspeth was simply the result of the boredom he'd been experiencing of late—Amanda's sexual amusements notwithstanding.

Not to mention, the prospect of Elspeth staying in his parents' house was much too intriguing a scene to miss.

He didn't admit that he might wish to see her again because she'd been much on his mind since Newmarket. To admit that would have caused anarchy in a life devoted to casual amours.

He subscribed instead to the it's-sex-and-only-sex-driving-him theory.

He simply wanted to make love to the seductive little wife he'd played with in Newmarket. Since she would be gone in the morning, he was riding into London to avail himself of her sweet passions before it was too late.

It was a perfectly reasonable explanation.

* * *

After dinner, the small party at Westerlands House had retired to the drawing room for tea. As the hour grew later, the children had been kissed and sent off to bed with their nursemaids, and the conversation had turned to various contacts of the duke who might procure a suitable vessel for Elspeth in the morning.

"Admiral Windom will accommodate us, I'm sure," the duke remarked.

"Or Commodore Hathaway," the duchess suggested. "Isn't he in charge of the Mediterranean fleet?"

"Don't forget Harold's good friend, Bedesford," Betsy offered. "He was envoy to one of the sultans, although there are any number of sultans no doubt. But his experience could be useful in some measure."

"Come morning, we'll have my secretary deal with it." The duke smiled at Elspeth. "We can't have you sailing on some lightly armed merchant ship in those pirate infested waters. A vessel with heavy cannon—that's what you want."

Elspeth felt as though she'd stumbled into some snug little earthly paradise where her concerns were paramount, the company was congenial, and an apparent host of angels was catering to her every whim. Had not the duke harrumped from time to time like her papa had, she might have thought she was indeed dreaming.

There was no doubt from whence came Darley's captivating charm. His parents were enchanting, his mother—warm and natural, *au courant* on all the doings of society, willing to speak her mind on any number of subjects. While his father was everything a duke should be and everything the royal family was not—intelligent, masterful, patrician to the core, yet a fount of common sense. His smile was very much like Julius's, too.

"I believe a nice glass of Madeira would suit us now," the duchess announced, setting down her teacup. "Betsy, ring for a footman."

"The '74 Machico," the duke directed.

Before Betsy had moved more than two steps, the tall, gilded double doors suddenly opened and Darley walked in booted and spurred, the scent of the summer evening wafting in behind him.

"Sorry I'm late." He singled out Elspeth with a smile. "A pleasure to see you again, Lady Grafton."

"And you as well, Lord Darley." She was surprised her voice sounded so normal when the object of her dreams these many weeks past was suddenly standing before her.

"You rode, I see," his mother observed, taking in her son's windswept hair and dusty boots. "Have you had your dinner?"

If a flask of brandy on the ride in counted, he had. "I'm not hungry, *Maman*." He began stripping off his gloves when he would have much preferred plucking Elspeth from her chair, carrying her upstairs, making love to her in the nearest bedchamber and being done with it. Not a reasonable option, of course. He handed over his quirt and gloves to a footman who had appeared at his side, anticipating him. "A brandy," he murmured. "Bring the bottle."

"We were about to have a Madeira," the duchess offered.

"Then Madeira, too," he said, dismissing the servant with a nod.

"The '74 Machico," the duke proclaimed to the footman's retreating back. He offered Darley a seat beside him with a wave of his hand. "What brings you into town?" he blandly inquired, although his son's fixed regard for their blushing guest was answer enough.

"Mother's note, of course," Darley said as mildly as his father, taking the offered chair, for it gave him an ideal view of Elspeth. "I'm sorry I didn't arrive in time for dinner."

"We'll have something brought up for you," his mother volunteered.

He smiled. "That's not necessary, *Maman*." Although, Elspeth could use a meal, Darley thought. She looked thinner. Did that negate any concern about a pregnancy or was it too soon to tell? Not that it was a major issue for him. This was, after all, a man's world and pregnancies were of slight account.

So his parents had sent for him, Elspeth reflected, not sure whether to be flattered or piqued. Did they think her available? Was the Ton so familiar with artifice and illicit liaisons that Darley had been invited to take his pleasure of her? Or had their invitation been mere courtesy?

"Betsy tells us you've been at Langford these many weeks," his mother said, making conversation in an effort to wrench her son's gaze from their guest who had taken a sudden interest in her teacup. "How is the fishing?"

He suppressed a laugh. But taking his mother's cue, he said with suave urbanity, "I haven't had time to fish. I've been busy following the events in Parliament." That Amanda's fiancé's letters detailing the workings of government had come with great regularity the past fortnight, allowed him to speak with a moderately clear conscience. "Apparently, the king's bilious fever has everyone in an uproar. The Tories are scrambling to retain power, the Whigs are hoping for bad news." He smiled. "Chaos is the order of the day." He could afford to be polite. Elspeth wasn't going anywhere tonight. He just had to wait until his parents took to their beds. "Was your journey south tedious, Lady Grafton?" he pleasantly inquired, choosing the subject in lieu of the weather that was unremarkable.

"Actually, no, it wasn't." Her cheeks were a resplendent pink and had been since he walked into the drawing room, her gaze focused somewhere in the vicinity of his waistcoat buttons. "We traveled very fast."

"How *is* your brother?" He recalled his mother's mention of him in her note. "Better by now, I hope."

"We don't know."

"She's much concerned, Julius, as you would suspect," his sister interposed, holding his dark gaze for a moment in pointed warning. "Her last report was not comforting."

"I'm sorry. Forgive me. What have you heard of his condition?"

As Elspeth explained the little she knew, he took note of the bracelet she was nervously twisting around her wrist. It was the

one he'd given her. Not that it should matter. After all the jewelry
he'd given women, he shouldn't care one way or the other. But
strangely, he felt as though it marked her as his. As though her
wearing it gave him some proprietary rights. A thoroughly outrageous supposition, of course, when he'd come here simply for a
fuck.

Which thought immediately brought his erection up. He
crossed his legs in an attempt to conceal his arousal, skin-tight
chamois breeches a liability at a time like this. "Perhaps I'll have
a cup of tea while I'm waiting for the brandy," he said, uncrossing
his legs and leaning forward to reach for the teapot, hoping this
family evening wouldn't be too protracted.

"You *are* hungry," his mother said. "Don't argue, darling. We'll
have something brought up for you."

He had no intention of arguing, grateful for the small flurry of
activity as his mother rose to ring for a servant, her chatter as she
crossed the room drawing everyone's attention. Pouring himself a
cup of tea, he sat forward with his forearms on his thighs, the cup
balanced on his fingers, hoping he'd survive the evening without
embarrassing himself.

The last time he'd been out of control like this, he'd been fif-
teen and one of his mother's friends had been flirting with him at
an afternoon musicale he'd been dragged to. Lady Fane had cor-
nered him at the back of the room while all eyes were trained on
the Italian soprano and whispered, "Meet me upstairs in five
minutes."

Not that their liaison hadn't been both enjoyable and enlight-
ening that summer.

But he was past the irrepressible randiness of his youth.

Or so he'd thought.

"There now," his mother said, returning to her chair. "You'll
have something to eat in no time. I expect you've been living on
claret and sandwiches at Langford."

"More or less," he said with a smile.

"We've been discussing who might be helpful in finding a vessel for Elspeth's voyage to Morocco," Betsy interjected, taking

pity on her brother, the cause of his discomfort highly visible from her position. "Do you know of anyone who has information on the best ships sailing that route?"

"Malcolm knows captains who sail that part of the world. He makes all my purchases of Spanish wines. By the way, the San Lucar sherry is excellent this year."

"Malcolm is Julius's secretary—a lovely young man with impeccable manners," the duchess explained to Elspeth. "I don't suppose he's in town," she added, turning to Darley.

"He's at Langford, but I could send for him." The marquis glanced at the clock. "It's not too late yet."

"Then do, by all means." The duchess smiled at Elspeth. "You can't imagine what an incredible aptitude Malcolm has for"—she fluttered her hands—"arranging things. Give him a task and it's accomplished in a thrice." She smiled. "For which Julius is constantly grateful, aren't you darling. Malcolm can transcend the most complete chaos."

Darley smiled faintly. "You make it sound as though I live constantly at sixes and sevens."

"Let's just say you survive in an unsettled milieu that would exhaust most of us, darling. Do be a dear, though, and go send a message to Malcolm before it becomes too late."

Betsy jumped up. "Let me. Julius is drinking his tea."

Darley gave his sister a grateful look. "Tell him to bring my sea charts," he noted as Betsy walked away. "Some routes are better than others this time of year."

"*You* could take Lady Grafton to Morocco," his mother said. "Now, why didn't we think of it before. The *Fair Undine* would suit perfectly."

"My schedule doesn't allow, *Maman*."

"I can't imagine what you have to do that can't wait a few weeks."

"I wish I could, but I can't," he said, offering Elspeth a polite smile.

"Please, Lady Westerlands, I couldn't possibly impose on Lord Darley," Elspeth quickly interjected. "There are any number of vessels plying the waters south that will suit."

The duchess gave her son a censorious look. But, regardless her sympathy for Lady Grafton's misfortunes, she knew better than to press him. He did very much as he pleased. "I'm sure the commodore will be more accommodating," she did say, however, reaching over and patting Elspeth's hand. "The duke has done him any number of favors."

"I'd prefer not burdening anyone with my plight," Elspeth murmured. "I'm already too much in your debt." She smiled. "Charlie's extremely capable. He'll find us a ship in the morning."

"Nonsense," the duke said. "I'll take care of it. Where's that damned Madeira?"

The duke's tone was such that everyone understood he would brook no interference.

A small silence ensued.

The duchess sniffed her displeasure of her son.

The duke shouted for a footman.

Elspeth tried to disappear into the settee.

Only Darley seemed unaffected by the exchange, pouring himself another cup of tea, stirring in three spoons of sugar, then adding a fourth and stirring some more.

Two footmen appeared almost immediately in the wake of the duke's shout, one conveying Darley's dinner on a silver tray, the other bringing in the brandy and Madeira. Betsy followed on their heels, after having sent a message to Malcolm informing him he was needed at Westerlands House. Darley ate moderately and drank less so, seeming intent on emptying the brandy bottle; the Madeira drinkers sipped the savory nectar in a more leisurely manner and the remainder of the evening passed in an atmosphere of strained affability and/or highly charged emotion depending on the individual.

It was all Elspeth could do not to shake, so agitated was she by Darley's presence and the intensity of his gaze. She often had to be addressed twice before hearing the question put to her. And when she answered, her attempts at conversation became increasingly brief and disjointed while her surreptitious glances at the clock became more frequent.

For his part, the marquis was in such an intolerable state of rut, he wasn't sure he'd survive this drawing room farce without exploding in some highly inappropriate way. Sheer will kept him in his seat when he'd thought a hundred times of snatching up Elspeth like some highwayman, throwing her over his shoulder and spiriting her from the room. As to his conversation, any of his friends would have wondered at the taut, unusual silence in a man known for his wit and repartee.

As the tall case clock chimed eleven, and his mother finally said, "It's getting late and Elspeth has to sail on the morrow," Darley felt such profound relief, he actually sighed aloud.

The duchess tossed a cool look his way at his gaucherie, came to her feet and held out her hand to Elspeth. "Come, my dear, Betsy and I will see you to your room."

As the ladies left the drawing room, the duke met his son's gaze over the rim of his glass. "You mother has taken on the role of duenna."

Darley dipped his head. "So I see."

"I commend you on your restraint. A novel situation for you, I expect."

"As you say," Julius replied with a tight smile. "But *Maman* would have rapped my knuckles had I misbehaved."

"The lady intrigues you, I gather."

"Apparently so."

"You're surprised."

"Vastly."

"What do you intend to do about it?"

Darley's brows rose. "I hardly intend to tell you."

"Don't offend your mother."

"Meaning?"

"Exactly that. She likes the gel. Although who wouldn't with her sweetness and beauty, not to mention the tragedies she's endured in her young life."

Darley met his father's gaze. "Am I being warned off?"

"I wouldn't presume to tell you what to do at your age. But you might *reconsider* taking the lady to Morocco. You have nothing to do beyond your usual debauch as you well know. I'm not expecting you to declare yourself to her."

"I'm relieved," the marquis drawled, "since she's already married. But allow me to refuse for reasons of my own. For one, I'm not inclined to spend weeks at sea with a woman." He shrugged. "It's too close quarters. And you heard her. She's quite willing to make her own plans."

The duke examined the liquor in his glass for a moment. "Perhaps you're right. She has an innocence about her though, doesn't she." He shook his head. "It's distasteful to think of her married to that blackguard Grafton."

"The marriage was never consummated if it makes you feel any better."

"Ah . . . I see. Indeed." He shrugged faintly. "I must be getting old. Hers isn't the first arranged marriage by any measure."

"Money for beauty," Darley murmured. "A custom old as man."

The duke tossed down the rest of his drink, set his glass aside and came to his feet. "How's Grafton's health? Might she be a widow soon?"

"You're taking an inordinate interest in someone you've just met."

The duke's brows lifted faintly. "Perhaps you have more taste than I give you credit for."

"Pray, don't start making plans for me."

"Now why would I do that when you've been fucking to your heart's content for lo these many years."

"I'm comforted you haven't turned mawkish in your declining years."

"Loving someone is the greatest of joys, my boy." The old duke smiled. "I hope someday you'll be as lucky as I."

"Just not too soon," Darley observed. "I believe I still have five years before I reach the age when Cupid's dart struck you."

"A word of advice," the duke murmured. "Love doesn't appear at your convenience. Sleep well," he added with a flicker of his brows.

"Since *Maman* likes her so, Elspeth must be in the Queen's Room?"

"Your mother put her there because *you* seem to like her so."

"She couldn't have known. I wasn't here."

His father smiled. "You know mothers. They know everything."

Chapter

23

The flickering light from the wall sconces illuminated Darley's passage up the broad staircase and down the carpeted hall to the Queen's Room that overlooked the garden behind the house.

Standing in the hallway outside the door, he listened, very much hoping he wouldn't hear his mother's voice.

But only silence met his ears.

Then the sound of Sophie's voice drifted faintly into the hall, answered by Elspeth's softer tones.

He suddenly wondered if it had been a mistake to have come into town. Perhaps what he wished to do wouldn't be of benefit to him after all. Since Newmarket, he'd experienced only discontent—for reasons he'd chosen not to acknowledge. And now that he was here, would a night with Elspeth be a remedy for his discontent or simply add to his affliction?

Walking away, he came to rest before a Palladian window at the end of the hall. Surveying the moonlit parterres below, he debated returning to Langford. The previous hours playing the gentleman had been frustrating. He'd been living a life of self-indulgence too long to sit in a drawing room drinking tea and exchanging small talk when his aching cock was demanding surcease.

Merde. He blew out an exasperated breath. Maybe he should cut his losses and decamp.

There was a possibility that Elspeth would turn him down even if he stayed. And she had every right to. Women took issue with being discarded, as he well knew.

He smiled faintly. Then again, placating women was his strong suit. One didn't gain a reputation for amorous adventure without acquiring a facile repertoire of conciliatory phrases along the way. And Elspeth wasn't here long enough for his honeyed words to have any major consequences.

So if he wanted a night of sex with the voluptuous Lady Grafton, it looked as though the old mainstay of suave flattery was on the agenda. Perhaps even a hitherto unpracticed sincerity might be of use.

Which called into question what exactly he was sincere about? Other than sex.

While Darley was contemplating this newfound notion of sincerity, Sophie was tucking Elspeth into bed. "You can say no to him," she asserted. "Don't think you can't."

Elspeth ran her palms over the coverlet, her eyes downcast. "He may not even bother to come."

"Oh, he'll bother, you can be sure o' that."

"It *was* lovely seeing him again." Discounting all the obstacles and hindrances that should have deterred her blind adoration, she uttered a small covetous sigh. "Didn't he look terribly handsome and grand?"

"Handsome he might be and grand as a prince, but he's naught but trouble in the end, sweetling. I know how much you missed him, though, so you won't hear no platitudes from me."

Elspeth smiled at her old nanny. "If platitudes would have solved my heartache these weeks past, I would have embraced them willingly."

"I know, I know," Sophie murmured, patting Elspeth's hand. "It's yer life for you to choose yer poison and that's a fact. Not that my Lord Darley wouldn't be mighty sweet goin' down. As for me own personal taste, I'm gonna have meself a cup o' tea. Charlie's in the kitchen waitin' for me to give him the story on yer visit with the duke and duchess. Sleep tight," she added, giving Elspeth a kiss on the cheek.

"I'm not going to sleep a wink when he's in the *same* house," Elspeth whispered, putting her palms to her hot cheeks. "Just think—he's *here* somewhere!"

Sophie winked. "And probably on his way to see ye right now."

Elspeth laughed. "Then go, go," she ordered, teasingly, shooing her maid away with a flutter of her hands. "Go this instant."

After descending the servants' stairway, Sophie entered the kitchen. The large room was silent, the fire in the grate burning low, the candles on the table a soft flickering glow in the darkness.

Charlie nodded as she approached. "He came, I hear."

"And she's faint from longing, the poor dear," Sophie noted, taking a seat at the table opposite the coachman. "When everyone knows he's a rake and a rogue and bound to break her heart all over agin." Reaching for the tea Charlie had poured for her, she shook her head. "There's no talkin' any sense into her, though."

Charlie shrugged. "The gentry have their own ways about 'em. They make their own rules, they do, and they're not the ones for me or you. Mayhap one night with him will at least bring her some peace. She's been right heartsick since he left."

"Poor baby. And a man like him what has his pick of all the ladies in the Ton, they say." She pursed her mouth. "But she wants him, there's no way around it. Mayhap you're right about a night with the rogue bringin' her some content. You and me both know there could be a right bitter end to our journey what with death knockin' at poor Will's door. Ef'n the handsome lord can make my lady happy for a few hours"—Sophie shrugged—"who am I to say it's wrong?"

* * *

While the servants were discussing the merits and liabilities of Darley and Elspeth's liaison, the main players were debating their options.

No one had come in or out of the room, Julius noted, which meant Elspeth might or might not be alone. As he recalled, her maid didn't sleep with her, though. If Sophie was there, she'd be in the dressing room, he decided, counting the topiary yews in the garden below for the eighth time.

While Darley was counting yews, Elspeth nearly had made up her mind to go find him, her only deterrent the colossal size of Westerlands House. The duchess had mentioned *thirty-some* bedchambers.

She could ask a servant where Darley was sleeping, she supposed.

How desperate would that be?

And embarrassing.

As the minutes ticked by, Elspeth finally came to the conclusion that neither embarrassment nor desperation would matter if she didn't return from her journey. And that possibility was very real. The voyage entailed enormous risks. The oceans and weather could be treacherous, pirates were rampant on the African coast, Morocco was nominally ruled by the sultan in Constantinople, but the local potentate governed autocratically. The only source of English authority was a single consul in Tangier.

When faced with issues of life and death, questions of propriety or embarrassment appeared less significant.

Or—completely inconsequential.

Tossing aside her covers, she slid from the bed and reached for her dressing robe.

He wasn't about to count the topiaries for the ninth time, Darley decided, as though he'd reached some level of self-discovery.

Turning on his heel, he strode toward the Queen's Room.

Fuck it.

Or fuck her.

Or fuck himself, perhaps, but he wasn't going to stand out in the hall like some bloodless fool.

Reaching the door of the Queen's Room, he pushed it open and walked in, the door shutting behind him with a soft click.

Elspeth spun around, eyes flaring wide, her dressing robe clutched to her bosom.

"Are you alone?" the marquis asked, gruffly. "Not that I care." Diplomacy apparently had given way to raw feeling.

She drew in a sharp breath, his rough voice bringing back a flood of unwanted memories. "Don't talk to me in that tone." Free of Grafton, she would *remain* free and against such hardened principle, adoration was forfeit.

He almost smiled at her feistiness when she was so small and he was not, when this was his home. But he was here because of some irresistible force he could no longer ignore and this time when he spoke, his voice was mild. "Forgive me. I spoke out of turn. Let me begin afresh." He took a small breath, beset by a novel sense of solemn purpose. "I've missed you for a very long time. I've tried to forget you"—he smiled ruefully—"without success. In fact, I'm feeling more than a little deranged at the moment for want of you."

A faint smile lifted her mouth, his candor enchanting. "You've been much on my mind, too," she said, weeks of longing equally culpable in her acquiescence. She held out her dressing robe. "See—I was about to go looking for you when I had no idea where to look."

"Then you're happy I walked in," he drawled, back on familiar ground, a woman wanting him a constant in his life.

"Against my maid's advice, I might add," Elspeth noted.

His lashes lowered infinitesimally. "I'm guessing my mother would prefer guarding your virtue, as well."

"So then." She tossed her robe on a chair and gave him a mischievous glance. "What are we to do against these twin forces of decorum?"

His smile illuminated the room, perhaps the universe. "I say we do as we please." His brows rose. "When do you sail?"

"On the morning tide." She glanced at the clock. "That gives us six hours."

He didn't move for a moment—after weeks of discontent—the elusive goal was at hand. He exhaled softly. "Do you know how long I've been thinking of this?"

"Since Newmarket for me," she replied, giving herself high marks for composure when she could so calmly understate the violence of her feelings. "I vastly enjoyed our time together there."

"Those days have become my gold standard for pleasure," he said with utter honesty.

"I expect you tell all the ladies that."

"Never," he said, surprising himself—sweet lies had always been his currency in dalliance.

"I think it's time you lock the door," she affirmed, as though she'd stamped his response with her seal of approval.

"In a hurry?" His smile was assured.

"Do you know how many weeks it's been since I saw you last?"

"Five weeks, three days, six and a half hours, give or take."

"Then don't toy with me," she purred, his ticking off the days and hours more seductive than the most ardent love poem. Not that she was naive enough to expect incorruptible sincerity at a time like this. Especially from a man like Darley whose sole interest was pleasure. But tonight, her interests were the same.

Because tomorrow she faced the great unknown.

And the day after that might never come.

The marquis was already locking the door to the hall.

She watched him as he went about locking the door to the dressing room as well, his beauty notorious, his bold virility the stuff of legend.

A tiny shiver raced up her spine.

Tonight he was hers.

He moved with a lithe grace, his spurs jingling faintly as he walked. His dark gleaming hair tied back behind the high collar of his riding coat, the black superfine tailored to the inch across his broad shoulders, his embroidered waistcoat smooth as silk over his hard, taut stomach. Then he turned and her breath caught in her throat at the sight of his rampant erection straining against the soft leather of his breeches.

Her cheeks instantly flushed, a throbbing deep inside commenced, the pulsing rhythm echoing in her ears. As he approached, an immeasurable gratitude filled her senses. How long had she waited for this? How often had she dreamed of seeing him again? "I want you to know how pleased I am—how grateful that you came tonight." She smiled. "In fact, a word of warning might be in order." She held out her trembling hands. "I fear I may be insatiable or demanding or both."

"I warn you as well," he murmured, reaching her, pulling her close, brushing her mouth with his. "After waiting so long, I take no responsibility for my actions. Hit me hard if you want me to stop."

"I didn't think I'd ever, *ever* see you again," she whispered.

"I've been drinking my way through my cellar trying to do just that." He lifted his head and grinned. "Unsuccessfully as you see."

"I'm really, really glad for that." Her eyes filled with tears.

"Hush, hush—don't cry—don't," he murmured. "I'm here . . . I came . . . we're together again." He licked away the tears sliding down her cheeks. "Tell me what you want and I'll do it."

What she wanted she could never have, but hiccuping through her tears, she stammered, "I—don't . . . want to think . . . about tomorrow . . . that's what . . . I want . . ."

"Then we won't," he said, husky and low. "I'm going to kiss you and you're going to kiss me back and—"

"A second after that . . . you're going to make love . . . to me." Rubbing her eyes with her sleeve, she sniffled and, bleary-eyed, met his gaze. "And that's . . . an . . . order."

He was already pulling up her night shift, more than pleased to dispense with foreplay—her order for immediate sex commensurate with his own inclinations.

She readily lifted her arms, after the long evening in the drawing room longing for him—for this, her partiality was for speed.

"I know I should be demure and modest, grateful for your notice, but—"

"Good God, no," he said, cutting her off. "Why would I want that?"

"Because females shouldn't be forward," she replied, her voice muffled by the fine cambric sliding over her head.

"*Au contraire*, I'm damned glad you are and even happier that I found you again," he said with more vehemence than he intended.

"So I don't have to apologize?"

"For wanting to fuck me?" he said, dropping her gown on the floor. "I don't think so." Sliding his hands around her waist, he lifted her onto the bed, her new slenderness even more evident without her numerous petticoats and ruffled gown. "You've definitely lost weight. Have you been sick?"

"Only so much as pining for you is a sickness." She smiled. "I rode for hours every day, trying to forget you."

"I drank instead." He slipped his watch chain through his waistcoat button hole and set the time piece on the nightstand. "Did your diversion work? Mine didn't. Although the liquor trade is certainly richer for my misery."

Her heart did a little flutter. "You were miserable without me?"

"Damned miserable." He was surprised at his candor, although her leaving in the morning no doubt allowed him greater honesty.

"I thought of nothing but you for all these *endless* weeks," she murmured. "I apologize for my indelicacy. I know no one speaks of love in situations like this, but I found myself thinking in those terms. Don't take alarm," she said, as he suddenly went motionless, his coat halfway off his shoulders. "I declare my feelings in the most innocent way. I'm leaving in the morning, as you know." She shrugged. "How can it matter what I say?"

His thoughts exactly, although he wasn't so green that he'd say so. "Then frankness is the rule tonight," he facetiously remarked. "A novelty in my world."

"I rather thought it was," she said with a smile, pleased to see him resume his undressing.

Elspeth was sitting on the edge of a gilded bed designed to complement the room's fashionable Zucchi interior. Taking in her swinging feet and sunny smile, she looked so much like an innocent child, she seemed out of place in this sumptuous, imposing room, Darley mused.

Or perhaps she was a breath of fresh air in this modish interior, like some lovely pink-skinned nymph or fey sprite from mythical climes.

That the Queen's Room was only volunteered for the most distinguished guests should have given him pause. But tonight he took no care that his mother had earmarked Elspeth for that special favor. Even while he suspected her reason why.

Instead, he understood there was enormous latitude allowed him—them—tonight with their hours together finite.

He'd never felt such freedom.

Which might have given him the license to say, "I thought you might be pregnant and had come to town to confront my parents."

Her eyes flared wide. "I would never have such nerve." Her expression suddenly took on a speculative cast. "And yet you came."

"As you see." He didn't elaborate. He couldn't—not understanding himself, why he'd come in spite of that liability.

"What would you have done if I *had* been pregnant?"

He shrugged, dressed in only his breeches now. "Probably nothing."

"Because you wouldn't have to." She shouldn't allow herself to be distracted by his physical beauty when his answer had been so crudely blunt, but she was. He was stunningly male—corded muscle, raw strength, a face handsome as a god's.

"You *are* married," he pointed out in another forthright observation, although he felt a rare proprietary satisfaction in knowing that he'd been her first lover.

His dispassionate statement was also quintessential male.

"That's true," she said, aware of the rules that governed society. Men were exempt from responsibility unless they were brought into court. Not a normal practice in the aristocracy where scandal was never openly acknowledged. "I could have named you father, however." Her voice took on an accusatory inflection. "You would have had to assume some monetary responsibility."

"What makes you think I would have contested my paternity?"

"I should be grateful for that, I suppose," she muttered. "But then money isn't an issue for you, is it?"

He sighed. "I'm sorry. I've made you angry." His dark gaze met hers. "Should I go?"

"Because I'm *not* pregnant? What would be the point?"

"I'll apologize at least," he said, trying to make his way through this potentially explosive exchange. "The world can be cruel, I know."

"Because it's a man's world," she said brusquely.

He half lifted his hands in a gesture of surrender, defenseless against her assertion. "I don't know where to go from here. If you have any suggestions . . ."

"I might. It depends."

"On?" His gaze was watchful.

"On whether you're afraid to make love to a woman who might speak more bluntly than you're used to." She gave him a speculative look. "After weeks spent riding in Yorkshire, I'm not inclined to be self-sacrificing. Nor can I see how rules and conventions particularly matter now. Whether I take you to bed or not is only my business and yours." Her brows arched faintly and she suddenly smiled. "So?"

"You don't have to ask me twice." He stripped his breeches off with lightning speed. "In fact," he said with an answering smile, "I'm not so sure I would have left regardless of your wishes."

"Your arrogance becomes you. You know that, don't you?" In her heart of hearts she knew she couldn't have turned him away.

"I know nothing of the kind. But that you want me, pleases me immeasurably."

"Good." She patted the bed, worldly custom discarded for more pleasant endeavors, the brevity of their time together always in the forefront of her mind. "Come give me pleasure for I might be without it for a very long time."

"You look more fragile than I remembered," he observed, moving the few steps to the bed. "I'll be careful not to hurt you."

"Don't worry about me. All I want from you are sufficient orgasms to sustain me during the long, lonely weeks at sea."

"Tell me how many," he whispered, tumbling her back and following her down. "And we'll see what we can do . . ."

He was as good as his word, making love to her with incredible sweetness, in contrast to his recent interlude at Langford where sex had been sex had been sex—pure and simple.

Tonight was different.

Tonight, he inhaled love with his kisses without recoiling in alarm. Tonight, he dared to say, "Call on me when you return. Let me have the pleasure of meeting your brother."

"I will," she said, wanting to with all her heart, even while she knew she couldn't. If she were fortunate enough to return with Will, she could never, never see Darley. Because if once she did, she knew she'd be lost. To be a kept woman would break her spirit.

He was on his absolute best behavior in every way, carefully gauging Elspeth's responses as they made love, watchful, attentive, wanting to maximize her pleasure, concentrating all his ingenuity and sexual talent toward giving her deep-felt satisfaction.

He found their night of passion startlingly meaningful.

It was tantamount to distilling the decade or more of his prurient experiences into a concentrated affection so pure it caused him to reconsider his father's recent homilies about love.

Not that he was going to throw over the traces and take on a new persona. But he had to admit, there was something intrinsically satisfying about making love to a woman who involved your senses and not just your cock.

Feelings of affection notwithstanding, a rake of long standing isn't so easily converted into a pattern card of propriety and in the course of the night, he forgot his poetical fancies in the more familiar rapture of orgasmic release.

And much, much later when they were both half dozing, Elspeth snuggled closer and murmured something in her sleep.

He brought himself awake at the sound of her voice, struggling against his drowsiness after his fortnight of little sleep and less rest at Langford.

Her lashes fluttered open as though she too was attuned to his movement.

"More?" he politely inquired, his voice husky with fatigue.

She smiled and shook her head, her eyes shutting once again.

He forced himself to stay awake for a time, solicitous of her needs, gallantly willing to assuage her passions if she so desired.

But her breathing soon settled into the gentle rhythm of slumber.

And only then, did he fall sleep.

Chapter

24

At first light, Darley gently eased out of bed, taking care not to wake Elspeth. Standing at the bedside, he gazed at the lush, sleeping woman who had redefined sensation for him, who had changed forever his definition of passion. Then the mantel clock struck the hour and shaking away a singular feeling of regret, he picked up his breeches and quietly left the room.

Minutes later, he was shaking his secretary awake.

"I'm up, I'm up," Malcolm muttered, his eyes still shut.

"We have to chart a course to Tangier for the *Fair Undine*. I'll meet you in the library in five minutes."

The young man's eyes snapped open. "Are you sailing to Tangier?"

"I'm not, but you are." Darley turned at the door. "Lady Grafton requires an escort. Do you want coffee or tea?"

"Coffee. When are we sailing?" Malcolm had swung out of bed and was shoving his night shirt into his breeches.

"This morning—with the tide. You don't need shoes. Come, bring the charts," Darley ordered over his shoulder as he walked away. "I'll have your coffee waiting."

Before the men had fully unrolled the sea charts, they were joined by the duke, faultlessly dressed and shaved, unlike his partially dressed companions who looked the worse for wear.

"I've been waiting for you two to wake up," he said, waving over the footman who had walked in with the tray of coffee.

"It's early yet," Julius replied. "And my yacht is always ready. Time isn't an issue."

The duke met his son's gaze. "You're taking Lady Grafton on the *Fair Undine*?"

"No. Malcolm is."

"Is there any possibility you might change your mind?"

"No. Nothing's changed since last I spoke with you."

"I see. Does she know?"

Julius's lashes lowered marginally. "We didn't discuss sea voyages."

The subject was closed. The duke understood. At least Julius was sending her off in relative luxury, the *Fair Undine* well above the standards of any merchant craft. "You might like to add some extra cannon," he suggested. "The coast of Africa is a sea lane for the pirates and they're becoming more bold. An East India merchantman was attacked last month. A rarity for so large a ship."

"I expect the richness of the cargo enticed them," Julius noted. "The *Fair Undine* will be less tempting. And it's well armed. Any added weight will only compromise her speed." Darley's yacht was one of the fastest vessels built, his racing records unbeaten since '85 when the *Fair Undine* had first taken to the water. That ability to outsail the competition would be useful on the Barbary Coast.

"You know best," his father remarked. Julius was a sailor of note. Since his youth, he'd been in love with the sea, buying larger and faster craft as he aged, winning all the premier races by the time he was twenty.

In the following half hour, while Darley and Malcolm charted the course to Tangier, the duke served as observer and coffee pourer. He also jotted down a number of items to send along for Lady Grafton's comfort: a case of champagne; fruit from his conservatory; some good English beef; his own special blend of tea.

Fortunately, Julius had a chef on board to ease her journey. For entertainment, he added some of Julius's bloodstock books to his list. Elspeth had briefly viewed the collection last night, but there hadn't been time to do more. And lastly, he scribbled, plenty of ice to keep the champagne chilled. "Should I send along some extra staff with these supplies I'm adding to the cargo?" he inquired, not sure the *Fair Undine's* personal retainers would be adequate for a lady.

Julius looked up. "Send whomever you like."

"Do you have room?"

One dark brow arched upward. "What do you have in mind?"

"A few servants to see to the lady's comfort."

"A few?"

"That's what I'm asking you. What quarters are available?"

The marquis shrugged. "There's room. Do what you like." If Malcolm hadn't been there he would have said more; his father was taking too much interest in one of his paramours.

Then Malcolm reclaimed his attention, pointing at the approach to the harbor at Tangier. "Do we go in alone or hire a pilot?"

"The charts aren't accurate for that part of the coast. Hire a pilot." Darley blew out a breath and stretched, the muscles of his upper body flexing and un-flexing in a smooth, supple flow. "I think that does it. Tell Captain Tarleton he's free to alter the route. This is only a suggestion."

"Yes, sir, and I'll need that letter to the consul."

Julius turned to his father. "Would you write one? Your name will lend more weight. Elspeth will require help with her brother and consuls in backwaters like Tangier, *can* occasionally be little tyrants."

The duke smiled. "I shall be suitably pompous."

"You might mention your friendship with the king."

"Good idea. I *won't* mention your friendship with the Prince of Wales, however."

Julius grinned. "Very wise." The dissolute escapades of the

prince were not held in high esteem by those in government. "Although a note may not be necessary. Most consuls are gracious to anyone from home."

"We'll consider it insurance. Lady Grafton's task won't be an easy one and if her brother is already dead . . ."

"The poor girl will be inconsolable," the duchess finished as she swept into the room in a rustle of lilac silk. "Although what chance does he have of surviving in such an insalubrious climate?"

"He's young," Julius noted, rolling up the charts. "He may overcome the bad conditions."

"One can but pray." His mother sighed. "Such a shame, as is Elspeth's need to travel so far." She indicated the charts in Julius's hand with a dip of her head. "I see you've been surveying the route."

Darley twined a leather strap around the roll. "Yes. We only await the tide."

"We?" The duchess's face lit up.

"Not *that* we, *Maman*," the marquis corrected, handing over the roll to his secretary. "*Malcolm* will see Elspeth to Tangier. She'll be in capable hands."

The duchess made a small moue. "You disappoint me."

"It can't be helped."

His mother sighed, the likelihood of coercing her son long gone. "Should I wake Elspeth or is she awake?"

"She's sleeping, but I'll wake her." Thin-skinned and edgy, Darley wasn't in the mood to put up with his mother's nonsense.

The duchess didn't contest his gruff reply—or perhaps she had ulterior motives. Perhaps she was hoping her son would be overcome by tender feelings on seeing Elspeth again and change his mind. "Is there time for breakfast before Elspeth leaves or will the tide not allow?"

"Send breakfast up. Then Elspeth can sleep a little longer. We'll meet everyone downstairs in an hour. Alert the captain," Darley added with a nod to Malcolm. "He still has time to lay in additional supplies."

Darley's yacht was always at the ready should the marquis feel a sudden impulse to travel abroad. Awkward entanglements with his female companions often motivated such decisions, a fortnight or so away from England usually sufficient for a paramour's anger to subside. Or at times, when his amusements paled or the pace of his life became too frenzied, he would take to the sea, looking for respite from his ennui in the vast reaches of the ocean.

Chapter
25

Elspeth came awake on Darley's return, as if sensing his presence the moment he walked into the room.

She smiled. "You're up early."

"Malcolm and I charted a course to Tangier," he said, moving toward the bed.

A rush of excitement spiked through her senses. Dare she hope Darley would see her to Morocco?

"Malcolm will take you in the *Fair Undine*. He's supremely competent. You couldn't be in better hands."

Except yours, she thought, swiftly cured of fanciful dreams. She should have known better. "Thank you for your generosity," she said instead. "I'm in your debt."

"Rather I'm in yours," he murmured, coming to a halt at the foot of the bed. "For all the pleasure you've brought me."

She wasn't able to so suavely respond, her emotions trembling on the brink after last night. But those courtesies relating to the offer of his yacht were more easily uttered. "How kind of you to offer the *Fair Undine*," she said. "If I can repay you someday for the use of your yacht, I surely shall."

"Repayment is unnecessary. It's my pleasure to assist you." In the grip of an unfamiliar restlessness, he glanced at the clock.

She saw the direction of his gaze. "Is it time?"

"Soon. I took the liberty of having a bath readied for you." He smiled, although not with his normal ease. "Water is always at a premium at sea."

Elspeth sat up, understanding she must comport herself with dignity. Darley would never mistake amorous pleasure for anything more than it was, *nor* would he welcome maudlin sentimentality. "Sophie must be waiting for me," she said, throwing aside the covers, and reaching for her robe.

"She is." He couldn't help but look, his gaze drawn to her lush form as she slid from the bed. But just as quickly, he looked away, her nudity triggering a host of unwanted sensations. "Breakfast will be here when you've finished."

"You think of everything." Her voice was arch.

His brows rose at her tone. "We try." He wasn't about to acknowledge any hint of temperament. Last night had been memorable; he didn't wish their remaining time together to be acrimonious. "I'll dress while you bathe and then bring back the sea charts to show you over breakfast."

She forced herself to observe the social graces as urbanely as he. She was deeply in his debt. Nor could she take issue with a man who had given her so much pleasure just because he wouldn't take her to Morocco. "Forgive me," she, slipping her arms into her dressing robe. "I didn't mean to act like an ingrate."

"There's nothing to forgive. You're absolutely perfect," he said, gallantly, relieved to see her pull the front of her robe over her plump breasts and silky mons before he lost control. "Since our time is somewhat limited," he said with a faint smile, "might I suggest you bathe quickly."

How smooth he was at avoiding emotion. How accomplished. Taking a lesson from his bland affability, she smiled back as she looped the belt on the dressing robe. "I look forward to your sea charts. Twenty minutes?"

He dipped his head. "Twenty minutes."

She looked back before she entered the bath chamber for she hadn't heard the bedroom door open or close. He was still standing where she'd left him, his expression shuttered, his fingers curled over the spine of the footboard, the strain on his arms visible in the taut disposition of his shoulders.

When she turned, he abruptly smiled and blew her a kiss. Then bending to pick up his boots, he strode from the room.

How unyielding he'd looked standing there. Austere, distant. Until that beguiling smile had flashed with practiced skill. A shame she'd not the strength to withstand his glorious charm. But then, what woman had?

She told herself she wasn't going to cry now that it was over. Crying was useless in any event. Nor did she wish to give Sophie the chance to say, *I told you so.*

She would deal with her loss like a mature and sensible woman.

But the instant she entered the dressing room, she burst into tears and ran to her old nanny.

Sophie held her close, gently stroking her back, whispering into her hair, "There, there, my pet—you'll feel better soon . . . it just takes time. Hush your tears, my sweetling. There're better days ahead. We'll find Will and bring him home safe and make a happy life for you both."

If only it were true. If only Sophie could make everything right again like she had in the past, Elspeth thought, sobbing into her nanny's shoulder. But life wasn't as simple as it was when she was a child. A sweetmeat or a kind word, or a ride on her favorite horse wouldn't make all her sorrows disappear.

And no matter what Sophie said, she wasn't going to feel better soon, because her heart was breaking.

And finding Will and bringing him home safe was a fearsome, daunting journey—with no guarantees.

She was tired to the bone, her nerves on edge, every sensation heightened after last night. But crying wouldn't solve any problems. No matter how many rivers of tears she shed, she wasn't assured of either Darley's love or Will's safety.

She must compose herself. Drawing in a deep breath, she stepped away from Sophie. "I'm done crying," she said, offering a tentative smile. "I'll be fine soon. I'm just short of sleep."

"Poor baby. Anyone can see that you're tired. Get in that there big tub over yon," Sophie said, beginning to untie Elspeth's dressing robe, "and rest while I bathe you."

"He's sending us to Morocco on his yacht." A simple, declarative statement, as devoid of emotion as she could manage. "With his secretary to see to our welfare."

"I heard." Sophie slipped the robe down Elspeth's arms. "Everyone's scurrying about downstairs."

"It's very nice of him to lend us the *Fair Undine*." She was trying to focus on the positive, trying not to let her voice break.

"Yes, it be right nice. I expect it's a fine yacht. He means well I suppose," Sophie said, her upper lip curling with disdain as she slid the robe free.

"Don't be vexed. I didn't expect even that."

"With them like the marquis, you're sensible not to expect much. They think of themselves and always have. I don't mean no disrespect—that's all they know . . . doing what they like." Sophie tossed the robe on a gilt chair.

"While we haven't had that advantage."

"Or disadvantage if'n you ask me," Sophie retorted, waving her charge toward the tub. "If you're too selfish, you sell yerself to the Devil as I sees it."

"That may be." Although Elspeth was reluctant to criticize Darley when so many men of his class were no better and many, like her husband, were much worse. "In any event, we must hurry," she observed, moving forward, her mood a modicum more cheerful. It helped to put things into their proper perspective—Darley a veritable angel compared to Lord Grafton.

At the thought of her surly, hot-tempered spouse, Elspeth almost felt a wave of relief at departing England, provided she found Will in good health—knock wood.

Once she left England, Grafton couldn't touch her.

How gratifying to consider that freedom.

"Tell me Will is feeling better," she said, stepping into the steaming water, needing comfort from the unsettling circumstances surrounding her brother.

"He is and that's a fact," Sophie replied on cue.

Elspeth sank into the soothing warmth. "And we won't be seeing Grafton again."

"Praise God and all the cherubs in heaven, we won't. Now, hold up your hair, my pretty, so it don't get wet. There's no time to dry it."

Chapter
26

Darley was seated at a table placed before the window, sipping his coffee when she walked into the bedroom.

Setting down his cup, he came to his feet with a smile. "You look refreshed. That color becomes you." She wore a simple gown of a chestnut colored lute-string with ecru lace collar and cuffs, the somber shade vivid contrast to her pale skin and golden hair.

"Thank you. I feel refreshed. And thank you for thinking of the bath."

"My pleasure." He held out a chair for her as though they were acquaintances of long-standing, as though they breakfasted together often. "I hope you're hungry. *Maman* ordered enough for a regiment."

"I'm starved," she replied, surveying the vast array of food as she sat.

"Coffee or tea?" Taking his chair across from her, he indicated the two pots. "Tea as I recall."

"Yes, please."

"Half milk, two spoons of sugar. Did I remember?"

"Perfectly." They'd had tea during Newmarket week.

"I don't know your tastes in breakfast. Please, help yourself."

He'd bathed too, his hair still wet, unlike hers that Sophie had

kept dry and tied at her nape with a bow. He wore a blue superfine coat, his linen pristine, his neckcloth impeccably tied, his
waistcoat and breeches both tan and simply tailored. Fighting
back the inclination to throw herself into his arms and passion-
ately declare her undying love, she clasped her hands in her lap
against the impulse. How embarrassed he'd be if she so forgot
herself.

His gaze met hers, reacting to her sudden silence. "Would you
like me to serve you?"

"Thank you, yes."

He looked up at her tone, about to pick up a rasher of bacon.
"Are you feeling well?"

She forced a smile. "I'm just tired. I'll sleep once I'm on
board."

"I shouldn't have kept you up all night. I apologize."

"I kept *you* up. You needn't apologize."

"In any event, you made me very happy."

She wouldn't have used so tame a word. She would have used
a thousand highly charged superlatives to indicate her feelings.
But this was the Ton. This was Lord Darley sitting across from
her—a man who only amused himself with women. She must be
as well-behaved as he. "You made my stay in London delightful.
I shall remember last night with fondness."

Why did her mannered phrases annoy him? Why wasn't he
pleased she was dealing with their farewell with poise? Hadn't he
always been averse to females who made unnecessary scenes on
parting? Didn't he dislike lovers who made demands? Yes to all
and yet . . . he would have wished her to feel a little of what he
was feeling.

He would have preferred her to feel as—he searched for the
appropriate word—and finally settled on *wretched*. As *wretched* as
he.

Merde.

This mawkishness would never do.

He needed a drink.

Pushing away from the table, he murmured, "They forgot my

brandy," and walking to the door, opened it, and beckoned to a footman hovering nearby.

Just the prospect of a drink calmed him, or perhaps having diverted the troubling direction of his thoughts was sufficient to alter his mood. Restored to a more familiar frame of mind, he was once again able to converse about nonentities with savoir faire.

And once the brandy arrived, his sensibilities were fully restored to the casual neutrality he preferred.

They spoke of everything and nothing as they ate. He unrolled the charts, showing her the route with the tip of his knife, making sure she understood that Malcolm was available for all her needs.

"Just ask him for anything at all. He's very resourceful."

She didn't suppose press ganging the marquis and bringing him on board his yacht would be considered one of Malcolm's duties. "Has he been with you long?" she asked in lieu of the unspeakable.

Darley thought for a moment. "Almost ten years. He came to me from Edinburgh with the highest recommendations and has lived up to them and more." It was amazing how the brandy calmed him. He could look at Elspeth and appreciate her beauty and charm without wanting to keep her with him in London.

At the phrase, *keep her with him*, he felt his breath catch in his throat for a moment. Good God—he'd never, *never* considered keeping anyone, in London or elsewhere, any tender thoughts from the previous night put to flight by the cold light of day. He'd always avoided permanence like the plague. Long-term relationships were anathema to him. *Merde* and bloody hell. He needed another brandy. And perhaps a hasty *adieu*. He glanced at the clock.

"Is it time to leave?" Elspeth, too, was feeling the strain of having to converse calmly when she didn't feel in the least calm, when the man she most wanted didn't want her. Even when his mother had tried to pressure him last night, he'd refused to go to Morocco. Not once but twice.

"Perhaps it *is* time," he crisply said, setting down his glass.

She instantly came to her feet as though jerked upright by puppet strings. "Thank you again for everything. You've been most kind."

Rising, he spoke in equally bland tones. "If you ever need anything on your return, don't hesitate to call. And all best wishes on your brother's health."

"Thank you." What more could she say when the air was taut with tension. She eyed the dressing room door. "Perhaps I should fetch Sophie."

"I believe she's downstairs. Come, we'll join her." He held out his arm, as a gentleman would at an assembly and she took it like a lady would who had nothing better to do than stroll with a casual friend.

And dictated by convention and circumstance, they remained in their respective roles as they made their way downstairs.

Darley's family was chatting while they waited in the entrance hall. Sophie, Charlie, and Malcolm were biding their time near the door.

The farewells were brief. The marquis saw to it, guiding Elspeth from one member of his family to the next as though they were passing through a receiving line.

Very near collapse, Elspeth was grateful for his haste. Maintaining her composure through sheer will and the knowledge that she would soon be gone, she politely offered thanks to her hosts.

The duke, duchess, and Betsy were gracious, cordially extending their hospitality on Elspeth's return, saying all that was expected in the way of good-byes.

Polished and urbane to the end, Darley escorted her outside where the duke's gleaming black coach and four was waiting. After handing her in, he held her fingers for a lingering moment, then smiled, and stepped away so her servants and Malcolm could enter. After everyone was seated, a flunkey shut the door, the crack of a whip rang through the air and the carriage began to move.

Leaning forward, Elspeth gazed out the window and waved at

the family standing on the porch. Then sitting back, she steeled her expression to a sangfroid she was far from feeling. Vowing not to cry in front of Darley's secretary, she forcibly turned her thoughts to the coming journey.

"We should have a fair wind for sailing," Malcolm observed, pointing at the duke's standard indicating he was in residence. It was tossing in the breeze at the top of the main cupola.

"Yes, I see. I'm looking forward to the voyage," Elspeth said, as though she were about to embark on a pleasure cruise.

As though all was agreeable in her world.

"As I understand it, you're from Edinburgh," she observed. "I've been there often for the races."

"My family didn't race, but I've been to many since coming to work for the marquis. Including those in Edinburgh," Malcolm replied, taking pity on another of Darley's discarded lovers and carrying the majority of the conversation in the course of their drive to the docks.

Cast off Lady Grafton may be, Malcolm reflected during that drive, but the marquis's actions suggested he held her in singularly high regard despite his having taken French leave. Not only had Darley left Lady Bloodworth stewing at Langford, but he'd hied himself off to London when he'd scarcely been outside his bedroom for weeks.

And now the offer of his yacht?

It was unprecedented.

The marquis never allowed ladies on board the *Fair Undine.*

Ladies were bad luck at sea, he'd always asserted.

An interesting business, this.

One he'd have considerable time to ponder during the long days at sea.

Chapter
27

Professing to have some business to attend to, Darley immediately quit his parents' house where he would have been assailed by collective expressions of displeasure, and made for the sanctuary of Brooks. The hardened gamblers and drinkers would still be left from last night's revels, while those cooler heads who had slept in their own beds would be there to read the morning papers.

Above all, he didn't wish to be alone with his thoughts.

He needed distraction, diversion, a good dose of brandy and the familiar environs of his club to remind him that the pattern of his life was unchanged.

And so it seemed—for the moment he stepped into the card room, he was greeted by a loud halloo and there was Charlie Lambton with a drink in hand, waving to him from a chair by the window.

Ah—the balance of life was confirmed.

"You obviously spent a quiet night," Charlie said on his approach, flicking a finger between Julius's smart attire and his own rumpled evening clothes.

Julius cocked a brow. "While you look like you might have slept here."

"I did eventually. Earlier in the evening, I made use of the Countess Aubrey's bed," he said with a grin.

"Because her husband was chasing after the fair Perdita I presume." Dropping into a chair, Julius signaled for a waiter.

"Exactly so." The viscount lifted his glass slightly. "The countess needed consoling."

"She consoles herself with regularity and"—the marquis's voice took on a sardonic note—"considerable diversity."

"Which accounts for her—shall we say . . . expertise. Lavinia has a very special charm."

"An acrobatic charm."

"Indeed," Charles said with a wink. "She could put a circus rider to shame."

"I pray there were no horses involved."

"Only the randy Stanhope stud."

"I'm relieved," Julius murmured.

"You—scruples?" The viscount gave his friend a skeptical look. "Since when?"

"When it comes to animals, I suppose. I'm a purist; I like my fucking simple." The marquis glanced up as a waiter approached. "A bottle of brandy," he said, then shot his companion a questioning look. At a nod from Charlie, he held up two fingers. "Make it two."

"Gossip has it you've been playing the hermit at Langford with Amanda for amusement. You're lucky Francis Rhodes is so busy kissing Pitt's ass he doesn't care."

"Dealing with Francis doesn't require luck. He'll kiss anyone's ass as long as they have wealth or power and I have both." He shrugged. "In any event, Amanda's at liberty to make her own decisions. She's a widow, not some innocent maid."

"So my friend," Charles drawled, "what woman of note lured you into town when you've refused to move from Langford for weeks?" With Julius it was a given; a woman had to be involved.

"Lady Grafton."

His surprise plain, the viscount pushed himself upright from his lounging pose. "Here? In town? With or without her depraved spouse?"

"Without. And she *was* here. She sails on the morning tide." Darley's voice was neutral, each word quietly deliberate.

"For?"

"Tangier. Her brother was put off there with others of his regiment who had come down with a fever on their way to India."

Charlie grinned. "Then she needed consoling as well, I suspect."

The marquis took a millisecond to answer, Charlie's notions of consoling wildly different from what had occurred last night in the Queen's Room. "Call it what you will," he said, repressing the surge of emotion generated by heated memory. "Let's just say, it was worth the ride into town."

"When will she be back?"

"Who knows." Julius lifted one shoulder in the merest shrug.

"In that case, are you back to Langford or did Amanda take issue when you deserted her?" Waiting until Darley took his brandy glass from the waiter, he added, "Amanda had to have been pissed when you walked out."

The marquis drained half the brandy, let the liquor soothe his senses for a moment. "If she was pissed," he said at last, "I didn't notice."

"You didn't bother noticing, you mean, when your prick was taking you to London."

"Possibly. But Amanda is always open to an apology in the form of a bank draft for her gambling debts. She plays too high."

"As do you."

"It's not too high if you can afford it."

"And if your père is sympathetic."

"Papa lived as wildly in his youth. How could he not be sympathetic?"

The viscount snorted. "I should be so lucky. Since my father found religion in his old age, his memory seems to have deserted him."

Darley smiled. "My father had a run-in with some divine of the church who consigned him to the devil and since then he's spurned theological dogma. He won't be turning to God any time soon."

"How fortunate for you"—Charlie grinned—"and the gambling dens you frequent."

Julius lifted his glass in salute. "To my father's indulgence." He grimaced faintly. "With the exception of his perplexing attachment to Lady Grafton. He seems enamored of her."

"Speaking of enamored," Charlie observed. "Are you broken-hearted now that the lady's sailed?"

About to take a drink, Darley paused, his glass arrested just short of his mouth. "I *beg* your pardon?"

Charlie waggled his hands in speculation. "You just seem mildly subdued this morning. Not your usual rakish, devil-may-care self."

Having taken a draught of brandy, Darley rested his glass on the arm of his chair. "I'm tired, that's all. Lady Grafton kept me up all night and then I had to be polite to my parents this morning."

"Your *parents*! Are you telling me you fucked her in your *parents*' house!"

"That's where she was."

Charlie's brows rose into his hairline. "Why in hell was she *there*?"

"It's a long story. You needn't salivate. It's nothing titillating. Betsy discovered she was in town . . . invited her over and now my parents and Betsy adore Elspeth. In turn, they view me as a miscreant for refusing to escort her to Morocco."

"Devil take it! Why would you want to do that?"

"Exactly what I said to them, slightly more politely. Can you imagine weeks at sea with a woman?" Julius blew out a breath. "Hell on earth."

"Jesus—terrifying thought. Here," the viscount said, leaning over to pour more brandy in Darley's glass. "Drink up."

Darley knocked it back in a single gulp, liquor a long-standing remedy for any inconvenience. Then sliding into a sprawl in the worn leather chair, he surveyed the room with a gratifying sense of well-being. Insulated from the vagaries of the world, surrounded by friends, this snug, comfortable club was a stronghold of male prerogatives, a citadel of the status quo and in his case, a personal bulwark against any defilement of his profligate and highly satisfying way of life.

"Parents just don't understand," Charles said with withering scorn. "The reason we amuse ourselves with paramours and Cyprians is precisely because the arrangements are *transient*. If we wanted a permanent arrangement—heaven forbid"—the viscount shuddered visibly—"we'd submit to the shackles of marriage."

"*My* father had always understood that. Until he met Elspeth and apparently changed his mind. Why not take Elspeth to Morocco, he said. You don't have anything better to do."

"Christ. Why would he want to tie you to a lady you've slept with once or twice? Your father was a byword for vice. He should know better."

"I expressed those sentiments in slightly more tactful words. He wasn't moved. He began talking about happiness and love. I didn't listen exactly." The marquis reached for the brandy bottle. He needed another drink—or more . . . a bottle or two to blot out the images of Elspeth that inundated his mind every time her name came up.

He didn't want to think about her.

He didn't want to remember.

He wanted oblivion.

The sooner the better.

For the next half hour, drinking steadily, he almost convinced himself he was well on his way to reclaiming the normalcy of his life. Charlie could always be counted on to supply a running commentary on whatever debauch had recently occurred, several of their friends stopped by to converse, Darley and Charlie were invited to a masquerade that evening guaranteed to showcase a bevy of beauties well-known for their expertise in the boudoir.

There was talk of viewing a prizefight later that afternoon.

Then dinner at the club, the masquerade, the convivial company of his friends.

What could have been more ordinary?

He should have been content.

Happy.

Satisfied.

But he wasn't.

He was haunted by memories of golden hair and blue eyes and a smile that brought him immeasurable joy.

While his need to touch Elspeth everywhere—inside and out—overwhelmed his discretionary judgment with the force of a tidal wave.

And any satisfaction or happiness he might aspire to had become inextricably tied to a lush beauty from Yorkshire who loved horses and racing as much as he did.

Without her—he softly sighed into his brandy glass—he was discontent.

"Let's go take in that prizefight," Charlie suggested, breaking into Darley's glum reverie. "We could use a change of scene."

"I'll meet you there." Darley couldn't bring himself to move.

Coming unsteadily to his feet, the viscount swayed for a moment, then steadying himself, gave Julius a squinty-eyed stare. "You sure?"

"I'm sure."

"You don't look sure."

"Jesus, Charlie, you're not exactly seeing straight right now, but if you were, you'd see I'm completely sure," he muttered. "I'm just going to have another few drinks here and then I'll join you."

"Don't forget, I'm going to introduce you to that pretty Kelly lass tonight. She's new on the Drury stage and so dew-fresh you can practically inhale the scent of the country when you're near her."

The marquis gave his friend a cynical smile. "Dew-fresh? Now there's a novelty on the stage."

"And all the more interesting for that singular asset," Charlie said with a grin. "You'll like her."

"I'll meet you in an hour."

"At Broughton's gym?"

"Precisely."

But after Charlie left, Darley drank two quick drinks, as though his friend's departure had activated a sudden cataclysmic groundswell of urgency. Then increasingly restless, he drank a third. About to pour a fourth, he hesitated, set the bottle down and called for pen and paper.

When a footman delivered the items, he scrawled a few quick lines, folded the sheet, addressed it to his parents, handed it to the flunkey and exited the card room in swift strides. Descending the stairs in a run, he rushed through the door hastily opened by a servant, and turning to the doorman on the porch outside, briskly ordered, "Get me a hackney. Something fast. I'm in a hurry."

Chapter

28

The crew of the *Fair Undine* was working frantically to unfurl the sails, the captain and his first officer overseeing the spirited activity from the quarterdeck when Darley swung aboard—the gangplank literally pulled up behind him.

Charlie saw him first, from his perch on the starboard rail. "We got ourselves another passenger," he murmured, giving Sophie a tap on the shoulder as she stood beside him.

"Lord have mercy," she murmured, understanding the significance of Darley's behavior; he knew the extent of the journey they were undertaking.

"Our lady might be smilin' right soon, I'd say. He ain't tellin' the captain to trim no canvas."

In fact, the breeze was beginning to fill the sails, the yacht slowly easing out into the river.

They watched Darley exchange a few more words with the captain; it looked as though he was giving some orders. Then the marquis turned away and made for the companionway.

"Wouldn't you like to be a fly on the wall right about now?" Charlie said with a grin.

"You hush." Sophie scowled at her companion. "Ain't none o' our business what our lady does."

"I didn't mean no harm. I jus' meant she's gonna be happy she is."

Darley didn't knock on his stateroom door when he reached it, too impatient after hours of drinking to wait.

Too driven.

But a moment later, he stood arrested on the threshold of an empty cabin.

"Elspeth!" His voice resonated in the small space, an uneasy note underlying the single word. According to the captain, she was supposed to be here. Improbable images of ladies drowning themselves out of melancholy filled his brain. Brandy induced, no doubt, but vivid nonetheless.

Uneasy, he swung around in full search mode, one foot already in the passageway when he heard a voice drowsy with sleep.

"You changed your mind."

He spun back at the familiar sound, apprehension giving way to joy. There was Elspeth in the doorway of his dressing room, looking slightly dazed.

"I must have fallen asleep." Still drowsy, her delight at seeing him was muted.

Stepping back into the room, he shut the door, selfishly immune to nuances of tone when the prize he sought was safely found. He smiled. "I thought you might like company to Tangier."

The ship was moving! Elspeth realized, a rush of joy out of all proportion to Darley's casual statement overwhelmed her. She knew better than to express her giddy delight, however, from *The Tatler*, her model—misguided though it might be—for manners in the Ton. "I would indeed enjoy some company," she said with what she hoped was equal casualness. That she would enjoy his company with all her heart remained unspoken. "Although I very much appreciate Malcolm's assistance as well," she added, lest he think her ungrateful for the aid he'd offered her. "He's most charming."

"Charming?" Darley growled and instantly aware he sounded

like a jealous suitor, corrected himself. "Forgive me. I spoke out of turn. I've had a drink or two this morning."

"I hope you won't wish to turn around once you sober up." Levelheaded after months of dealing with her husband's drunkenness, she didn't take issue with Darley's temper, confining her remarks to more pertinent matters. "Having to return to London would delay me unnecessarily as well as put my brother at further risk."

He gave her high marks for poise. She wasn't easily shaken. "You needn't worry," he said, his voice deliberately mild now. "I won't delay you. I felt the need for a change of scene and Tangier was as good a place as any."

"I thought perhaps someone was giving chase," she noted, his precipitate appearance calling to mind the famous Rowlandson print of Darley being hounded by a pack of ladies. He was famous for decamping when a paramour became too enamored.

"My creditors are all paid off," he answered lightly, pretending he didn't understand her question. Not about to admit *he* was the one giving chase. "I believe I'm safe at the moment."

As if a man of Darley's fortune had creditors. But she didn't belabor the point. "One last caveat if you please," she did say though, fearful he would compromise her schedule when he was less in his cups. "I wouldn't want you to wake up tomorrow and change your mind about—"

"I'm not your husband," he noted, gruffly. "I know what I'm doing."

"Now it's my turn to ask forgiveness. I didn't mean to offend you."

"You couldn't," he pleasantly replied. "There's nothing remotely offensive in you," he added, moving toward a chair and gracefully disposing his lean frame into a lazy sprawl, as though making himself comfortable for the long journey ahead. "You are, my sweet"—he smiled at her across the small distance that separated them—"the most flawless creature on God's green earth."

"Now I know you're drunk,"—her voice was droll— "when I

hear such fulsome flattery." A man of fashion such as he—well-dressed, well-behaved, capable of the most suave cajolery—had played this game a thousand times before.

"I could be ruthlessly honest in my assessments if you wish," he offered, his gaze amused. "I could begin with that dour gown of yours."

She smiled. "Perhaps I'd prefer exaggeration after all."

"You realize you're on my yacht, with my captain and crew," he drawled. "So perhaps what you prefer or don't isn't of consequence."

"I'm very glad you're smiling as you say that."

"And I'm very glad to have you to myself for several days. I would be even more delighted if you'd leave that doorway and come closer."

"How close?"

"Need you ask?" he murmured, huskily.

She felt a shiver race up her spine, the invitation in his voice reminding her of other days and other nights when she'd heard him speak thusly. And now, she thought, trembling faintly, he was her prisoner, as it were, on this sleek yacht for the foreseeable future.

Taking note of her agitation, the flush rising on her cheeks tantalizing, he looked forward to making love to her. Which thought brought to mind the baubles he'd acquired at a quicksilver detour to Grey's on his way to the docks. "I brought you something. Come, look." Reaching into his coat pockets, he drew out his hands and held them out, palms down, his fingers curled into fists.

Her brows came together in a slight frown, uncomfortable with his usual largesse to his paramours. "I don't need anything from you."

"That may be, but I need things from you and this is my way of offering you thanks." He smiled. "In advance."

"Like you would a courtesan." A small pettish sniff punctuated her remark.

"No, like I would a woman who is about to bring me to some

outland I had no intention of visiting," he said, coolly, letting his hands drop to his thighs. "It's very different, I assure you."

"I apologize once more." His disclosure was both startling and pleasing in the extreme. "I shouldn't let my temper get the better of me," she said, her smile conciliatory. "Especially when you're drunk."

"I'm not drunk," he muttered. "It takes more than a bottle of brandy to do that."

"Can we agree you're less than sober?"

He shrugged, a faint smile softening his reserve. "Very well. I'll admit to perhaps—feeling good. Very *much* better, as a matter of fact, since coming aboard." His smile broadened. "Now, be a dear, and take this from me." He lifted his hands slightly. "Consider it a peace offering. I should have come with you from the start."

Concessions from a man of Darley's repute were outrageously seductive, although he might know as much. "Yet you refused your parents' coercion," she declared, as though she didn't have a shred of sense. As though Sophie was right about her deplorable lack of tact.

His mood was more tolerant; he didn't take offense. "I expect that's why I chose not to go."

"Among other reasons," she said with the unappeasable female appetite for analyzing the men they love. "You don't do things like this, I suspect."

"Like what?" This time, his tone was guarded.

Anyone with half a brain would have taken note of the pitch of his voice. "I heard Malcolm tell the captain I was aboard on your orders," she said, undeterred by pitch or tone. "Apparently, you have some rule about females on your yacht."

He made an indistinguishable grumbling sound deep in his throat and in lieu of an answer, nodded at his closed fists. "Do you want these, or should I give them to Sophie? They'd look better on you."

That was clear; she wasn't going to get an answer. "I shouldn't," she said. "If I were more saintly, or less curious"—Elspeth sighed delicately, already moving from the doorway, intrigued despite her best intentions—"I'd say, give them to Sophie. She deserves them more than I."

Darley's lashes lowered marginally. "I doubt it."

Oh, dear—the iniquitous truth. She came to a stop. "So this is for services rendered—or for future services?"

"No, it's a token of my affection, if you must know," he groused, a faint scowl creasing his forehead. "And a more graceless recipient I have yet to see."

"Allow me to question men like you bearing gifts."

"Men like me?" Her moods were shifting with mystifying swiftness, or perhaps he was drunker than he thought.

"Don't be obtuse, Darley. You're a byword for seduction." She made a small dismissive gesture. "I expect gifts are often involved in your pursuits."

She wouldn't care to hear the truth—that he was pursued, not the other way around and no gifts were required other than those he dispensed in the way of sexual satisfaction. "Would you like a note from my priest expressing my sincerity?" he sardonically murmured.

Her gaze was cool. "Very clever, I'm sure."

"Fuck it," he growled, tossing two handfuls of glittering jewelry in the direction of the bed. "I don't beg." Surging to his feet, he stalked to his liquor cabinet, swung the door open and grabbed a bottle.

Elspeth's eyes flared wide at the dazzling trail of jewelry scattered from the chair to the bed—ear bobs, bracelets, brooches, a string of diamonds and pearls, a very large, blood-red ruby ring that had come to rest against the bed pillows.

Jerking out the cork, Darley upended the bottle over a glass and impatiently waited for the rising liquor to reach the rim—the liquid gurgle the only sound in the silent room.

She couldn't have taken anything so expensive anyway, she thought.

Why couldn't Elspeth be like other women, he irritably reflected, lifting the filled glass to his mouth and draining it.

She should apologize. She should also be less difficult when Darley was obviously going out of his way to be agreeable.

He'd made one helluva mistake leaving London! *Merde* and bloody hell! Exhaling softly, he refilled his glass, drank it down and poured another.

Perhaps she'd spent too many evenings watching her husband drink himself into a stupor or maybe Sophie was right—she'd never learned to be compliant. "Isn't that just like a man," she snapped. "Drinking solves everything."

He swivelled around. "It's either this," he said through gritted teeth, "or something you'd find considerably more distasteful."

Her spine went rigid. "Such as?"

"Jesus, Elspeth, such as anything I damn well please. This is my yacht; you're here on my sufferance. And I outweigh you by seven or eight stone." He sighed. "Look, I shouldn't have come, but I'm here. And I promised you I wouldn't turn back. So what in bloody hell do you want me to do?"

"Perhaps deal with this like an adult?" Even as she spoke, she realized how insufferable she sounded.

The knuckles on his fingers holding the glass turned white and he quickly set it down before the glass shattered. "Perhaps we should discuss this later." Like in ten years he thought, striding toward the door.

"I wouldn't blame you for turning back," she whispered, suddenly filled with remorse, her petulance mortifying, so out of character and disgraceful she was at a loss to explain it. Could she blame her months with Grafton for her rudeness?

If only she could.

But her unreasonable hostility couldn't be laid at Grafton's door. That rash folly, the seething tumult in her brain had to do with Darley. She wanted him too much. Or maybe she didn't want him enough to accept him on his terms.

Or maybe she didn't know *what* she wanted.

Except, silly fool that she was, she wanted her love returned.

She wanted him to *love* her—not likely, that.

What was particularly humiliating was that she'd become exactly what she didn't wish to be—simply another in a long line of women warming Darley's bed.

If swearing would help, she'd swear to the heavens, if reason would make him hers, she'd debate the issue to infinity, if pleading would serve her purpose, she'd do it and willingly. But her brain was beyond the required cleverness and, emotionally bankrupt, exhausted, she yielded to despair and slowly crumpled to the floor in a pouf of chestnut brown silk.

Lying on the carpet, she fought to suppress her tears, desperately trying not to break down completely. And for brief moments she succeeded—until that first tear spilled over and the dam broke.

He'd turned when she'd spoken, his hand on the door latch. He watched her collapse but didn't move, not sure he wished to involve himself. She'd already caused untold tumult in his life, effecting major changes in his way of life—like this fucking, disastrous voyage to Tangier, for one. Not to mention the shocking impact she'd had on his family—evoking lectures on love and happiness from his father, bringing chastisement from his mother.

Seriously debating the folly of responding, he pursed his mouth, inhaled, blew out a breath and briefly questioned his sanity for being here at all. Then, swearing softly, he shoved the door shut, knowing what he was about to do went against his better judgment and every tenet by which he'd previously lived.

He walked slowly to where she lay—as though some unseen hand might sensibly deter him from his path before it was too late. None did. Coming to rest beside her, he bent over and he lifted her up in his arms. And in that act, knew his life had irrevocably changed.

There was no visible portent, no flash of light or trumpet call indicating an occurrence of great moment. Yet as he stood in the middle of his stateroom with Elspeth in his arms, he understood that he had taken on a new responsibility for which he'd previously considered himself unfit.

A not entirely disagreeable responsibility, he decided, gazing down at the lady who had brought him so far from home. Far from it. "If you like, you can give the jewelry to Sophie," he murmured, lightly teasing, hoping to staunch her weeping. "I wouldn't want to make you unhappy."

At the kindness in his tone, her eyes opened, and lifting her tear-stained face, she offered him a heart-wrenching smile. "I don't—deserve . . . you," she whispered.

"We probably deserve each other," he replied, alluding to a connection between them without a qualm—apparently heedless of his shocking admission, for he went on to say with a smile, "Rumor has it I can be intractable."

"No—no, never." He had been like a veritable savior to her. "I will apologize—for my—petulance . . . every day till 'Tangier," she murmured between sniffles. "I promise."

He knew what he wanted instead of apologies, but wisely held his tongue in this most delicate of situations. "You've been under enormous strain," he said instead, carrying her back to the chair and sitting down with her on his lap. "Rest now, and we'll decide what to do later."

"I'll do whatever you want me to do," she breathed, her lashes fluttering gently downward as she spoke, a gratifying peace inundating her body and mind, Darley's forgiveness a soothing balm to all that had disturbed her. And in seconds, she was deep in slumber, as though their heated contretemps had sapped her last bit of strength.

He held her close as she slept, her soft breathing a comforting pianissimo, the lilac scent of her hair fragrant in his nostrils, her warmth against his body sweet bliss when he'd not thought himself likely to appreciate so simple a pleasure.

He was content.

Happy.

He was also infused with a new determination to ease and assuage the difficulties facing her. She'd struggled too long against the misfortunes of her life. He was here now to offer aid and comfort. For a man who had long avoided entanglements, he found himself singularly pleased that he had the means to see to her future.

They would find her brother and carry him home.

And if there was time, he'd bring back the horses Bachir had purchased for him since his last trip.

Elspeth and her brother could have their pick of the blood-stock to set up their own stud. It would give Will a living and please Elspeth in the bargain. More importantly, if they were comfortably settled in their own home, Elspeth wouldn't have to return to Grafton.

He busily made plans as she slept, wishing he could summon Malcolm to begin drafting a list of necessities. There was that small estate for sale, near his stud in Gloucestershire. He would have Malcolm make inquiries. The manor house and barns needed repairs but Malcolm was competent when it came to dealing with builders. He handled all the construction on Darley's properties. Elspeth would need a trainer too, of course—someone good. Perhaps some of their old stable staff might still be available.

His mind raced from project to project and when she woke some time later, he greeted her with a smile.

"I have a plan," he said. "Listen."

Chapter

29

By the time he'd finished his explanation, her heart was racing from a byzantine jumble of hope, fear, and dismay.

"Well?" he said, expectantly.

"I don't know what to say." She didn't wish to argue again, but how could she possibly take so much from him without compromising herself in the eyes of the world. Not that she wasn't aware of the possible scandal already attached to her name. But what she was doing now, she was doing for her brother. It wasn't for profit. As for her love for Darley, that was a private matter. But if she allowed him to do what he wished to do, she would be branded as a woman under Darley's protection. And once she took that step, the world she'd lived in would be forever closed to her.

"Say, you like the idea, and we'll do it."

"Could we talk about this later?"

"You don't like it."

"I do."

"But?"

"Honestly?"

"Of course, honestly," he said, smoothing a curl behind her ear. "It's your life."

Which was the issue at hand, was it not? Their lives were separate in every way. She took a deep breath. "Very well. I'm married as you know."

He frowned.

"So whatever you do for me," she went on, intent on being truthful, "will be viewed in a certain way. Not that I'm not deep in your debt already—for which I'm very grateful. But once we return to England . . . and should you do all that you spoke of for me, I would be quite alone in the world. Set apart, perceived as a woman of a certain stamp."

"You wouldn't. Do you know how many women live apart from their husbands—women of good family?"

She didn't. "There aren't any in Yorkshire."

"Don't tell me you're going back to him," he muttered.

"No, but I would prefer to make my own way regardless of where I go. It's a matter of pride and self-respect. And I don't require much. Will and I are content with a simple life."

"Doing what?"

"I thought we could open a village school somewhere."

"Will your brother agree?"

"I'm not sure," Elspeth replied, his question one she'd put to herself more than once. "But Will can find some other livelihood to help sustain us if he dislikes my plan."

"Let *me* be your livelihood. I'll finance your school. No one need know. You wouldn't even have to tell your brother if you didn't wish."

"And you would stay away?"

"No. Why should I have to?"

"Because no one would send their children to my school, if I was seen as your mistress. Come, Darley, you know how even a hint of scandal can adversely affect a woman."

"Not if their protector is powerful enough. The best homes are open to the mistresses of men of great fortune. They're invited everywhere." Like my parents' home, he wished to say.

"Please, allow me my reputation—if indeed any survives."

"You didn't bother with your reputation in Newmarket."

"I should have."

A sensible man, he chose not to further the argument. Why ruin what appeared to be a very pleasant voyage. Time enough to renew the subject once they returned to England. "You may be right," he said. "Society is far less forgiving to women."

"Exactly." She should have been pleased he understood. But she found herself suffering a twinge of regret that he had so willingly acquiesced. Not that she should have expected anything different. A man like Darley was capricious in his relationships with women.

"At least you're not subject to the censure of society out on the ocean," he said with a smile. "We're quite free of restrictions for a fortnight at least."

"How soon *will* we reach Tangier?" She shifted the conversation to a subject less fraught with contention.

"If the winds don't fail us, in two weeks."

"You know you have my eternal gratitude," she said with quiet earnestness. "I couldn't have done any of this without you or been ensconced in such comfort for my voyage." She might take issue with Darley's prodigal way of life, but she couldn't fault him for his kindness to her. "If there's any way within my powers that I can repay you some day, I surely will."

"Your company is payment enough," he smoothly replied, careful to keep any hint of innuendo from his voice. The lady was feeling vulnerable. Soon enough for seduction once her spirits were revived. "In the meantime, let's see about increasing our speed. I'll talk to the captain. And you could use a cup of tea, I'll wager," he added with a smile, standing up, and placing her on the chair. "I'll send in Sophie and be back shortly."

Leaving the stateroom, he set about his tasks, motivated by more than simple altruism. The sooner they reached Tangier— and hopefully found her brother still alive—the sooner they could return to England. Where he intended to put Elspeth under his protection one way or another. He preferred handling it openly but if she balked, he was more than willing to resort to surreptitious means. But he would have her. That he knew.

And having always lived a life of sweeping carte blanche, with

every privilege conferred, every whim allowed, desire and fulfillment were one in the same.

He would not be thwarted.

On finding Malcolm, he gave no explanation for his last
minute appearance, thanked him instead for escorting Elspeth
aboard and then gave him a number of commissions beginning
with seeing that Sophie was sent to Elspeth along with a tea tray
and two bottles of his father's champagne. "If you'll see to Lady
Grafton's servants during our voyage," Darley added, "as well as
the extra staff my father sent along, I'd be obliged." He dipped
his head. "And I'll thank you in advance."

The implication that he would be incommunicado was left
unsaid, but Malcolm understood. "You can count on me, sir. Your
father sent along enough rations to victual us all in some luxury"—
he smiled—"along with a sous-chef who has already had two
screaming matches with your chef, my lord."

Darley smiled. "It sounds as though you'll have your hands
full. Francois can be temperamental in the best of times. I wish
you luck. Although, I'm not overly optimistic with two prima
donnas in such close quarters. Do your best. I'm off now to press
the captain for more speed," he went on, dismissing chefs from
his thoughts. "Lady Grafton wishes to reach her brother post
haste."

Leaving his secretary's cabin, Darley made his way to the
quarter deck. After the captain and Darley exchanged some min-
imum courtesies, Darley came directly to the point.

"I'd like to reach Tangier in record time," he asserted. "And to
that purpose, I'd like to offer a bonus to every officer and crew
member. Say, triple pay. With a similar amount to each for a
speedy return voyage."

"Yes, sir," Captain Tarleton replied, already beckoning over
his first officer. "All the sail she can carry, Mr. Ashton," he said to
his lieutenant. He turned back to Darley. "She can fly, sir. We'll
have you in port in no time."

"Thank you. Lady Grafton is concerned for her brother's
health and every day makes a difference."

"I understand."

"She's hoping to reach him"—Darley paused—"in time."

"Yes, sir, I understand, my lord. It's a dangerous climate for foreigners. Please offer my sympathy to Lady Grafton. Tell her we'll run full out, sir."

Men were already swarming up the shrouds and out onto the yards, loosening more sails, the canvas dropping, flapping, filling with loud snapping sounds.

"The lady will be pleased. And we needn't be concerned with pirates for another few days, as I recall." The *Fair Undine* had begun to surge ahead as every sail went taut, the trim, thin-skinned craft slicing effortlessly through the waves.

"They don't prowl this far north, but once we gain the sea lanes off Africa, we'll have the lookouts on high alert. Not that anything can catch us, sir," the captain added with a smile. "This beauty has lightning speed."

"I wouldn't mention the word pirate in earshot of the women."

"No, sir. There's no need to alarm them."

"Very well—all is in order, then. My compliments," Darley said, with a slight bow. "I know we're in good hands."

Captain Tarleton was paid a handsome salary, so handsome he was able to live the life of a gentleman back home in Sussex. He would accommodate the marquis to hell and back even without a bonus. "It's my pleasure to have you aboard, my lord. And you needn't worry. If the winds hold, we'll have Lady Grafton in Tangier in under two weeks."

"Thank you. I'll tell her."

Darley took the companionway to the main deck in one leap and strode to the hatchway feeling uncommonly good. He'd made the right decision to quit London and come aboard. He hadn't felt this good—really . . . since Newmarket.

There was something to be said for the milk of human kindness.

It was incredibly uplifting.

Chapter
30

The following days couldn't have been more idyllic if Arcadia itself had been transported lock, stock, and pastoral landskip to the *Fair Undine*.

Darley saw to Elspeth's every whim, with gentle good-natured charm—a eunuch-like charm that first day—not even attempting to kiss her initially. She'd spoken of self-respect and pride; he wasn't obtuse.

But he hadn't had to long fear that celibacy might be his fate for shortly after that first tea, after he'd drunk two bottles of his father's champagne and talked idly of nothing for an hour or so, Elspeth had said, "How long are you going to sit way over there?"

"No longer than necessary," he'd replied, sliding up in his chair and smiling at her across the tea table. "You talked of me staying away; I wasn't sure."

She'd been resting against the back of her chair, relaxed after her tea, grateful for Darley's casual conversation. "Are you always so solicitous?"

"Usually not. You're a special case. As you see." He jabbed his finger at his chest. "I'm here and not in London."

She smiled. "Against your better judgment?"

He shook his head. "More against long-standing habit—and

that's different." He grinned. "Vastly different I might add. The sea air will do me good. Getting out of London will do me good."

"I'd rather not think about England until I have to," she murmured, "and I'd prefer not thinking of Tangier at all."

"I can help you forget," he said, softly.

"I know."

He leaned forward in his chair, but didn't rise, wanting her to decide. "We have time."

"Days?"

"Yes—eight or ten . . . maybe more."

"And you would be willing to play the gentleman—"

"For as long as you wish. I'm not in a hurry."

She smiled. "I might be."

He laughed. "Ask me why I'm not surprised?"

"So, my lord." She kicked off her slippers, crooked her finger and gazed at him with a sweetly provocative smile. "Show me this promised forgetfulness."

And he did while the *Fair Undine* raced south and the winds stayed strong and the staff and crew tiptoed past the marquis's stateroom where the door remained essentially closed—save for deliveries of food and wine, fresh linens and bath water.

Until the morning of the ninth day, one of the several lookouts who had been posted in both masts and to port and starboard at the bow and stern since passing the coast of Portugal, shouted, "Tangier off the port bow! Four or five leagues!"

By the time they'd taken a pilot aboard and had made their way through the shallows and shingle of the huge bay, Elspeth and Darley were dressed and standing at the rail.

"It's larger than I thought," Elspeth said, taking in the sprawling town spread out like an amphitheater before her eyes, the gently rising hills covered with white structures gleaming under the sun. "How will we ever find Will?"

"We'll go to the consul first. He should have some notion of where the sick men were housed."

"What if he doesn't?"

"Darling, don't worry. We'll find Will." If they hadn't been within sight and sound of everyone, he would have taken her in his arms. Her fear was beginning to show, her hands were trembling.

"Are you sure?"

"I'm sure," he said, ignoring their surroundings and placing his hand over hers as they rested on the rail. "Your brother is young and strong. He's going to be fine." At the lookout's cry, her apprehension had surfaced, taken hold and held her in its grip. Not that he didn't understand her worry. She would learn today whether or not her brother lived and all his platitudes aside, there were no guarantees in this outland. Doctors were in short supply, *good* doctors perhaps a meaningless term, while the sanitary conditions could be appalling if the navy had quartered the army troops with their usual disregard for humanity. "Come now, look on the bright side. Once we find your brother, he'll be back in England with you in only a week or two." He patted her hands. "You'll like that. He'll probably like it even more," he said with a smile.

"You're much too good to me." Her bottom lip was quivering even as she sternly warned herself against bursting into tears. The captain was only a short distance away, the crew notably curious about her since they knew of Darley's rule concerning women on his yacht. She didn't wish to embarrass herself and Darley both.

"On the contrary, darling, who is good to whom is decidedly in my favor, I assure you. And if there weren't so many people watching I'd give you a resounding kiss to prove it."

"Don't!" she quickly retorted, forgetting for the moment her larger concerns, her imminent tears staunched by a rush of panic.

"I'm damned tempted."

His mouth was close to her ear, the scent of his cologne, familiar and comforting; and if it were possible to stop time, she would have liked to capture this moment of closeness and warmth for eternity. "You may be tempted at some later date," she said, grateful for the distraction he'd offered. "One of my choosing."

"Consider me yours to command, my lady." He grinned. "And

I don't believe I've ever said that before. I hope you're suitably impressed."

She found she could smile. "I am and I thank you."

"You're very welcome. Look, they're lowering the gig. We'll be ashore in no time."

Chapter

31

The consul turned out to be an absentminded scholar more interested in his Greek histories than his consular duties in Tangier—as evinced by his pale complexion in this land of intense sunshine. But once he'd been coaxed from his books and had dithered over the Duke of Westerlands' letter of introduction, he set about with a well-intentioned, albeit bumbling ineptitude, to try to solicit the required information from his staff. The house servants were his only contact with the outside world since his secretary had retired to the more salubrious environs of London and a replacement had not yet arrived.

"And a damned bloody inconvenience it is not to have a secretary—pardon me, ma'am, for my imprecation—but curse it all I'm trying to translate Herodotus! I don't have time for state matters!"

Apparently the local staff had been left to their own devices for long periods of time for it took a lengthy interval to assemble them. When a considerable tribe was finally collected, they turned out to be of little use. From young children to ancients and every age between, they offered a blank stare or a shrug to all queries.

"Damn your slyboots eyes—all of you!" Consul Handley shouted, his color having risen to a bright red as the interrogation seemingly floundered. Turning, he jabbed his finger at a tall, narrow-nosed man. "Ismail, I order you to find these Englishmen!"

"Effendi, it is not possible." The man's voice was ultra soft in contrast to his employer's strident tone, his gaze half-lidded. "The city has swallowed them up by now."

"Find them or I'll turn out every one of your relatives within the hour, dammit!"

"I'll do what I can, Effendi, but I can't promise—"

"Just do it!" Consul Handley snapped. "Out, out, now, the lot of you! You have an hour, Ismail, or your grandmother sleeps in the streets tonight." The consul flicked his fingers, dismissing the wild assortment of retainers who began shuffling off in the same leisurely fashion in which they'd arrived.

Ismail—who appeared to hold the post of majordomo as well as family benefactor—put his steepled fingers to his forehead and bowed. "As you wish, Effendi. I'm yours to command."

"Yes, yes, I'm sure," the consul muttered. "We'll be needing tea for the lady and some of the good brandy. Quickly if you please." As Ismail left the loggia, Handley rolled his eyes and grumbled, "Who commands whom is moot as you see. Until my new secretary arrives on this uncivilized shore, I'm at Ismail's mercy. But come, come, sit. Hopefully we'll soon have some tea." He turned an expectant smile on his guests. "I don't suppose Herodotus is of interest to you?"

Handley's little burst of temper must have served its purpose, for Ismail returned to the jasmine scented loggia that overlooked the bay before they'd finished their tea and brandy. Having held counsel with his relatives first, he now offered up the information that was more or less common knowledge in the city. "An English ship was in port some weeks ago off-loading their sick. Two of the barbarians still live, Effendi," he reported. "The others died. Do you wish to visit their graves?"

The color instantly drained from Elspeth's face.

Quickly taking her teacup from her shaking hand, Darley set it on the table and leaning forward, spoke under his breath. "He may not know of what he speaks." Looking up, he queried Ismail in a normal tone, "Where are the two men who still live?"

"In a barbarian taverna on the waterfront."

"Take us there." Darley held out a gold coin that was plucked from his hand and disappeared into Ismail's *djellebah* with lightning speed.

"Naturally, I would accompany you if it were necessary," the consul said with such obvious insincerity, he didn't even bother to wait to pick up the book he'd carried in with him. "But I expect you wish to deal with this tragedy in private," he added, already rifling through the pages to find his place.

His sham courtesy aside, if the consul would have been useful, Darley would have insisted he accompany them. But it was obvious he didn't speak the local language, and was completely ignorant of his surroundings. Furthermore, his intimations of a tragedy weren't at all helpful to Elspeth's peace of mind. "We won't impose on your time," Darley noted, coming to his feet. "But we will need your servant to take us to this tavern."

The consul glanced up. "Yes, yes—go with the marquis, Ismail. And stay with him until you're dismissed." Mr. Handley waggled his finger at this majordomo. "I don't want you running away. Do you hear, you scoundrel?"

"Yes, Effendi. I hear."

"The natives are an independent lot, I'm afraid," the consul said with exasperation. "And not to be trusted. If I didn't have my books I would go stark raving mad in this savage place," he added, apparently subscribing to the aristocratic view that servants were deaf and invisible. "I wish you good fortune in your quest and a pleasant voyage home. Would that I could quit this hellhole," he said with a sigh, adjusting his spectacles.

His pleasant voyage home remark suggested the consul preferred not seeing them again, Darley understood. And while he'd been nominally helpful, it was clear why Mr. Handley was in Tangier and not in Whitehall with the power brokers of the diplomatic world.

The consul, however, was once again lost in his reading and oblivious to his visitors and their inferences.

Darley forwent an *adieu* that would have gone unnoticed and helped Elspeth from her chair. She was pale as a ghost so he slipped his arm around her waist to steady her as they walked from the room and through the meandering passages of the residence. On reaching their hired carriage, he lifted her mute form inside, took his seat beside her and gently drew her close. He couldn't bring himself to utter platitudes or offer her unwarranted hope on their silent drive to the docks. The odds were too much against them.

Elspeth was holding herself together by sheer will, not allowing herself to contemplate what lay ahead, or more particularly— what might await them at the waterfront tavern. Instead, she concentrated on the passing scene, mindlessly observing the houses and people, the bustle and activity of daily life, resorting to the pretense that they were only here in Tangier for Darley's horses.

And so she would pretend until she no longer could.

They finally came to a stop before an old, dilapidated structure, its door long gone, the windows no more than slits in the pise', sun-dried earth, lime and straw, exterior, the stench from within more fetid than the offal filled lane outside.

Ismail called down from his seat on the bench beside the driver. "Effendi, this is the offending den of iniquity."

"Stay here," Darley murmured, gently squeezing Elspeth's hand. "I'll make inquiries."

"No. I'm going in."

"It's not safe."

She met his gaze. "I don't care."

"There's no knowing who lurks inside." Or what horrors she might see. The navy's benevolence to their sick and wounded was a contradiction in terms.

"It's an English tavern."

"Maybe. I doubt Handley's man can be trusted. Take note, he's not getting down. Let me go in and reconnoiter." Pulling off the top of his cane, he drew out a lethal-looking blade. "If your brother's in there, I'll carry him out."

"Please, Julius, I don't want to argue."

She wasn't pleading, her expression obstinate, unyielding. And short of tying her up, he couldn't force her to remain in the carriage. "Promise to stay behind me at least. Ismail and I will go in first."

She nodded, but her mouth quivered faintly despite her determination to stay strong. With only two survivors of the many who had been put ashore, what lay inside might annihilate her last bit of hope.

Taking a woman inside such a pest hole was going to be a damnable problem, Darley thought, not to mention Ismail couldn't be trusted—no more than those inside. Pulling out a leather case from under the seat, he lifted the lid and took out one of the two pistols he'd carried from the yacht. Flipping the pistol grip toward Elspeth, he lifted his brows. "Can you shoot?"

"I have a few times years ago."

Not a comforting response, but he didn't exactly have a choice. "This might be heavy for you. Here." He placed the grip end in her palm. "Use both hands if you have to," he said. "You have two shots. Aim for the head and *squeeze* the trigger."

"Understood." She suddenly felt a very long way from Yorkshire.

Taking the second pistol from the case, he slid it in his coat pocket, and gave her a quick, reassuring smile. "To good news." Then he turned and opened the carriage door.

Lifting her from the carriage a moment later, Darley ordered Ismail down, his sharp tone inducing the tall native man to instantly drop to the ground. That the marquis wielded a long blade and looked as though he knew how to use it were only added incentive.

"Now, look lively," Darley said, shoving the servant forward. "We're here to see the English sailors. Explain our mission in whatever language will get results."

They entered the hovel, Ismail in the lead, followed by

Darley, with Elspeth close on his heels. Holding her pistol at the ready, her heart beating furiously from fear and apprehension, she prayed with all her heart that she hadn't arrived too late—and prayed even harder that one of the two men would be her brother.

As their eyes became accustomed to the shadowed interior, a burly man standing behind a makeshift bar came into focus, as did a motley crew of patrons seated at rough tables. Every eye regarded them with suspicion, every expression was writ large with cunning and guile. It was clear, these men lived by their wits.

At their entrance, conversation had abruptly ceased.

The silence was nakedly ominous.

Darley jabbed Ismail with the muzzle of his pistol. "Ask about the English."

Ismail's voice took on a deferential quality with Darley's pistol in his back and he addressed the man behind the bar in a blend of English and Berber.

"Well, well, lookee here," the barkeep crowed, playing to his audience in a heavy Cockney accent. "We got ourselfs a couple o' high flyers. And they be wantin' to see our lodgers." He bared his toothless gums in a villainous grin. "What's it worth, me pretties?"

"It might be worth your life." Darley lifted his pistol, pointing it directly at the man's head. "I suggest you move smartly."

The man's smile abruptly vanished, and a rumble of hostile murmurs reverberated in the dimly lit hut. "There's only one o' you," the barkeep growled, reaching under the bar for his truncheon. "The lady's sceered out o' her wits and that there savage with you is sure as hell gonna cut and run."

As if on cue, Ismail turned to flee.

Without shifting his gaze from the barkeep, Darley's blade came up, blocking Ismail's retreat. "I have two shots here that will blow your head off, so you might want to reconsider." Darley's voice was like ice, his aim unwavering. "And if anyone considers touching the lady"—he flicked his blade—"I'll slice their throat. Now then," he went on, silken authority in every syllable, "we're prepared to pay you handsomely if you carry the men that were left here outside." The edge of his sword pressed lightly against the Ismail's stomach to deter his twitching. "There's twenty gold guineas in it for each of you. Fifty, if you bring the men out in under two minutes."

It was a fortune to men who couldn't have earned that much in five years before the mast.

An instant scraping of stools on the dirt floor gave evidence of their avid interest. And each man jack scurried to accommodate the gentleman who spoke with the same voice of command as their former officers in His Majesty's navy.

Darley glanced over his shoulder. "Back up," he murmured. "Slowly. We'll wait outside."

Elspeth gladly complied, exiting the noxious stew into the blinding sun. As she squinted against the bright light, she offered up her last prayer—promising everything and anything if only her brother lived.

"Stand by the carriage," Darley murmured, nodding at Elspeth. "If you would be so kind," he added with exquisite courtesy, hoping to avoid an argument. So far so good, but they weren't out of danger yet. Should Elspeth discover neither of the men were her brother and fainted, he wanted her conveniently near the vehicle.

She nodded and did as he asked, her gaze on the tavern door.

Darley too, focused on that dark portal.

While Ismail furtively watched the marquis, fearful something untoward might occur, causing the pistol in his ribs to discharge.

In less than the prescribed time limit, two emaciated men were carried out by their arms and legs. Their clothing was stained and foul, their hair matted with filth, their faces so black with dirt it was difficult to make out their features. As they were dropped to the ground, neither corpse-like figure so much as uttered a groan, their eyes shut, their breathing barely discernable, the stench of death like a shroud around them.

For a fleeting moment, Elspeth couldn't bring herself to search their faces, terrified her worst fears would be confirmed.

Darley despaired as he surveyed the gaunt, wasted figures. Even if one was Elspeth's brother, both men were so near death there was little hope of their survival. He quickly ordered Ismail to fetch a transport wagon, then stooped down and began going through the men's pockets. Not that he was expecting to find anything of value. That would have been long gone. But perhaps some token would remain—a scrap of a letter or some written orders.

Finding nothing, he settled back on his heels and scanned their clothing, looking for some clue—an epaulette, the cast of a button, a tailor's mark. Both men were more than common soldiers, their clothes were of good quality.

Moving away from the carriage, Elspeth bunched up her skirts in one hand and squatted down beside Darley. "Give me your handkerchief," she murmured, understanding she might be clutching at straws, but the line of one man's brows nearly met over the bridge of his nose in a familiar pattern. Not that her brother was necessarily unique in that regard, she warned herself. But taking Darley's proffered handkerchief, she allowed herself a modicum of hope and began gently wiping the dirt from the man's forehead.

"They're both officers." Darley glanced at Elspeth. "I don't suppose you recognize either's tailor?" Their faces were so gaunt, any former resemblance had been drastically altered.

"Will's uniforms came from York. A seamstress made them."

A seamstress wouldn't have left her mark, Darley thought, flipping over a lapel. "Bond Street," he murmured, running his thumb over the embroidered label. "Schweitzer and Davidson." He recognized his tailor.

Elspeth's hand trembled as she continued cleaning. Bond Street meant that man was eliminated as her brother. She frantically searched the face of the youth she was succoring for some clue—any fragmentary indication that this ghastly apparition could be her brother.

The prostrate form abruptly twitched.

Squealing in surprise, Elspeth tumbled backward.

Darley caught her—just short of her landing in the muck of the street.

"Thank you," she murmured, regaining her balance. "I wasn't expecting him to move."

The man's eyelids fluttered.

Darley and Elspeth exchanged a glance. Was the man conscious or had the movement been a reflex?

"We're here to help you," Darley said, gently, leaning close. "We're English. We'll take you home."

They watched the man struggle to open his eyes, his lids twitching, his brows arching slightly—even so small an effort seemingly overtaxing his strength for he went inert again.

"You're safe now," Elspeth murmured, her voice catching, the man's painful attempt to respond to them, touching. "We'll take care of you."

A guttural croak issued from the parched lips and with a superhuman effort that jerked his thin chest and pinched his face, the man lifted his lids enough to expose the vivid blue of his eyes. "Sis."

It was scarcely a whisper—more lip movement than sound.

Then his eyes shut again and he lost consciousness—along with his sister.

But Darley was smiling as he caught his swooning companion. He was still smiling as he lifted her into his arms and moved to the carriage. Gently laying Espeth's insensate form on the seat, he shut the carriage door and set about paying the barkeep and his numerous patrons.

Shortly, Ismail returned with a wagon and driver, the sick men were carefully loaded aboard a makeshift pallet cobbled together by the barkeep and the small party took their leave. They were sent on their way by a round of cheers from the tavern regulars whose fortunes had all prospered thanks to Darley's gold.

But it was money well-spent, Darley reflected with Elspeth in his arms and the carriage slowly rolling toward the docks. Gambler that he was though, he wouldn't have bet a six pence on the success of their venture. In fact, the odds had been so astronomically *against* them, he was seriously considering the possibility of divine intervention.

And he was the least likely man to nurture such feelings.

But there it was.

In this outland, in that den of iniquity that had apparently killed off a good number of Will's fellow troopers, they'd had the most fortuitous stroke of random luck in the universe. He might be inclined to offer up a prayer of thanksgiving once they had the men aboard the *Fair Undine.*

He frowned.

Provided they lived.

Quickly quelling his frown as Elspeth came awake, he smiled at her. "You're a very lucky lady," he whispered.

"Will!" She jerked upward.

"He's fine. He's in the wagon ahead of us. That's why we're driving so slowly."

"Tell me he'll—"

"He's going to be fine," Darley replied smoothly. "Absolutely fine," he added, perjuring himself without a qualm. Whatever was within his power he would do to prove his statement true. "I was thinking though, Gibralter would be more suitable for his convalescence. It's close. The garrison will have a doctor. And once Will has recuperated, then we'll sail for England."

"I almost believe you when you sound so assured."

But she was smiling, not fearful. He was pleased he'd calmed her. "Your brother's young and strong. He'll be back to his old self in no time."

"I can't thank you enough, for everything . . . for your faith and support *and* your frightfully intimidating posture inside that tavern," she added with a grin.

"My pleasure, darling."

She would dearly love to be his darling, but too much yet intervened between wishes and reality. "How long before we reach Gibralter?" she inquired, deliberately shifting the conversation to safer topics.

"A few hours, no more . . . where we may all enjoy a pleasant holiday."

She smiled. "You make all things possible, don't you?"

"We do what we can," he drawled. An understatement from a man who had always bent the world to his will. And in this case, his efforts would be directed toward making a certain Elspeth Wolsey as happy as possible.

A not entirely unselfish gesture.

He expected his own reward in due course.

Chapter
32

While the *Fair Undine* was making for Gibralter, Lord Grafton was seated in Chief Justice Kenyon's chambers in Lincoln's Fields. He was accompanied by his barrister although he and Kenyon were old friends, and had already agreed by correspondence that Grafton's suit for divorce would be taken up by the lord chancellor with all due speed.

"The slut gets nothing from me, not a pence!" Grafton said, angrily. "And I want a bill to bastardize any children she might have! Darley's by-blows won't be inheriting my lands or title!"

"Suitable provisions will be made, I assure you," Kenyon replied. He was a man of staunch chauvinistic principles when it came to the role of women. Furthermore, he fully agreed with Lord Chancellor Thurlow's moralistic view that adulterous women were sapping the moral fiber of the nation. "We will see that a clause is inserted bastardizing any children conceived by your wife. We will also demand that she present herself before the bar of the House to be cross-examined."

"And her infamous lover as well! I want Darley publically humiliated!"

Kenyon lifted a restraining hand. "I may not be able to accommodate you in that regard. The Duke of Westerlands has considerable influence, including the king's friendship. As for your wife, however, she will stand before the court and be condemned before the world for her immoral behavior." That Grafton had a reputation for debauch was of no consequence to a man like Kenyon who subscribed to the time-honored double standard.

A man could do as he wished while a woman was to be subservient in all things. So it had always been and so it should remain.

That Lord Chancellor Thurlow and Chief Justice Kenyon were in opposition to the changing social needs, sensibilities, and moral values of the time that emphasized considerations of personal happiness rather than descent of property mattered not a whit to either of them. They intended to stand firm against the new, corrupt views of morality that were threatening to undermine the fabric of society.

"I want a criminal conduct suit instituted against Darley as well!" Grafton wrathfully declared. "He can pay for his cunthound ways with my wife!" The process of extorting compensation for a wife's adultery from her lover had superseded dueling as a means of retribution. Although it was relatively rare since it entailed high costs in legal fees. "I want thirty thousand and an apology from the prick!"

"Are you sure you want to do that?" The chief justice gave Grafton a searching look. There was still a degree of shame in acknowledging one's cuckoldry. Publically exposing a wife for her adulterous behavior on the other hand did not reflect on a husband's character.

Grafton bristled. "Of course, I'm sure. I insist on it! The rogue can make me richer, damn him! I want his thirty thousand and I want him to know he took on the wrong man when he fucked *my* wife!"

The barrister quietly sat in a corner while the discussion took place, more than willing to earn his fees with very little work other than having to listen to Grafton's endless tirades against his wife. In truth, the woman probably had good reason to take flight. Grafton was reprehensible. But Mr. Eldon, Esq. had a large family to support, he was building a discreetly elegant house in

Mayfair and the transgressions of the aristocracy were well out-side his critical censure.

Fortunately, between Chancellor Thurlow and Justice Kenyon, he would have minimal duties to perform other than filing the re-quired paperwork. And now that Grafton was planning on fleec-ing Lord Darley out of thirty thousand in compensation, perhaps increasing his fees wouldn't be amiss. The terrace behind the house his wife was insisting on was proving expensive.

It wouldn't be the miserly Grafton's money after all; Lord Darley was rich as Croesus.

Grafton made a restless gesture with his hand. "Are we done then?"

"For the moment," Kenyon agreed.

"Send notice to my club when you need me again. I'm in London for the duration. My men are posted at the docks so I'll know the second the slut sets foot in England!"

"We'll have everything in readiness for that eventuality. Are you expecting her soon?"

"God knows. She ran off to Tangier on Darley's yacht on some wild goose chase looking for her brother who's no doubt been in his grave these many weeks."

Kenyon leaned back in his chair, his gaze narrowing. "On Darley's yacht? With *Darley*?"

"Of course with Darley," Grafton snapped.

"Are you sure?"

"The fucker took her," Grafton said with venom. "My sources are reliable."

The recently disclosed bit of information surprised Kenyon. Lord Darley was known for the brevity of his affaires and an ocean voyage to Tangier spoke of a rather drastic shift in prece-dent.

Moral scruples aside, he might want to tread lightly in regard to this case.

He would tell Thurlow as much; the Duke of Westerlands was a formidable opponent.

"Although, I warrant Darley will be glad to jettison the bitch once he's back in London," Grafton said, spitefully. "He don't tolerate women for long."

"No doubt," Kenyon ambiguously replied. Grafton's assessment of Darley's behavior was similar to his own. However—take nothing for granted was his motto. He smiled thinly. "Why don't we meet again once I speak to Thurlow."

Grafton swung his cane toward the barrister. "Fetch my chairman!" he ordered brusquely.

Mr. Eldon rose to his feet with a nod and a smile, but Grafton's rudeness would cost him.

He didn't appreciate being ordered about like a flunkey.

Nor would he tolerate it for less than five hundred. And that was whether Grafton won his criminal conduct suit or not.

As he entered the antechamber, Eldon nodded to Tom Scott. "He's ready to go."

"Pissed you off, did he?" Tom said with a grin.

The barrister grimaced. "Is it that obvious?"

"Nah. He pisses off everyone."

"You as well?"

"Let's just say, I'm savin' for my future." Tom smiled. "He's drunk more than he's sober and if'n he's missin' a fiver or two now an' then—who's to know."

"Putting up with him is worth more than an occasional fiver, my man," Eldon said with feeling.

Tom's smile broadened. "I ain't sayin' how often now an' then comes up. I'm jes hopin' he lives long enough to get me my little farm."

"I wish you all the best."

"You wouldn't be happen' to know when Lady Grafton be comin' back?"

"No one knows. She's in Tangier with Lord Darley."

"Don't let old Grafton harm her none."

Eldon sighed, beset by a small dilemma of conscience. The money he'd make from Grafton's suit would be considerable. On the other hand, any woman who had to put up with Grafton deserved a medal, not a public divorce. "My guess would be that

Lord Darley, not to mention his father, the duke, will be better able to help Lady Grafton than either you or I," he said, placating his conscience and hopefully the chairman as well.

"If'n he will. Darley ain't exactly a pattern card for faithfulness."

"Perhaps in this case he might be. And Kenyon looked as though he was undergoing a change of heart at the news of Darley's involvement. He may not wish to become a party to Grafton's suit." The barrister made a living reading people. Clearly, the chief justice had been taken aback on hearing that Darley had gone to Tangier with the lady.

"Would Grafton have to give up, then?"

Eldon blew out a breath. "Not necessarily. But his chances of success would lessen considerably. He needs votes in Parliament for his divorce action to prevail and Kenyon and Thurlow are powerful in that regard."

"I might keep tabs on the situation, if'n you don't mind a question from time to time. I expect we'll be seein' each other again."

"No, certainly not. Ask away." Eldon had no loyalty to Grafton; he couldn't imagine who would. He tipped his head toward Kenyon's office. "I believe that bellow is for you."

"Ain't it lucky I'm the one what is young and strong," Tom Scott said calmly. "He can holler all he wants, but he can't do much else. Good day to you." And with a nod, he strolled toward the door, none too fast.

Chapter
33

During Britain's war with the American colonies, Gibralter had been under siege by the French and Spanish from 1779–1783, and while the town had been destroyed, it hadn't surrendered. After the peace of Paris, reconstruction had commenced, and as the *Fair Undine* neared Gibralter, the sparkling fresh face of a newly built town came into view.

Will and his compatriot, Lieutenant Henry Blythe, had been carried up to the deck on stretchers and after a bath, a short rest and some of Sophie's substantial broth and restorative tisane, the two young men were able to summon up enough strength to witness the approach to Gibralter.

Elspeth stood beside her brother, holding his hand, while Darley rested against the port rail some distance away. Until Will was stronger, he would play friend and host rather than lover to Elspeth. He had offered as much to her once they were aboard and she'd accepted with alacrity, thanking him for his gallantry in a situation of great delicacy.

"Until Will is feeling better and can more easily deal with the blunt realities of life, I very much appreciate your chivalry."

"I won't be completely unselfish if you don't mind," he'd replied with a smile. "I intend to rent us a villa. You will have your own suite of course for appearance's sake, but I would like to see you on occasion."

She smiled. "At night, for instance."

His mouth quirked in a cheeky grin. "I would find that highly gratifying."

"I warrant I would as well."

"I'm sure you would."

"Arrogant man," she murmured.

"Let's just say I've come to know what you like."

"Yes," she gently noted. "You have indeed."

"So we have a bargain?"

"Yes, but Will comes first."

"I understand."

And so it had been left, the remainder of the short voyage given over to more mundane pursuits having to do with the sick-room.

When the *Fair Undine* docked, Darley and Malcolm excused themselves to make arrangements for their housing and for the horses loaded aboard in their brief time in Tangier. Darley's agent had purchased six handsome stallions and even a mare, a coup— since prime mares were generally not sold.

"If it's possible to find some pasture," Darley said as the men strode up the hill to the garrison, "I'd prefer that. The horses have been cooped up in that livery stable in Tangier for too long. They need some open country."

"I'll see what I can do."

"After I introduce myself to the commander, I'll ask him whether he knows of a serviceable villa outside town. He might."

"Why don't we meet at the parade ground in an hour?" Malcolm lifted his brows in query.

"Fine. We'll compare notes. I'm looking for seclusion, a staff and"—Darley smiled—"a good view."

"We'll see what's left after the siege."

"Or what's been built. Check out the possibilities in Catalan Bay. We'd be well away from town over there."

"I'll make inquiries. How long do you plan on staying?"

"It's up to the lady. I have no plans."

Such a startling statement from a man who'd always been known for the brevity of his affaires was enough to momentarily leave Darley's secretary nonplussed. Quickly finding his voice, he said in as close to a normal tone as he could muster, "We're looking for a property to rent for an indefinite period of time, then." In the event he'd misinterpreted Darley's remarks, he decided to double check.

"Yes. The weather is delightful here. What better place for Elspeth's brother to recuperate. He's looking better already, don't you think?"

That was a very clear and precise "yes" to his query. "Her ladyship's brother looks remarkably improved considering so few hours that have passed," Malcolm replied, comfortable once again now that he understood the situation.

"Will is young. One is practically indestructible at twenty."

Darley had about ten years on Will Wolsey, a licentious decade that would have brought lesser men to their graves. "Your health is equally sound, my lord," Malcolm observed. "I perceive you as indestructible as well."

"I admit, Malcolm, I'm feeling a new lease on life. Boredom and ennui have quite deserted me." Darley smiled. "It must be the sea air."

"No doubt, sir," Malcolm diplomatically answered. Far be it for him to point out that Darley's previous sea voyages had not brought about such a striking or enthusiastic transformation. "In an hour then," he said, politely. They'd reached the garrison gates. "I wish you good fortune with General Eliot."

"He's a friend of my father, an amiable sort," Darley replied with the cheerful complacency so much in evidence since departing Tangier. "I expect he'll be helpful."

General Eliot was so pleased to see his old friend's son that he broke open his thirty-year-old brandy and the early part of their visit consisted of numerous toasts to their mutual friends. Once the courtesies concluded, Darley explained his reasons for choosing Gibralter as his residence for the foreseeable future.

"You're fortunate you found those men alive," the general observed. "The navy is a brutal service. They treat men as disposable. Flogging, for instance, for the veriest of misdemeanors." He grimaced. "I don't understand that. You can't trust a man once he's been flogged."

"I couldn't agree more. And that luck played an enormous role in our finding Lady Grafton's brother I readily acknowledge. As a gambler, I wouldn't have given odds on our success. But the young men seem better already. I'm vastly encouraged."

"They'll soon feel fit as a fiddle, I guarantee. Our climate is salubrious—sun and fresh sea air, excellent foodstuffs available from the Spanish village of San Roque over the border. I expect your ailing men will be fully recuperated in a fortnight. Now, as to your lodgings, I suggest you speak to a Mr. Barlow. My aide will give you directions. Barlow's the sort who knows everything that goes on in this garrison town as well as the surrounding countryside. He's a native if such a term exists for the hodge-podge of humanity who reside here."

"He sounds like he'd be useful to know."

"Indeed. If you need something done—Barlow's your man."

"Thank you for the suggestion—and for your excellent brandy. I have people waiting, so I shall take my leave." Darley came to his feet. "We'll have you to dine once everyone is settled in," he added with a bow. "And I'll give your regards to my father."

"As to that, should you have any mail you wish to send back to England, we'll put it in our diplomatic sack. It goes out with a deal of regularity since we have so many ships stopping here for provisioning. I shall look forward to dining with you." The older man shouted for his subaltern.

When his aide came running, the general gave him orders concerning Darley's needs and shortly the marquis was back outside in the dazzling sunshine.

* * *

Malcolm was waiting as Darley exited the parade ground and the men compared their information. Malcolm had been referred to the same Mr. Barlow, apparently a man of vast acquaintance.

They found him in a new building with offices on the ground floor and lodgings above, his desk placed so he had a clear view of the harbor. He was a small, wiry, middle-aged man of indeterminate heritage despite his English surname, his faint Andalusian accent common to the area. English was clearly his second language, but once he understood that the general had sent Darley to him, a smile replaced his wariness. Snapping his fingers, he ordered sherry from a young man who appeared at an inner doorway. "Our local sherry is superb," he said with a faint smile that creased his tanned face. "Tell me now, what type of accommodations would best suit you?"

Darley explained their requirements over a superb sherry, referring to Elspeth and Will as old family friends, briefly sketching out the details of their excursion to Tangier. "I would like something away from town for our invalids. They need fresh air and quiet."

"And you require pasture for your horses as well. Hmmm." Barlow ran his finger down a ledger page he'd been scrutinizing. "Might I suggest the property near Europa Point. A Spanish grandee built the house in the last century but it's been well-maintained. It has a spectacular view of Africa on a clear day, your invalids will have quiet and fair sea breezes. There's pasture for your horses such as it is this time of year, but if you have Barbs from the Atlas, they're familiar with our style of summer grazing."

"Is there a road?" Darley inquired. "The men will have to be conveyed in litters."

"There's a narrow lane, but it's serviceable. You shouldn't have any problems."

"It sounds very suitable. We'll take it. Can you have a staff sent there immediately, as well as stock the property with all the necessary supplies? Malcolm will handle the financial arrangements." Darley set down his sherry glass and leaned across the desk to shake Mr. Barlow's hand. "Thank you very much. I expect we'll leave from my yacht within the hour."

"Very good, sir. I'll have everything in order when you arrive."

"Thank you again," Darley said, coming to his feet and nodding at Malcolm. "I'll see you at the dock."

All was accomplished save for the mundane details that Malcolm could handle with his usual competence. Darley was in a fine mood as he exited the small office.

Things couldn't have gone more smoothly.

Elspeth's brother had been found and would soon be well again.

Gibralter was a suitably remote locale in which to enjoy Elspeth's delightful company.

And as though to put the final gloss on perfection, his Moroccan horses had been ready and waiting for transport from Tangier.

Lady Luck was indeed kind.

Chapter
34

The next fortnight was all that was good. Darley played the gentleman, seeing Elspeth only discreetly at night, the two ailing men prospered, becoming stronger every day, the new horses enjoyed the fresh air and pasture, and as specified—the view couldn't have been better.

The villa had been built on the heights north of Europa Point, the site having been designated by the Greeks as one of the pillars of Hercules. The African shore as well as panoramic ocean views were visible from the loggias, sea breezes tempered the summer heat, native stone pine and wild olive lent a romantic aspect to the rugged landscape. The staff Mr. Barlow had recruited was excellent, the food was precisely what recuperating patients required—fresh fruits and vegetables, good wines, the local stews, fish of all descriptions.

The small group spent lazy days playing cards, reading, swimming at Catalan Bay once Will and Henry were able, lingering over dinner each night—discussing politics, horses and racing, the next day's schedule—enjoying each other's company.

It was a time of calm and revitalization.

It was a pastoral paradise of good friendship and contentment.

It was charmingly humdrum—and *perfect*.

And so it would have remained had Darley not received a note from General Eliot one morning, bidding him to call at his earliest convenience.

"I'll go with you," Elspeth said. "Will needs more poultice for that sore on his leg."

"The General might want to drink. You know how garrison commanders are away from home. Do you mind?" There was something about the wording of the note that had caused Darley misgivings. The phrase, *grave matter* to be precise.

"No, of course not. If he keeps you long, we'll dine without you."

"Courtesy won't require I stay more than a few hours," Darley said. "I'll be home in good time for dinner. Give me the name of the poultice. I'll fetch it."

He left shortly, riding one of his new Barbs, a small list from Elspeth in his pocket, a sense of foreboding prominent in his thoughts.

The general had him ushered into his office the moment he arrived and pointedly said to his aide, "I *don't* wish to be disturbed." As the subaltern left the room, the general walked over to the door to the adjoining office and shut it. "People will listen," he cryptically remarked as he took a chair beside Darley. "I expect you could use a brandy. I certainly could."

None of which—actions or comments—did much to ease Darley's concern.

The general had already filled two glasses and handing one to Darley, lifted his glass. "To the king," he saluted, drank the brandy down and began refilling his glass.

"Perhaps we should discuss this grave matter you referred to in your note," Darley proposed, the general's discomfort only increasing his own unrest. Furthermore, whatever the problem, he preferred facing it sober.

"It was in *The Times*." General Eliot poured down the second brandy and topped off another glass.

"This matter you wrote of," Darley noted, hoping the general would remain coherent long enough to explain his summons.

"Yes." The general snorted in disgust. "A contemptible business—gossip," he grunted and tossed down his third brandy.

The general's face mirrored his distaste of the rumor mill. Personally, Darley didn't give a damn about gossip, but since others were involved this time he couldn't so cavalierly dismiss the inescapable curiosity of his fellow man. "You have the—article . . . or news item? The paper?"

"It came in the mail pouch this morning. Naturally, I thought you should see it immediately. Here." Eliot reached for a copy of *The Times* on a nearby table and handed it to Darley with a grimace. "Page six, "Society," second paragraph."

Obviously he'd read it more than once. Darley turned to the designated page, found the "Society" column and read:

> *Information has surfaced concerning an impending divorce suit against Lady Grafton by Lord Grafton. There is word that a crim con action against Lord Darley may also be instituted. Chief Justice Kenyon has refused to comment on the case. Lord Grafton has not been so reluctant. According to reports, Lady Grafton and Lord Darley are currently out of the country.*

Darley laid the paper aside, then leaned over and checked the date. Twelve days old. Picking up his brandy, he drank it down. "A startling bit of news," the marquis remarked, his gaze bland.

"I expect it is," the general replied with the same studied understatement. "Another?" He raised the bottle.

Darley held out his glass. "I appreciate you apprising me of the account. When does your next mail go to England?"

"Tonight. The *Enterprise* is scheduled to leave on the tide."

"If you would be kind enough to give me pen and paper, I'll send my father a letter. He can look into this for me."

Both men spoke with a well-mannered reticence.

"A damnable business," the general muttered. "My apologies for being the bearer of bad tidings."

"No need to apologize. I'm grateful for the warning."

"If there's anything else I can do for you, you need but ask. Anyone who's met Grafton can't help but be sympathetic to his wife"—the general's brows rose—"the third is it not?"

Darley nodded. "The other two are in their graves."

"My, my, you don't say," Eliot murmured. He cleared his throat and lifted his glass. "Give Lady Grafton my best regards, of course, and convey my good wishes to her."

The general had dined with them on more than one occasion and been charmed by Elspeth. Although, who wouldn't be, Darley thought with his own highly personal bias. "Thank you. I'll tell her. And if you could make arrangements for my letter to be hand delivered once it reaches London, I would be grateful."

"Of course, of course. Let me see to that paper," Eliot grunted, coming to his feet, glad to be finished with the embarrassing conversation. He had no doubts about the probability of a divorce. One had only to see Lord Darley and Lady Grafton together to know that they were besotted. He'd bet a year's pay, she wouldn't be going back to her husband. Although, with Darley's reputation for dalliance, whether *his* intentions were serious was another matter.

Not that it was any of his concern.

"McFarlane," he shouted as he walked to the door to the anteroom. "Come in here."

Darley was supplied with pen and paper, a private room, and per Eliot's orders, a bottle of brandy. The general considered this a drinking matter, although officers posted to distant locales were known to drink for a great variety of unlikely reasons.

The marquis kept his letter brief and to the point. His father would know what to do better than he. But Elspeth was to be protected at all costs. He stopped short of making a declaration of his feelings, habits of a lifetime not easily discarded. In all else, however, he was clear. Grafton would not be allowed to humiliate his wife. After sealing the letter, the marquis handed it to Eliot's aide and went to take leave of the general. "Thank you again for informing me of *The Times* item," he said. "I'll let you know our plans when we've decided our course of action."

"It's none of my business, I'm sure," the general said, tight-lipped. "Nor anyone else's," he grumbled. "But whatever you decide, may I say it's been a pleasure to have your small party here on Gibralter. Stay as long as you wish, of course. The im-broglios of London are far away and have nothing to do with us."

"So it has seemed these past weeks," Darley said with a smile. "We're grateful for the respite. I expect my father will deal with Grafton. If the lady wishes to stay, we will."

"Capital! Excellent! And why shouldn't you," Eliot replied with a wide smile. "We have everything here we need."

A valid point, Darley thought.

Provided one wished to remain an expatriate.

On his ride back to the villa, the marquis debated their op-tions—at base, reluctant to leave this sweet paradise. He couldn't recall when he'd been more content. So, option one: they could do nothing stay here and *do* nothing. Then again, they *could* re-turn, get counsel for Elspeth and see the divorce through—an idea of considerable merit since it would free Elspeth from her husband. As to the crim con suit against him, he was inured to embarrassment and more than willing to pay Grafton for the pleasure of taking his wife away.

But ultimately, it wasn't his decision.

It was Elspeth's life and thus hers to make.

She was the one who would be least able to bear the intense scrutiny that was bound to occur. Having been the cynosure of society for all of his adult life, Darley was largely indifferent to public censure.

She would have to decide, he resolved.

As he entered the house a short time later, Elspeth came run-ning from the library, threw her arms around him and gaily cried, "You weren't gone long at all! But I missed you vastly even then!"

Maybe they'd stay after all, he suddenly thought, overcome by a heady wave of happiness. "I couldn't stay away," he murmured, holding her close. "I had two drinks with the general and left."

She grinned. "Because you missed me dreadfully."

"For that exact reason," he said, grinning back. "I am desolate without you."

"Yes, yes, *yes!*" she exclaimed, rising on tiptoe to kiss him. "I've bewitched you completely."

"No argument there," he said, recognizing the artless truth in her remark.

"So then," she murmured with a mischievous smile, "what did you bring your enchantress from town?"

He softly swore. "I forgot about the list."

"Even Will's medicine?"

"Sorry, I'll go back right now." His hands dropped from her waist and he stepped away.

"No, no, it can wait." She pulled him back. "There's still a smidgen of medicine left. We'll go tomorrow when you don't have to visit with the general. You can take me to lunch at that little Turkish inn near the harbor where the baklava is so delicious."

"Very well—we'll go tomorrow."

"Now, tell me what the general wanted. Did he miss your company like I?"

"No. He had some news. Come, we'll go outside and I'll tell you."

Her brows came together in a faint frown, her gaze searching his face. "That sounded ominous."

"It isn't," he lied, or maybe not, depending on one's point of view. "Don't worry. It's nothing I can't take care of."

"I'm not sure I like the sound of any of this," she replied, worriedly.

"Really, it's nothing. You'll see." He smiled and took her hand. "We'll sit on the bench that overlooks the point."

When he told her, she went utterly still, her cheeks flushed bright scarlet. "I always knew he'd retaliate," she breathed.

"It doesn't matter." He took her hands in his. "A divorce will be a good thing. Think, darling, you'll have your freedom." The opportunity of having Elspeth to himself—unfettered by marriage—was undeniably appealing. The notion of a divorce increasingly attractive. Grafton's suit in Parliament would be a scandal—but fleeting, like all scandals. "We'll find you a good barrister, or if you wish to stay here, I'll have my father handle the matter. The divorce will be over before you know it."

"What if Grafton calls me to the dock?" She'd heard lurid tales of women who were brought before Parliament, the most intimate details of their lives trumpeted in the papers.

"Grafton won't do that. Or more aptly, we'll see that he doesn't."

She took a deep breath, looked away briefly, taking in the rugged, sun-drenched landscape, wishing they could stay forever in their secluded haven. "I suppose I always knew I couldn't simply walk away unscathed," she softly said, pulling her hands from his, clasping them tightly to hold down her panic.

"It's not a catastrophe, sweetheart." Darley spoke calmly, aware of her agitation. "I guarantee you, this situation is completely manageable." And where fine counsel and money didn't work, there were always other means of bringing Grafton to heel, he thought. The earl was far from a saint; there would be no need for scruple. "Let me take care of this for you."

She grimaced faintly. "Like everything else."

"You've said yourself how much easier it is for a man than a woman to make their way in the world. Let me handle this."

Like all females, she had few legal safeguards. The world was run by men, the laws written for them—particularly men of a certain class. She could count on Will's support, but he wielded little more influence than she without a penny to his name. And then again, Darley always made it so easy to acquiesce. She softly sighed. "This will implicate you as well. You understand that."

He smiled. "I doubt my reputation can be further subverted."

Her brows rose faintly. "I'm not so sure about that. You could be called to the dock as well."

"Let them."

He was completely unfazed; she admired his composure. Although a title and great wealth eased the uncertainties of life. But short of throwing herself on Grafton's nonexistent mercy, she didn't know what choice she had. Contending with a divorce action was very expensive. "I feel as though I'm contracting an enormous debt to you—"

"Nonsense," he interposed. "Anyone would be more than willing to help you." He smiled. "Although I'm pleased you've favored me with your friendship."

How agreeable his allusion to friendship; how ingratiating—and practiced. How charming.

Were that he were less lovable.

Or perhaps she more principled.

She sighed again, defeated on all fronts—by love, by fear of Grafton's reprisals, by her own abject poverty. "We'll have to tell Will," she said, surrendering to the inevitable. "About us . . . about this divorce action."

"Of course," Darley said with exquisite restraint.

"I confess, I'm more nervous about his reaction than all the rest."

"You saved his life, darling. I doubt he'll take issue with anything you do."

She made a small moue. "Women aren't allowed the same freedoms as men. I'm not sure how liberal his attitudes."

"He adores you. It's obvious. You worry too much. We'll tell him after dinner tonight; he'll be supportive I assure you."

"Do we *have* to go back?" Her hesitancy was plain.

"It's up to you."

"Truly?"

"Truly." Leaning back, he spread his arms along the back of the bench, pleased with the direction of events, the prospect of Elspeth's freedom extremely gratifying. "You decide and let me know what you want to do."

"You don't care if we stay here?"

"I don't."

"You might someday."

He shrugged. "Maybe. Should that time come, we'll deal with it. At the moment, I'm entirely neutral. The decision is yours."

Could he be any nicer? She was reminded again why he was

such a favorite with all the society belles. He was charming, amiable, more generous than any man she'd ever known—and she loved him much too much. Particularly when he was the least likely man to offer more than transient pleasure. Not that she'd expected he would.

Grateful for all that he had done and was doing for her, she cautioned herself against any undue expectations. Darley wasn't interested in permanence. Just because he shared her bed didn't make her any different from all the other ladies he'd made love to. "Why don't we decide what to do once we talk to Will?" she said, taking care to be as well-mannered as he. "My brother might have some ideas."

"Fine." He smiled. "You'll see; this will all turn out for the best."

Chapter
35

Henry Blythe was a year younger than Will and the type of young man who took pleasure in living life to the fullest. And now that he had his life back, of late, he'd taken to retiring early with one of the local servant girls.

Will had refrained from becoming involved in such amorous activities—not from lack of interest on the young maids' part— but because his heart belonged to Clarissa Burford in Yorkshire. They weren't formally engaged, but they had an understanding that when Will returned from India, they would marry.

So, shortly after dinner, when the port came out, Henry excused himself, as did Malcolm—who strangely for a Scotsman didn't drink—and the three remaining retired with the port to the sitting room.

The conversation was desultory at first. Elspeth was visibly nervous, while Darley wished he might lift her into his lap and comfort her. Since he couldn't, he took over her share of the discussion, comparing notes with Will on the various premier studs in England. Yorkshire had its share, the north addicted to racing, although several in and around London were top quality as well.

"I was thinking, I might try my hand at training once we return to England," Will said. "The army isn't going to want me with this leg of mine—or at least not for the moment. I'm going to have trouble sitting a horse for the foreseeable future." He glanced at his sister. "I thought I might approach Lord Rutledge. He knows what I can do."

She smiled. "I like your idea." She particularly liked that Lord Rutledge lived in the south.

"Good," Will said, lounging back in his chair, breathing more freely after her ready acceptance. "I didn't know how you'd feel about me living so far away."

Darley and Elspeth exchanged glances.

"What?" Will inquired. "Or rather, why don't you say what you want to say, Sis, and stop your fidgeting. You've been nervous as a cat all evening."

The lovers' gazes met again.

Darley would have spoken long since had he not been concerned about interfering.

"You tell him," Elspeth murmured.

Relieved, the marquis smiled reassuringly at Elspeth, then turned to her brother. "You must know that I hold your sister in high esteem."

Will suppressed a grin. "I rather got that impression."

"And naturally she's been concerned about your health or we would have spoken sooner."

"I understand." Will shot Elspeth a sympathetic look. "You needn't be so distrait, Sis. Whatever you do is fine with me. In fact, you could dance with the devil himself and I'd say bravo. I owe you my life," he softly said, "and I'll never forget it."

"You owe Julius more than I," Elspeth maintained. "Without him, I'm not sure I would have succeeded in rescuing you."

"I'm in your debt, of course," Will noted, lifting his glass to Darley in salute. "I know how much you've done for both of us. And if it will make this conversation any easier, I'm well aware of your relationship." He smiled. "All the tiptoeing around at night did not go unnoticed. I wish you well. I wish you both"—his pause was infinitesimal—"whatever you want." Aware of Darley's reputation, he didn't expect any posting of the banns.

"Thank God," Elspeth blurted out. "I didn't know how you'd

feel about"—she fluttered her fingers—"this . . . well . . . ir-regularity."

"No offense, Darley," Will said drolly, "but anyone's an improvement over Grafton."

The marquis laughed. "I'm not sure that's a compliment, but I shall take it as such."

"And so it was intended." While he knew of Darley's prodigality, he also knew that all the women in the marquis's past remained his friends.

"We do have another bit of news as well," Darley remarked. "Your sister thinks it disastrous. I do not. But you should know what has recently transpired in London. We learned via an item in *The Times* called to my attention by General Eliot that Lord Grafton has begun a divorce bill against your sister. Excuse me." Quickly rising from his chair, he walked to Elspeth who was beginning to tremble, plucked her from her chair, sat in her place and set her on his lap. "Everything's going to be fine," he whispered, holding her gently in his arms. Looking up, he met her brother's gaze. "Tell her this can all be managed. She's terrified."

"You'll be well rid of Grafton. I should never have let you marry him in the first place." Clearly disturbed, Will restlessly ran his hands through his golden hair so like Elspeth's. "It was selfish of me and that's the plain truth. Sis always took care of everyone after Mama died," he explained. "I shouldn't have let her keep doing it when I was old enough to help. I owe you my life in many ways, Sis, and on my honor, I'll start taking care of *you* now."

Darley found himself disinclined to let her brother assume that role. Not that he was about to initiate an argument now. Time enough to settle who was taking care of whom once they reached England. "I'm sure your sister will be able to negotiate a living from Grafton in the divorce settlement," he offered. "As for this divorce bill, I've already sent a letter to my father. He can deal with the procedural process. Elspeth isn't sure she wishes to return to England."

"You *don't*?" Will caught himself. "There I go again being selfish. If you don't want to go back"—he swallowed hard—"I'll stay here with you."

Elspeth smiled for the first time that evening, her brother's offer so obviously forced. It reminded her of him trying to be well-behaved and share his peppermint sticks as a child. "If you wish to go back, Will, please do. I'm not certain I may stay anyway; my feelings are in flux."

Will's relief was patent, but scrupulously polite. He suggested, "Why don't we just wait and see for a time. Nothing's pressing, is it?"

"Not in the least," Darley replied. "I endorse your proposal. We have no need to make any hasty decisions. Is that better, now?" He dipped his head and met Elspeth's gaze. "We have all agreed—there's no urgency."

"Thank you." She smiled, feeling ever so much better, Will's acceptance a huge obstacle overcome. While the suggestion that they take their time about making a decision, suited her irresolute mood to perfection.

And so it was left for over a week, while the small party continued to enjoy their holiday. The general came to dine twice, offering his hearty approval of their plan to extend their time on Gibralter. They went sailing often on Darley's yacht, exploring the local coastline, anchoring off shore to swim in the azure sea, picnicking on deck, coming back each night with deeper tans and happy hearts and a cheerful acceptance of their unencumbered life.

Until Elspeth woke one morning feeling nauseous. "It must be something I ate," she said, sitting up in bed, trying to hold back the bile rising in her throat.

"The squid we had at dinner, perhaps," Darley suggested, although the greenish cast to her skin gave him pause. "I'll call a doctor," he said, "just to be safe."

He was already walking to the bellpull to summon a servant when she uttered a muffled squeal, leaped out of bed and dashed for the chamber pot.

Wiping her face with a damp cloth afterward, Darley helped

her back to bed. "We need a doctor. Don't argue," he gruffly said, cutting off her protest. He'd seen the serious effects tainted food could have on a person and in this summer heat, spoilage was much more prevalent.

"A cup of tea first, please," she whispered, her face still tinged with green, the contrast stark against the white linen. "With sugar."

"I'll ring for a maid." He had no intention of leaving her, although he was slightly encouraged that she felt well enough to ask for tea. "Would you like toast with it or maybe some cake?"

She made a face.

"Fine. Just tea."

"I'm feeling much better," she murmured as he returned from summoning a maid and sat on the edge of the bed beside her. "Perhaps I'll have a bit of toast after all and maybe some ham— just a wee bit—and one of those juicy pears we had yesterday."

He felt his stomach muscles relax, a palpable relief washed over him and in that revelatory moment, he understood that he could no longer delude himself about the nature of their liaison. It was not like all the rest. Elspeth's sudden attack had frightened him. Scenarios of disaster had raced through his mind— ones where he thought he might lose her. People died of lesser things—expiring of lung fever after a walk in the rain, contracting a mortal infection from a small cut, dying from the flux after drinking bad water.

"We'll stay home today," he said, intent on her recovery. "You should rest. And I'll taste your food first, just in case. I have a cast iron stomach." After years of drinking and debauch in which he was always the last man standing, he knew of what he spoke.

After the maid arrived, breakfast soon appeared, and to Elspeth's amusement, Darley assumed the role of food-taster. The food was judged safe, they both ate a hearty breakfast and by the time the doctor who had been called appeared, Elspeth was in fine good spirits.

Elspeth's symptoms were explained.

The doctor nodded his head, took her pulse, listened to her

heart and deferentially said, "If the lady will allow and my lord agrees, I will proceed with a brief examination."

Darley looked at Elspeth, she at him and still concerned, Darley said, "I think you should, darling."

"Very well." The doctor had come from town, a not inconsiderable journey.

The marquis stayed in the room while the doctor examined Elspeth, not inclined to leave her unattended with another man no matter how elderly. Add jealousy and possessiveness to his novel feelings.

The examination wasn't lengthy, although it was of an intimate nature. When the doctor had finished and washed his hands, he returned to the young couple who sat side by side on the bed, holding hands.

"May I offer my congratulations," he said, smiling. "My lady is with child and in excellent health."

Elspeth felt her breakfast coming up.

Darley grinned.

And before another word could be uttered, Elspeth jumped up and raced for the chamber pot.

Chapter

36

The Duke of Westerlands had heard of Grafton's divorce suit. Who in London hadn't. But he'd not heard from his son until the *Enterprise* docked and Darley's letter arrived at his door.

After sharing the news with the duchess, he sent for his solicitor.

"Julius didn't say if he was coming home," his wife noted, as unconcerned as her son about any scandal having to do with the divorce.

"I gather it's up to Elspeth."

The duchess smiled. "What a lovely thought. We must expedite Lord Grafton's divorce bill. You should talk to the king?"

"I will. He owes me a favor or two, and the prime minister will do the king's bidding. Pitt can quietly and expeditiously steer this bill through Parliament."

"Pitt *should* do His Majesty's bidding. He's become very wealthy thanks to the king's favor." The duchess folded her hands in her lap and offered her husband a complacent smile. "It looks as though dear Elspeth will soon be free of that villain Grafton—oh, dear." She sat up straight. "What about the public testimony?"

"Don't worry about public testimony." The duke's lidded eyes took on a predatory gleam. "It won't happen."

"What of Grafton's apparent need for revenge in that crim con suit against Julius? Can he be stopped there as well?"

"Naturally." The duke's voice was soft. "Grafton will be silenced one way or another. Crighton can apprise me of the legalities, but if those should fail, I'll deal with the earl myself."

The duchess relaxed against her chair back, her worry lines erased. "I knew I could count on you—as always. It's a shame this disagreeable divorce has to be dealt with. But," she added, cheerfully, "the fact that our son has finally fallen in love is quite, quite delicious."

"I'm not sure I'm ready to stake money on Julius being in love," the duke noted, drolly.

"Of course he is. All the signs point to it. You must admit he's never gone out of his way for a woman before—and now he's sailing to *Tangier*? Really, darling, if you weren't a man you'd know these things."

"I'm sure you're right," her husband said, having learned long ago not to argue with his wife when it came to matters of the heart. She could sniff out a love affaire like a bloodhound. "Do you have any feelings about when we might see our son again?" he inquired, his gaze amused.

"Tease me if you will, but mark my words, Julius will return with dear Elspeth before too long. Which reminds me," she briskly added, "I must consult with Betsy about dear Julius's wedding."

The duke chuckled. "Perhaps we should see the lady divorced first."

"I expect you to handle that—and please—in all haste if you will. I was thinking a wedding before the summer is over would be delightful—when the flowers are still plentiful . . . you know, all the lovely lilies are at their peak then."

The duke laughed. "I'll tell the king he must hurry right along because my wife is concerned with the fleeting nature of summer blooms."

"Tell him whatever you want," she said, lightly. "So long as he sees that Pitt takes care of this divorce quickly. Now if you'll excuse me," she said, rising in a rustle of aquamarine silk, "I have myriad plans to make."

She turned at the door, her smile reminding him of that first smile he'd seen across a meadow fence years ago—the one that had instantly curtailed his bachelor existence. "One more thing. Be a dear and invite the king and queen to Julius and Elspeth's welcome home tea when you talk with him."

"A tea?"

"Yes, the one I have to go off and arrange." Her fair brows came together in a small frown. "A shame we don't know exactly when they'll be back from Gibralter." Her smile appeared again. "Never mind. Tell the king we'll give him fair notice whatever the date."

"Pulling out all the guns are we? A public affair with the king and queen in attendance?"

The duchess's brows rose. "He's our son, darling."

"Indeed." The duke smiled. "I'll see that Their Majesties come."

When the duke's solicitor arrived shortly after, he explained the process through which a divorce bill passed. First an investigation by a Committee of the House of Lords takes place, the main burden of the investigation falling on the law lords. It was normal for the second reading of the bill to take the form of a full trial, with personal testimony of witnesses and cross-examination of them and of the petitioner. If the bill of divorce survives the Committee of the Lords and a third reading, it goes to the House of Commons, where it is examined by a Select Committee on Divorce Bills made up of nine members. A majority of these are laymen, but all current and former law officers of the Crown are also included. Should the bill be accepted by the Commons, it would be returned to the House of Lords, rarely with amendments, and in due course become law.

"It will be almost certain that Lord Darley and Lady Grafton will be called before Parliament and forced to testify."

"No," the duke said, firmly, twenty generations of D'Abernon nobility bolstering his surety. "That's not acceptable. Neither Lady Grafton nor my son will testify. I won't have it. They may not even return to England in time. Now then." He clasped his long, slender hands on his desktop and leaned forward, his dark eyes so much like his son's, piercing. "Here's what I need from you. Assemble whatever team of barristers you require to deal with this case. I want a full report on Grafton's plans in regard to this proceeding by the end of the week. I'm sure you have access to people who can obtain that information for you. In the meantime, I shall visit the king and solicit his help in moving this bill through Parliament. My preference would be a quick vote and passage without any fanfare or notoriety. I'm not naive enough to expect that to happen without suitable pressure being put on those who might oppose my wishes. Grafton may or may not be our only adversary. Is that all clear?"

"Yes, Your Grace, perfectly clear. I will report back to you by week's end."

"Sooner if possible."

"Yes, my lord." Crighton was a man of considerable consequence in his field, but in the duke's presence, he always felt like a first year law clerk.

"Very few people have any personal sympathy for a man like Grafton. I expect Kenyon and Thurlow are on one of their moral crusades, but in this case, they've taken on the wrong man. You have my permission to express my opinions on that matter to them should the occasion arise. I don't tell Thurlow and Kenyon how to live their lives and I expect equal courtesy in return."

"Yes, my lord. I will so convey your message. One question, my lord," he said, needing to know the answer whether the duke liked it or not. "Should Lady Grafton and Lord Darley not return to England, might I ask where they would reside? It's a territorial matter—having to do with England's sovereignty abroad apropos the divorce."

"They're in Gibralter at the moment, but that's for your ears only. I don't wish it bruited abroad. They may not stay there in any event."

"If they don't return, my lord, might I suggest they consider somewhere outside England's jurisdiction. For their own safety, my lord."

"I certainly hope you're not expecting problems," the duke gruffly noted.

"If the Chancellor and Chief Justice are involved, there's a likelihood that their minions in Parliament can be brought into line—for the vote, sir," the solicitor added, hesitantly.

"Rest easy, Crighton. I'll take care of Thurlow and Kenyon."

The duke's voice was chill as the grave. Mr. Crighton was under the distinct impression that whatever obstacles might lay in Lord Darley's path would be handily crushed by his father's influence and power. "Very good, sir."

"I wish you a pleasant day, Crighton, and cheer up." The duke smiled. "The king and Pitt outrank Thurlow and Kenyon, not to mention that drunken blackguard, Grafton. All will proceed nicely, I assure you," he said at the same precise time that Elspeth was dead certain *nothing* in her life was going to go nicely from this moment forward.

Chapter
37

When Elspeth had run into the dressing room, she'd slammed the door shut, in either haste or more likely temper, Darley thought, if he'd properly interpreted the condemnatory look she'd flashed at him as she dashed by.

But he preferred dispatching the doctor before confronting Elspeth and to that purpose, he thanked the man for riding so far, accepted his congratulations once again and sent him to Malcolm to be paid.

Then repressing the grin that threatened to remain permanently etched on his face, he walked to the dressing room door and opened it.

"Don't you say a word! Don't you dare SAY—ONE—WORD!" Elspeth glared at Darley as she stood before the washstand, a wet cloth in her hand.

He stood motionless in the doorway, although he surveyed her slender form with a new scrutiny.

"And don't look at me like that!" she sniped, whipping the wet cloth at him.

He caught it, let it drop to the floor and spoke despite her fiat. "I know I should say I'm sorry, but I'm not. I'm pleased about the child."

"Easy for you to say," she hissed. "You're not the one who's having this child. You're not the one who will live the rest of her life—not to mention the child's—with scandal dogging your heels!" She took a deep breath for she'd been screaming at the end and exhaling, spoke in a less vehement tone. "I know it's not your fault completely. This pregnancy required two participants." She grimaced. "But I'm not feeling real reasonable right now. I want to blame *you*! I want to scream my outrage to the skies! But mostly," she said with a sigh, "I wish everything could go back to the way it was before." Dropping into a nearby chair, she wrinkled her nose at him. "It's a little late for any of that, though, isn't it?"

"I suspect it is. But then I'm no authority on pregnancy."

She shot him a narrow-eyed look. "Please—a man of your profligacy? Acquit me of stupidity."

"Nevertheless, it's true. I don't leave by-blows behind."

"Then, pray tell, how did I get so lucky? Am I to understand you changed your customary habits for me?"

"It seems I have. But then everything with you has been different."

She snorted. "Don't try to gull me."

"I'm not; I understand your frustration. It's—"

"You can't *begin* to understand my frustration," she snapped, interrupting him. "You haven't the slightest notion what I'm feeling."

"At least, let me make amends. That I can do."

"In case you haven't noticed," she curtly replied, scowling at him, "it's too late for any relevant amends."

"I meant, we could marry."

She gave him a caustic look. "But for the fact that I'm already married," she said, her voice heavy with sarcasm, "your offer would be delightful."

A tic fluttered high over his cheekbone, but he kept his temper. "We could marry after your divorce," he said with exquisite restraint.

"Which may never occur." Her gaze was cool. "I wasn't born yesterday. You needn't perform some mummery for me."

"It's not mummery. I mean it."

"Maybe this moment you do, but a man like you?" Her brows arched high. "The betting books wouldn't give odds of Lord Darley marrying"—she blew out a breath—"nor would I."

"You know all this, do you?" he queried, his voice ultra soft.

She shut her eyes for a moment. "I don't know what I know," she whispered, exhausted, overwhelmed.

"*I* know *one* thing," he said, about to utter what would have been only weeks ago considered a lunatic thought. "I know I love you."

"You don't know what love is." A man like him? She wasn't that naive.

"I know what it isn't."

She snorted softly. "There's an understatement."

He was surprised at his equanimity. He was the least likely man to let a woman berate him. With anyone else he would have been out the door long ago. "*You* might think about whether you love me and if you are even mildly inclined to favor me with your affection, we could make a home for this child. Think about it at least." This from a man who had been London's most confirmed bachelor. "Should you agree to marry me, it would give us added reason to expedite your divorce."

She groaned, having forgotten that horrendous problem with the more daunting prospect of motherhood facing her. "You can be sure Grafton's going to be vicious about this."

She looked very small in the large chair and no longer waiting for permission, he moved across the room, drew her to her feet and held her in a loose embrace. "This isn't a catastrophe," he said, encouraged that she hadn't resisted him. "It's wonderful that we're having a baby. I want this child and more than that"— he dipped his head so their eyes met—"I want to make you happy. And you needn't worry; I won't let anyone hurt you, nor will I allow any scandal to touch you or our child."

She made a small moue. "If only the world were so benevolent."

"Not a soul will dare take issue." He pulled her closer. "I give you my word. We'll see that your divorce goes through in record time and then we'll marry—in the chapel at Windsor if you wish."

"God, no! Nothing so public!" she said with alarm.

He grinned. "Is that a yes?"

"With all the problems confronting us, even if it was a yes it should probably be followed by a very large *maybe*."

He liked the way she'd said *us*. He wouldn't have thought it possible so small a word could make him feel so triumphant, when in the past any intimation of *us* would have been anathema. "I'll gladly take any kind of yes," he said, as though he'd been a bona fide romantic all his life. As though the other Lord Darley had been some alien creature. As though having a child had always been his fondest wish.

Such was the transforming nature of love.

"Let's tell your brother," he asserted, eager to broadcast the news to the world. The power of love together with his normal unbridled self-indulgence were a potent combination. Taking her hand, he took a step toward the door.

She pulled back. "Must we?"

His smile was benign, his current mood in charity with the entire world. "Darling, sooner or later Will's going to wonder why your belly is getting bigger."

She glared at him. "I don't find that amusing."

"Let me reword that. He would rather hear this from you than from someone else." His brows rose. "You know how servants talk and with the doctor's visit this morning . . ."

She groaned. "I'm not up to decisions right now."

"I'll take care of every little problem, don't worry about a thing. All you have to do is eat and sleep, stay healthy for our baby and give me a smile from time to time."

"You're much too cheerful about this entire matter," she grumbled, testily.

"It must be love," he said, not questioning his impulses, nor had he ever, this scion of privilege. Neither did he question Elspeth's feelings toward him—arrogance perhaps, or simply recognition after years of female adulation. "Come, now, we'll tell your brother and Malcolm and—everyone—Henry, Sophie, Charlie. We'll relay the news in one fell swoop. Since Will already knows of the divorce, he'll be pleased, I suspect, about our marriage plans. And since you're apt to be sick from time to time, they're going to know about the baby soon enough anyway."

Not feeling as confident as Darley about the world's view of their relationship, she muttered, "You tell them—and I'll see everyone . . . say, tomorrow."

He laughed. "You can have your pick of my Barbs if you come with me now when I deliver the news."

She was shocked at how venal her instincts, the thought of owning one of those swift ponies so tempting she immediately began rationalizing away her apprehensions. "I couldn't," she said. "Really, I couldn't," she added more firmly as though the repetitive avowal would bolster her virtue.

"Of course you can. What do you think of the black mare? She's fast, she has impeccable lines and with those hindquarters, she's going to be quick off the start. She'll suit you to perfection."

"You're tempting me sorely," Elspeth murmured, her cheeks flushed with excitement.

"That's my intention, darling. Now pick one and then we'll go wake everyone."

Chapter

38

The following days were lively with activity, both in London and on Gibralter. The Duke of Westerlands spoke to the king, who in turn spoke to Pitt. Mr. Crighton gathered his colleagues and spies and set in motion the opposition to Grafton's lawsuit. The servants at the villa busily packed, making ready for their imminent departure, while the captain of the *Fair Undine* put in supplies for the voyage home. General Eliot shared a last convivial evening with the party on Europa Point and a week after the announcement of the new addition to the Darley family, the *Fair Undine* weighed anchor and set sail.

Orders were given to make landfall at Dover rather than London. Hoping to avoid a possible scene with Grafton—for Elspeth's sake—Julius thought it wise to take a coach into the city. In addition, he wished to protect Elspeth from the legal prerogatives of her husband. The earl could, with impunity and the full protection of the law, carry off his wife, hold her captive and do anything to her short of murder. The patriarchal right to "discipline and punish" a wife was not in question. If there was any doubt, a judge's verdict on a case in 1782 resolved the issue. He declared that, if there was a good cause, a husband could legally beat his wife so long as the stick was no thicker than his thumb.

When Elspeth questioned the reason for landing at Dover,

Darley blamed it on the tides. And as they lingered over dinner at the last posting stop before London, he prevaricated with regard to her query about their staying so long. "You look tired," he said. "Why don't we rest for a time before we move on?"

She *was* tired. In fact, it seemed she was tired all the time lately; she didn't further question Darley's motives. It felt much too good to rest in an upstairs bedchamber, as it did to be coddled by her indulgent lover. She was coming to accept his ready forbearance to her every whim with an equanimity that worried her at times. "You're spoiling me," she would often say, feeling guilty, to which Darley would reply with a disarming smile, "I'm allowed. I'm going to be a father."

When she dozed off, he let her sleep, deliberately delaying their departure, wanting to reach the city under cover of darkness, hoping to slip into town undetected. They left when she woke some time later, and close on ten o'clock, two nondescript, hired carriages quietly entered the mews behind the Duke of Westerlands' house.

"Are you sure we'll be welcome?" Elspeth had asked, more than once on their voyage home. "I mean, under the circumstances."

Darley had reassured her in every possible way.

But even he hadn't anticipated the excitement their arrival would occasion, and once Elspeth's pregnancy was announced, the degree of exuberance and delight was unbounded. After much ebullient hugging and kissing and congratulatory exclamations, the duchess and Betsy whisked Elspeth away, tut-tutting that she shouldn't be on her feet so late at night, that a nice glass of warm milk was just what she needed and once she had a good night's rest, they would begin making serious plans for the new Westerlands baby.

The men retired to the duke's study and over brandy exchanged a condensed version of events that had transpired since last they were in England. After another drink, Will and Henry, who were still not completely recovered from their illness, were shown to their rooms. Shortly after, Malcolm returned to his quarters and Darley and his father were left alone.

"I gather you're pleased with the turn of events," the duke said, surveying his son's permanent smile as he sprawled in a chair opposite him.

Darley's grin widened. "I didn't think it possible to feel this good."

"I could say, I told you so, but I shan't," his father said, his eyes alight. "Instead I'll offer all best wishes to your child." The duke raised his glass.

"Thank you." Darley lifted his goblet and drank his brandy down. "With the future of my child in mind," he murmured, setting his glass aside, "tell me how goes Grafton's divorce bill."

"Pitt is shepherding it through Parliament." His father smiled. "I spoke to the king. It shouldn't take long."

"I thought you might pay a visit to His Majesty. How soon, do you estimate, before a settlement is reached?"

"Another month or so; there're various readings in both houses. Ostensibly, the legalities must be observed."

Darley frowned. "Unfortunately, time has become an issue."

"I understand. I'll speak to Pitt's secretary tomorrow and exert some pressure. By the way, your mother is planning a tea with the king and queen in attendance. A welcome home for you both, as it were."

Darley grimaced. "Elspeth will find such an event daunting, I'm afraid. She doesn't view the world with the same degage attitude as we. I wonder if the tea might be postponed? Should she take sick before Mother's friends, it could raise eyebrows and Elspeth's stomach is exceedingly queasy at the moment."

"I'll speak to your mother." The duke shrugged. "But I warn you, your *Maman* is intent on clarifying Elspeth's position as a member of this family."

"Perhaps in a few weeks," Darley suggested, stretching, beginning to feel the effects of the late hour and several brandies. "Nothing can be done before morning anyway. We'll discuss it then. We've been up since dawn and"—his brows flickered—"Elspeth is waiting."

His father smiled. "May I say, it's gratifying to see you so happy. As to the divorce, I'll handle that. You needn't concern yourself. Now go. The mother of your child is waiting."

And so it was left that first night back in London, the duchess's tea party in flux, the need to expedite the divorce agreed on, father and son pleased to have the family intact once again—with the latest addition and possible heir bringing a new level of excitement to the Westerlands household.

Elspeth was sitting up in bed when Darley entered the bedroom, waiting, unable to sleep without him beside her. Overwhelmed by neediness, at the mercy of her quixotic, skittish emotions, his presence was becoming indispensable to her.

A shocking admission from a woman long familiar with taking charge of her life. But there it was.

An undeniable fact.

Like the baby.

"You look pleased to be home," she said, smiling.

"I am. How are you managing all the hubbub?" He knew how shaky her moods were of late.

"I'm a bundle of nerves, but glad to be back in England."

"Rest easy, darling," Darley said, sitting down to take off his boots. "You have a phalanx of Westerlands to guard you with my mother, perhaps, your most redoubtable champion." Pulling off one boot, he dropped it on the carpet. "She's planning a tea to welcome us home—with the king and queen in attendance to staunch any rumors."

"God, no!" Eyes wide, Elspeth shook her head.

The second boot followed the first. "I said as much to Father—knowing you wouldn't welcome such an event right now. I'll speak to Mother in the morning. She can plan it for later."

"Forgive me for being so timorous, but I really can't face a public spectacle. I know your mother means well, but the KING! I'd collapse in a puddle on the floor."

"So long as you don't throw up on him," Darley teased, dropping his socks beside his boots.

"I'd probably do that as well. Please, please, *please* promise me you'll change your mother's mind."

"Perhaps we can keep her happy buying baby clothes instead," he replied, pulling his neckcloth free and tossing it on a chair.

"I'm not sure that's any better in terms of avoiding scandal. Could we remain slightly more private until the divorce is final?" Elspeth pleaded. "I know you don't care about scandal, but I'm not so thick-skinned."

"I shall restrain my mother, rest easy," Darley soothed. "We'll find something else to amuse her."

"You're much too good to me." Elspeth could feel her anxiety dissipate.

"I could be even better if you like," Darley said with a grin, standing and unbuttoning his buff silk waistcoat.

"Oh, good." Elspeth smiled. "I was hoping you weren't too tired."

"That's not likely with you waiting for me." Elspeth had been even more amorous since her pregnancy, her condition apparently heightening her desires. The voyage home had been a fortnight of lush, boundless passion.

"I absolutely adore you." Pulling the ribbon free at the neckline of her nightgown, she offered him a winsome, pink-cheeked smile. "Vastly, excessively, feverishly"—she winked—"impatiently."

He laughed. "If you continue in this amorous mood, soon there won't be any point in leaving the bedroom." Coat and waistcoat were swiftly discarded.

"I can't help it. I'm sorry." Slipping off her gown, she pushed down the bedclothes in readiness, shameless in her need.

"I'm not complaining." Loosening his neckcloth, he pulled the crushed linen and his shirt over his head, let them fall at his feet, unconsciously smoothing his hair back afterward as he habitually did. "I'm more than happy to clear my schedule in

order to stand stud to you." He grinned. "Actually—enthusiastic."

"How very nice—since I can barely keep my hands off you.
No one ever mentioned that pregnancy makes one so *lascivious*."
She waggled her fingers, beckoning him closer. "I *need* to touch
you. We haven't made love all day—not for hours and hours and
hours."

They'd been in transit and she'd fallen asleep at the inn, but
he tactfully chose not to cavil. Instead, he obligingly moved to
the bed, unbuttoning his breeches in transit. "Consider me at
your service now," he said with a smile, stepping out of his
breeches. "And for the foreseeable future."

"Lovely, lovely, lovely," she whispered, her gaze fixed on his
splendid erection. "Is that all for me?" she purred.

"It's always for you," he murmured, this man who had for-
merly considered fidelity unthinkable.

She shifted over slightly as he climbed into bed, her quick
movement conspicuous in the bobbing bounce of her breasts.

"Is this all for me?" he said, echoing her words, lightly tracing
the high plump curve of her breasts with a fingertip as he settled
into a lounging sprawl beside her.

"Later." Pouting prettily, she wiggled her bottom. "I want you
first."

He watched her heavy breasts sway as she moved, their bur-
geoning size highly erogenous, the fact that he could take credit
for their delectable, ripening fruitfulness further arousing. "I
have to suck on these first. Consider it practice for the baby." It
was newly fashionable for society ladies to nurse their children.

"No, no, no," she remonstrated, with a little moue. "I want
you."

"You don't mean me, you mean *this*." He lightly rapped his
turgid cock.

"Yes, yes, that."

"Only if you let me suck on you first." He didn't know if her
eagerness was more provocative or the fact that his cock held her

in thrall. "It won't take long," he said, softly. "And afterward, you can have me inside you all night."

"All night?" she whispered, the tantalizing thought sending a fevered heat coursing through her body.

"I'll keep you stuffed full of cock until you're faint from coming. *Afterward,*" he whispered. "After you let me suck on you."

"Yes, yes." How could she say no? She was in continual rut and had been since Gibralter, insatiable, lustful, craving sex as though she were in the grip of some love potion that had been meted out with her pregnancy.

"Sit here," he murmured, easing her higher against the pillows. "Five minutes," he said. "Look at me."

She wrenched her eyes from his rigid, upthrust penis.

"Can you wait?"

"No."

"You have to." Bending the world to his will was a long-standing habit that even love had not wholly tamed.

She shivered, yielding to the promise of greater pleasure. "Hurry."

Her large breasts had almost doubled in size even so early in her pregnancy, her nipples deepening in hue, elongating, the substantial weight of each plump globe significant. She would need a new wardrobe soon to accommodate their size, he decided.

Darley's impulses weren't entirely selfish; if anyone knew best how to bring a woman to climax, the marquis had long held that title in the club betting books.

Devoting himself first to one breast and then the other he suckled with a tender, expert proficiency—hard, but not too hard, tugging gently so the pleasure flowed downward to each quivering nerve, concentrating on his task with a flair for delicacy. In quick succession, his erstwhile fiancée was brought to a panting, manic hysteria and two seething climaxes.

She was definitely on an orgasmic hair trigger.

He still had two minutes left.

But she'd collapsed from the wild ferocity of the spasms, every sensation, every perception fiercer now, overwrought and exaggerated, as though her body was no more than an oversensitive vehicle for sexual passion.

He lay beside her, waiting for her fevered senses to cool, offering up his appreciation to whatever gods had brought him to this point. He found himself grateful in a measureless way. Genuinely happy.

"How do you always know?" she whispered after a small interval, turning her head to smile at him.

He smiled back. "How can you always forget how good it feels?"

"Luckily, I have you to remind me."

"You can be lucky again whenever you wish," he said with a grin. "I'm here to service your every whim."

"Give me a minute, although in my current insatiable mood, don't expect any lengthy respite."

"I believe I can keep up," he drawled.

Her gaze narrowed. "I'm not sure I like that insolent assurance."

"Since I met you, I seem to have acquired a substantial sexual appetite, I meant."

"How smooth, my lord," she murmured, sweetly. "However, I shan't take issue since I need you rather desperately."

He liked that about her. She was a practical woman, not given to coy dissimilation like so many women he'd known. "Just tell me when our new little mama is ready for more," he cheerfully said.

"I'm holding you to your promise. You said all night."

He grinned. "Feeling renewed, are we?" Coming up on one elbow, he ran an exploratory finger up her inner thigh.

"A little higher," she whispered, shutting her eyes, a flush beginning to color her cheeks.

As his finger slipped inside her dewy heat, she blissfully sighed.

"I'm really glad to be home," she breathed.

He was too.

Rolling over her a moment later, he settled between her thighs and entered her with a supple shift of his hips, sliding in with frictionless ease. She was slick as silk, and just snug enough to afford them both an acute, spine-tingling thrill. In the grip of her new nymphomania, she was always overeager and impatient; he in turn knew how to pace himself after so long in the amorous lists.

She came almost immediately, but as promised, he didn't move and before long, she came again.

Opening her eyes a short time later, coming back from the blissful fringes of quivering rapture, she gazed up at him with dewy-eyed adoration.

He flashed her a smile, allowing himself to move now that she was semi-coherent again. Stripping the ribbon from his nape, he arched his back, and pulled back his hair that had fallen in his face. Clubbing the unruly tendrils into a rough queue, he tied them up with a few, economical twists.

"Are you mine?" she suddenly said, wondering how many times in how many boudoirs he'd brushed his hair from his face after sex.

Dropping back onto his forearms, he shifted his hips faintly. "Do I feel like I'm yours?" he whispered.

She smiled. "You feel very, very nice indeed."

"And you feel like the mother of my child"—he grinned—"as well as my future wife."

"Wouldn't that be grand," she breathed.

"It *will* be grand," he said with absolute certainty. "My word on it."

Such utter confidence was vastly erotic, Elspeth reflected, an aphrodisiac as it were—like some relentless symbol of maleness and phallic power. Or maybe just everything about Darley would always be erotic.

Although, she probably wasn't the first woman to think so. "Tell me you'll love me always," she insisted, her moods wretchedly unstable of late. "Lie if you have to."

He grinned. "Honestly?"

She hit him hard.

He didn't even flinch. He only smiled more. "I shall love you, my sweet, until the end of time. I swear. Feeling better now?"

"Yes." She grinned. "Although—"

"Don't say it. I know. You'd like to feel just a little bit better."

"I just adore how you can read my mind."

This wasn't the time to point out that she wasn't the first impatient woman he'd known. "It must be kismet," he said instead, with charming finesse.

And so the night progressed, Darley in his most obliging mood, Elspeth needing his love and reassurance more than ever with her sexual urges seething at fever pitch.

Both of them delighting in their mutual carnal appetites.

Both pleased to be home.

Chapter
39

It was impossible to curtail gossip, especially when the tale was so titillating, when the most confirmed bachelor in all of England had finally succumbed to love. With those belowstairs privy to everything that transpired abovestairs, the news quickly passed from servant to servant, house to house like wildfire.

Elspeth's pregnancy was common knowledge by tea time the following day.

It hadn't helped that she'd immediately thrown up the morning after her return.

No more than the duchess's orders to her chef that Elspeth have whatever food she wished at any time of day had concealed her indelicate condition.

And the reason for the duke's call early that morning to Pitt, had swirled through the Ton like a whirlwind.

So Chief Justice Kenyon wasn't surprised when Lord Grafton was wheeled into his office that afternoon, the earl's face purple with rage. "The damned slut is pregnant!" he screeched, before Tom Scott had even closed the door behind him. "I want this divorce stopped! I won't let Darley have the satisfaction of seeing his child inherit, damn his bloody hide! The bitch and her spawn can rot in hell as far as I'm concerned, but she'll *remain* my wife!"

"I wouldn't recommend you flaunt the king," Kenyon counseled, Pitt's brokering of the divorce an open declaration of the king's support.

"Screw the bloody king!" Grafton shouted. "I don't care if God himself is sponsoring the damned bitch!"

Kenyon shot a fleeting glance at Mr. Eldon who was sitting in his usual chair in the corner.

Eldon's shoulders lifted faintly, as if to say, *What do you want me to do?*

"Now, now, Lord Grafton," Kenyon asserted, having reversed his previous moral stance on hearing of the king's interest. "We must face facts here. The king is not to be gainsaid, as you well know, regardless of either your or my personal feelings. He is the king and as such, the supreme authority in the land."

"Like hell he is! We have a damned Parliament so the king isn't the supreme authority for Christ's sake! I'll have you know the earls of Grafton have resided in England for five centuries longer than those damned upstart Hanoverian Germans! And if you think I'm going to be threatened by some king who can't even speak bloody English, you're sadly mistaken! I will disown that slut's child though—see to that, damn you, and I will also see that that libertine Darley rues the day he fucked with me! Do you understand! I'm going to make them both wish they'd never crossed my path! They're going to suffer for eternity for what they did to me! And if you can't handle this, damn you"— Grafton gasped for air—"I'll . . . go—somewhere—" The purplish cast to his face took on a blackish hue as he struggled for breath, his eyes bulging with the strain. Clawing at his throat, trying to loosen his neckcloth, his lips moved soundlessly as he choked and gagged. A terrible rasping sound came in the wake of his desperate exertions and a moment later, the earl started shuddering and jerking in the grip of a violent seizure.

"I'll take care of this," the chief justice crisply declared, waving Eldon from the room. "Wait for me outside. Speak to no one," he ordered, the threat in his words unmistakable.

The moment Grafton's solicitor was gone, Kenyon locked the door and, leaning back against the oak panels, dispassionately watched and waited as the figure in the Bath chair thrashed about in its death throes.

Earlier in the day, when he'd heard of the Duke of Westerlands' visit to Pitt, Kenyon had spoken with Lord Chancellor Thurlow. Their decision to aid Grafton in his divorce suit no longer seemed prudent with the king taking such a personal interest in the affair. Since both men had careers to consider and neither was uninitiated in the patronage system that governed a man's rise to prominence, they'd agreed that thwarting the king's will would be unprofitable.

One divorce case wasn't worth their future.

And *now* it seemed their problem had been solved, the chief justice observed, adjusting his shirt cuffs, the sudden silence in the room deafening.

He waited another ten minutes in the hushed chamber, just to be certain the body was completely lifeless. He wished to confirm—without a doubt—that dead men tell no tales.

After what he considered a circumspect interval, he unlocked his office door and called for his secretary. "An unhappy occurrence has befallen Lord Grafton," he said. "His lordship has succumbed to a sudden apoplexy. The poor man was never the same after his last illness," the chief justice added with feigned sadness. "Notify the late earl's chairman to take away the body and have Pitt notified as well. Tell the prime minister that, as of now, we will be withdrawing Lord Grafton's divorce suit from the schedule in the House of Lords."

Chapter

40

The duke received the news of Lord Grafton's death almost immediately, Chief Justice Kenyon conveying the facts with ingratiating swiftness in a letter delivered by his personal servant.

After perusing the message lavish with toadying phrases of esteem, the duke sent for Crighton. He wished a full understanding of all the legal ramifications before raising needless hopes for his family.

"With the earl's death there are no longer any obstacles to Lady Grafton's marriage," Crighton declared, pleased to be the bearer of such glad tidings.

The duke's gaze drilled into his solicitor. "How sure are you?"

Crighton looked pained. "Your Grace, I would never offer unsound advice. I assure you, the lady is entirely free of any hindrances. In fact, she might be the recipient of a widow's portion on her husband's death."

The duke waved his hand in a dismissive gesture. "No one needs Grafton's money."

"The lady might not agree, sir." Few people had the Westerlands' wealth.

"Yes, yes, I see. It's up to Elspeth, of course. Now then, on to more pleasant things." Rising from his chair, the duke came around his desk and taking Crighton's hand in a crushing grip shook it vigorously. "Thank you for all your work. I expect we'll be seeing you soon in regard to a marriage settlement. It's a very, very fine day, isn't it?" he said, smiling brightly.

And then, the solicitor relayed to his colleagues a short time later after he returned to the offices of Crighton, Addington, and Morley, the duke shocked him by embracing him, a mark of such favor Mr. Crighton's heart was still beating wildly from the honor. As if that momentous measure of both the duke's esteem and high spirits wasn't enough, the duke also compensated him with a purse from his own hand with enough guineas inside to buy spacious new quarters for their law firm in the very best section of the city.

"Not that I don't understand the duke's jubilation," Mr. Crighton explained. "Lord Darley seemed most unlikely to marry and the duke is no longer young. To see a grandson born before he dies would gratify him, I'm sure, as well as assure the continuity of the ancient dukedom."

A pithy appraisal of the duke's state of mind.

But then Crighton had been with Granville D'Abernon since before he assumed his ducal title.

At the conclusion of his meeting with Crighton, the duke walked from his study to the middle of the magnificent gilt and marble entrance hall and raising his voice to what could only be characterized as a bellow, summoned the household.

Everyone immediately understood that something of rare moment had occurred.

The Duke of Westerlands was not an overtly demonstrative man.

The duchess and Betsy were in the duchess's sitting room mulling over a guest list for the future tea.

Darley and Elspeth were lying abed, as they had been for most of the day.

Will and Henry were perusing a Tattersall flyer for an up-and-coming thoroughbred auction with Malcolm jotting down their choices in a small ledger.

The servants were momentarily rooted to the spot, so shocked were they at the sound of the duke's voice raised above its usual moderate timbre.

Brief moments later, however, the residents converged from all parts of the house and assembled in the entrance hall, their expressions ranging from simple expectation to fear.

"I have excellent, excellent news," the duke announced. "Most excellent," he repeated with a wide smile to those standing beneath the high domed ceiling adorned with various mythological figures cavorting on Olympus. "Any obstacles to a marriage between Julius and Elspeth have been completely nullified by the sudden death of Lord Grafton. I just received word of his demise and Crighton has assured me no legalities remain to interfere with the marriage. Naturally, the loss of any life is regrettable, although in this case perhaps less regrettable than some," he added. "Having said that"—a sudden smile animated his aquiline features—"might I suggest we decide on a wedding date."

"Tonight," Darley replied, without charity in regard to Grafton.

"Tonight?" Elspeth gasped.

Darley's brows lifted infinitesimally, a flash of amusement gleaming in his eyes. "I hope you're not going to back out."

"A small ceremony in the Rembrandt Room would be lovely," the duchess interposed, finding it impossible to refrain from speaking when all the daunting problems impeding the marriage had summarily vanished. Furthermore, she'd known Grafton's first wife; no one could possibly mourn his loss. "Do say yes, darling," the duchess cajoled, smiling at Elspeth.

Elspeth looked at her brother who grinned back and said, "Why wait?"

She had no reasonable answer to so simple a query. Certainly, Grafton's death didn't affect her decision. She only felt relief that he and his cruelty were gone from her life.

"It's up to you, darling," Darley murmured, graciously, when he would have preferred bringing in a minister before another minute passed. He kissed her lightly on the cheek. "You decide."

His eyes glowed with love, while her love for him was infinite. And certainly their child deserved a mother who was less indecisive. "The Rembrandt Room sounds very nice," she said.

"Wonderful, my dear!" the duchess proclaimed, putting period to any further equivocation. "Now if you'll excuse me"—she gestured at her husband and daughter—"us," she added with a smile. "Come, everyone," she added, encompassing the whole of the servants with a wave of her hand. "We have much to do." Just before exiting the hall, she turned back. "How does tenish sound?"

"Eight," her son counterposed, Elspeth's bedtime earlier since her pregnancy.

"Eight, it is!" the duchess trilled and dashed away, a crowd of servants in her wake.

"I think they like you," Darley said, grinning.

"I rather think they despaired of you ever marrying and aren't taking any chances."

"Just so long as *you* take a chance with me," he said, pulling her close. "I'm content."

"How could I not when I'm so deeply in love I can't live without you."

"Nor me without you. An astonishing phenomenon, I might add. It makes one wonder whether fairies and elves exist as well, for love seemed equally fantastic to me a short time ago."

"Finding myself in a veritable fairy tale at the moment, I'm quite willing to believe anything."

"Believe this." He grinned. "We're getting married."

"People will talk, won't they? About the unseemly haste so soon after"—she couldn't bring herself to utter Grafton's name.

"It doesn't matter what people say." Although several of his friends were going to lose heavily. The general consensus in Brooks's betting book was that he wouldn't marry for at least another five years.

"People will count on their fingers, too, I suppose."

"Let them."

She grinned. "You make it all sound so easy."

"It will be, darling," he said, the prerogatives of generations of ducal ancestors and wealth fostering his assurance. "I guarantee."

They were married that night by special license, with only the family in attendance, the sensational news causing more excitement than the king's last fit of insanity.

Every paper in town vied to have the most provocative headline: "The Runaway Marriage"; "The Lucky Bride"; "Darley Snared"; "Quit Him And Fly With Me (Death Takes A Hand)"; "The Briefest Of Widowhoods."

Naturally with the scent of scandal so much in the air, everyone claiming the faintest acquaintanceship called at Westerlands House the following day, only to be turned away. The family had retired to the country for an indefinite period of time.

In the following months, the young couple remained secluded at one of several estates owned by the duke or the marquis, finally choosing to settle at Oak Hill in Lincolnshire where the marchioness was delivered of a son in February.

The family remained in the country through the summer, where their young son thrived, as did their love for him and each other. When Parliament opened again in the fall, they returned to town and the duchess's much postponed tea with the king and queen in attendance finally came to pass.

The Marchioness of Darley was more beautiful than ever, everyone agreed. Gossip had it she was once again with child, although even the closest scrutiny wasn't able to confirm the rumor. But what was certain was her husband's continuing affection; he never left her side that afternoon, their fondness for each other quite unnatural, many in the Ton opined.

But Darley had always lived his life unencumbered by the shibboleths of society and so he continued, immune to both gossip and censure.

In time, their family expanded to include two sons and two daughters, their racing stud became the best in the land and the Darley name became synonymous with winning thoroughbreds bred from the best Barbary bloodlines.

It was a life of great contentment and joy.

With nothing to mar the perfection.

Until decades later, after the Battle of Waterloo, the new Lord Darley came home a changed man.

He'd been in the thick of battle at Quatre Bras, wounded twice and left for dead.

His parents despaired for the soundness of his mind at first.

Until one day he met an actress.

She was highly unsuitable, of course. Or so some would say.

But she made him smile when he'd not done so for months.

Her name was Annabelle Foster.

Don't miss Lucy Monroe's
WILLING
available now from Brava . . .

His dark eyes narrowed. "Are you okay?"

"Yes, but I can't seem to get my feet to move."

"You're nervous."

What had been his first clue? The way she equated making love for the first time with death by drowning, or the deer-caught-in-the-headlights look she knew was in her eyes? "I shouldn't be. I'm not a child."

"But you are innocent."

"Only physically." She'd heard and seen things women married for forty years would never experience.

He shook his head, his mouth twitching at the corners. "Your heart and your mind are very innocent still, no matter what you think you know."

"Oh, really?"

"Yes."

That sparked another set of worries that kept her feet firmly glued to the floor outside their room. "Won't you be bored making love to me, seeing as how I don't know anything?"

"Josette, I could spend the entire night just looking at you and not get bored." His tone wasn't reassuring so much as bewildered.

Which was actually pretty comforting. Later, she would probably feel flattered and special, but right now she just felt relief. At least something about this was new for him too. "I take it you've never been that way with a woman?"

"No." And if the frown on his face meant anything, he didn't like it.

"It's a first for both of us." She couldn't help the satisfaction that laced her voice.

He let out an impatient breath. "It's not going to be anything if we don't get out of the hall."

She sighed and looked into the room. It was a suite. She could see the bedroom through the sumptuously decorated sitting room. It was like a room out of time, the colors and décor from a bygone era.

"It's a pretty room," she said without moving.

"Not as pretty as the woman I'm bringing into it." Before she knew it, the decision was being taken from her as he swept her up in his arms and carried her inside.

"This isn't our wedding night," she said breathlessly.

"I know that."

"But you just carried me over the threshold."

"It was the expedient thing to do."

Perhaps, but she liked the sensations zinging through her body as a result of being held securely in his arms. She looped her arms around his neck and buried her face in the warmth of his chest. He smelled so different than she did, but it was a good different. Masculine.

Maybe she wasn't as lacking in the feminine department as she thought she was. At least she now realized she smelled like a woman, not a man. She should have caught on to that sooner, as much time as she spent around male soldiers, but she couldn't ever remember actually focusing on the scent of one before.

He carried her through the sitting room to the bedroom beyond and her breath caught in her throat.

Did he want to make love right now, just like that?

Of course he did. She was his obsession. It wasn't the romance of the century or anything schmaltzy like that.

Then another scent, one very different from Daniel, invaded her senses. Roses.

She lifted her head from his chest and looked around them.

The room was filled with flowers—red roses, white roses, yellow roses and even lavender roses. They were everywhere. Swags of dried orange blossoms hung off the ornate head and footboard of the antique bed too, but the thing that caught her attention and kept it was a white silk gown spread over the burgundy velvet bedspread.

"Daniel?"

He looked down at her, the hardened mercenary she knew him to be not quite hiding the man who cared enough to make this night special. "It's your first time. I want you to remember it for all the right reasons."

Tears filled her eyes and she couldn't get a sound out past the big lump in her throat.

He let her down and stepped back, seemingly unconcerned by her display of emotion.

"I'm going to take a walk. I'll be back in a while. The bathroom is through there." He pointed to a door on the opposite side of the room. "Take your time getting ready. I'm not going to rush you tonight, in any way."

She was still quivering from the promise in that last comment when the outer door closed.

When Daniel came back to the room a half an hour later, the door to the bedroom was still shut.

How much longer would she be?

He'd promised not to rush her, but he wanted her with a hunger that left him feeling hollow and achy inside. Calling his need for her an obsession had been pure fact. If she had turned him down, he would have been on a collision course with spontaneous combustion.

The closed door mocked his promise of patience. He wanted to pound on it and demand to know how long it took to put on a nightgown, but he had just enough self-control left to keep him seated on the oversized Victorian sofa.

This was too important to mess up with impatience, even if it was born of desperation.

She'd waited twenty-six years to share her body with a man. After their talk in the park, he understood that better, but still found it difficult to believe a woman as sexy and beautiful as she was could have remained innocent so long.

If Daniel had been one of the soldiers going through Tyler McCall's training camp, Josie would have gotten educated about men and their desires a lot earlier. He would never have allowed the older man's threats-slash-promises to deter him from pursuing a woman he wanted as much as he wanted Josie.

The handle turned on the door to the bedroom and he surged up from the sofa. The door swung inward and she came out, the sheer white silk gown clinging lovingly to her small curves.

His breath caught and he had to clear his throat to talk. "You look beautiful."

"Thank you for the gown. It's the prettiest thing I've ever worn."

The exclusive boutique owner he had called earlier had followed his directions to a T. The nightgown was designed along the lines of a medieval dress. Its bell shaped long sleeves floated gently around Josie's slender arms, and the skirt whispered against the smooth skin of her legs. The high waist tucked in just below her breasts, accentuating them.

He ached to taste the dark nipples peeking out at him from behind the sheer silk. He wanted to put his mouth right over each one, making the fabric wet and transparent and her nipples hard and tight.

Familiar sensation brought his sex to full attention as the images in his head grew increasingly erotic. "It'll look even prettier off you."

Take a look at MaryJanice Davidson's
hilarious new novella
"Cuffs and Coffee Breaks" in
VALENTINE'S DAY IS KILLING ME
available now from Brava.

"**W**ell, this is it." Julie Kay tossed her keys on the kitchen counter. "Home sweet hell."

"It's nice," he commented, glancing around the small house she rented from her brother-in-law. "I used to live in Inver, back when I was a student at the U."

"Yeah, what, six weeks ago?"

"Oh, you're hilarious."

"I hate apartments. I always feel like a bee in a hive. So when my brother-in-law moved into a bigger place, he let me rent this one. It's worked out for everyone."

"Mmm." Scott was prowling around the living room and dining area like a big brunette panther. "I have an apartment, and I know what you mean. But I'm almost never there."

"Where are you?"

"Work, usually. That's why I was really glad when you decided to go out with me. I mean, I have *no* social life."

"But you're so . . ." Gorgeous. Delicious. Fabulous. Tall. ". . . smart."

He shrugged. "I was always the tallest kid in my class, *and* the skinniest. But I was bad at sports. So who'd want to go out with a big gork like me?"

Oh, I dunno, anyone with half a brain?

"Uh, let me see if I can find something better than my old cardigan." She turned to go into her bedroom, but he came up behind her and put a hand on her shoulder, gently turning her around.

"It's fine," he said. "It's the least of my problems, believe me. What the hell am I going to do about that poor guy at the restaurant?"

"Uh . . . well, I . . . uh . . ." Blue eyes were filling her world, her universe. They were getting closer and closer. There was nothing else: no house, no living room, no cardigan, no dead guy.

She felt his lips touch hers and she put her arms around him— she could hardly reach, his shoulders were so broad. Her mouth opened beneath his and his tongue touched hers, tentatively and then with more assurance, licking her teeth and nibbling her lower lip. She pulled, and the cardigan was on the floor, and her hands were running across his fine chest, and—

(*Dead guy, dead guy!*)

She yanked herself away. "Stop that! This is totally inappropriate!"

"Hey, *you* kissed *me*."

"I did not!" Oh, wait. Maybe she did. "Well, it doesn't matter. This isn't the time or place."

"I *know*. That's why I didn't kiss you. Although, I have to say," he added cheerfully, "I've been dying to all night. But you're right, this isn't the right time. Bad sweetie."

"Oh, like you were really fighting it!"

"It seemed rude to give you the brush off," he said, sounding wounded. "You know, me being a guest in your home and all."

"Well, never mind that. Let's stay focused. Put your sweater back on."

"I didn't take it off," he grumbled, but did as she asked.

"Let's figure this out. We have to be back there in fourteen hours. So, if you didn't kill the guy—"

"Charley Ferrin."

She gasped. "You know him?"

"No, no." He held his hands up, palm out. "Calm down, don't have a coronary."

"I'll have one if I damned well please!"

"It's not like that. Detective Hobbes told me his name. I swear, I have no idea who he is. The name meant nothing to me."

"Okay, okay." She forced herself to calm down. He was right, this was no time to burst a blood vessel. "So, if you didn't do it, who did? Who had a motive and could do it quickly, and avoid the cops, and stick you with a murder charge?"

"Honey, I got nothin'. I've been trying to figure it out all night. I was minding my own business, waiting for you, and the next thing I know, I'm wearing handcuffs. And not in a good way."

She felt the blood rush to her face as she pictured him cuffed to her headboard. "All right. Did you overhear any arguments? See anybody fighting? Anything weird at all?"

"No."

"Come on. There must be something."

He shook his head. "No. And no, and no. I told the cops all this already."

"Well, now tell *me*," she snapped.

"Don't boss me!"

"I'll boss you if I like! If it wasn't for me you'd still be rotting in jail!"

"The hell. My lawyer would have vouched for me."

"Yeah, I could tell what a great job he did by the way it took him *hours* and *hours* to *not* show up."

"Listen-mmph!"

She had kissed him again. What was wrong with her?

"Not that I mind," he gasped, extricating himself from her grip. "But, again, don't you think this is a little inappropriate? Given the circumstances?"

She got up to pace. "Of course it's inappropriate, it's nine kinds of inappropriate! What the hell is wrong with me?"

He opened his mouth, but she beat him to the punch. "I'll tell you, it's this fucking holiday! It's killing me! It's making me act in ways I would never normally act! God, I hate it, I hate it, *I hate Valentine's Day!*"

Here's a scintillating peek at
Sylvia Day's "Stolen Pleasures"
in her new anthology
BAD BOYS AHOY.
Available February 2006 from BRAVA.

British West Indies
February 1813

He'd stolen a bride.

Sebastian Blake gripped his knife with white-knuckled force and kept his face impassive. If the beauty in front of him was to be believed, he'd stolen *his own* bride.

He watched as her chin lifted with defiance and her dark eyes met his without fear. She was tall and slender with blond curls tumbling down from a once-stylish arrangement. Her lovely watered-silk dress was torn at the shoulder, revealing a tempting display of creamy breast. There was a sooty handprint marring her flesh, and unable to help himself, Sebastian reached out and rubbed the offending mark away with gentle strokes of his thumb. She stiffened and lifted her bound hands to knock his away. He met her gaze and held it.

"Tell me your name again," he murmured, his hand tingling just from that simple contact with her satin skin.

She licked her bottom lip and his blood heated further. "My name is Olivia Blake, Countess of Merrick. My husband is Sebastian Blake, Earl of Merrick and future Marquis of Dunsmore."

He lifted her hands and stared at her ring finger, noting his crest etched in the simple gold band she wore.

He scrubbed a hand over his face and turned away, striding to the nearest open window for a deep breath of salt-tinged air. Staring out at the water, he spied the debris from her ship bobbing in the waves. "Where is your husband, Lady Merrick?" he asked, keeping his back to her.

Hope tinged her voice. "He awaits me in London."

"I see." But he didn't, not at all. "How long have you been married, my lady?"

"I fail to see—"

"How long?" he barked.

"Nearly two weeks."

His chest expanded with a deep breath. "I remind you that we are in the West Indies, Lady Merrick. It is impossible that you were married only a fortnight ago. Your husband would not be able to await you in England if that were true."

She was silent behind him and finally, he turned to face her again. It was a mistake to have done so. Her beauty hit him with the force of a fist in his gut.

"Would you care to explain?" he prodded, relieved he sounded so unaffected.

For the first time her bravado left her, her cheeks flushing with embarrassment. "We were married by proxy," she confessed. "But I assure you, he will pay whatever ransom you desire despite the unusual circumstances of our marriage."

Sebastian moved toward her. His calloused fingers caressed the elegant curve of her cheekbone and entwined in her hair. Her breath caught, and her lips parted in response to his gentle touch. "I'm certain he would pay a king's ransom for beauty such as yours."

Through the smoky smell that clung to her, he could detect the arousing scent of soft woman, warm and luxurious. He reached for the blade strapped to his thigh and withdrew it.

She flinched away.

"Easy," he soothed. Sebastian held out his hand and waited patiently for her to step forward again. When she did, he sliced through the rope that tied her hands together and sheathed his knife. He rubbed the marks on her delicate wrists.

"You are a pirate," she murmured.

"Yes."

"You have taken my father's ship and all of its cargo."

"I have."

Her head tilted backward on her slender neck and she gazed up at him with melting chocolate eyes. "Why then are you being so kind to me, if you intend to rape me?"

He caught her fingers and placed them on his signet ring. "Most would say a man cannot rape his own wife."

She glanced down and gasped at the heavy crest that mirrored her own band. Her eyes flew up to his. "Where did you get this? You can't possibly . . ."

He smiled. "According to you, I am."

Olivia stared up into the intense blue eyes and felt certain her heart would burst from her chest. Her mind faltered, stumbling over the shocking revelation that the notorious Captain Phoenix was claiming to be her husband.

She backed away from him in a rush and he reached to steady her when she almost fell. A whimper escaped as his touch burned her skin. The day's events had shaken her, but it was the gorgeous face of the infamous pirate that made her weak kneed.

Tall and broad shouldered, his presence sucked all of the air from the tight confines of the cabin. His black hair was unfashionably long and the darkness of his skin betrayed how much time he spent outdoors. He was wild, untamed—a man of the elements.

She'd watched, fascinated, as he'd swept onto her ship and taken command of it within moments. Phoenix had executed the attack with brilliant precision—not one man was seriously injured and no one had been killed. Having spent most of her childhood on her father's ships, Olivia recognized singular skill when she saw it.

The way he'd used his sword and barked commands, the way loose tendrils of his hair had blown across his face, the way his breeches delineated every stretch of his muscular thighs . . . she'd never experienced anything so thrilling. So exciting.

Until he'd touched her.